ROUGH LANDING

I gripped the rails at my sides so hard that no one, not even the huge alien porracci, could have pried my fingers loose. The air buffeted us from side to side as we dropped on an extremely steep glide path, but that's normal. The idea is to get the drop ship on the ground as fast as possible, giving the enemy no time to target you with ground-to-air missiles. It doesn't take much to do lethal damage to an airsled.

We hit the ground, but not hard enough to burrow in. The sled skidded along the turf as compressed gas jets slowed us down. The terrain provided more breaking. We could hear underbrush, maybe even small trees, snapping and scraping the sides of the sled—the last part of the ride always seems to last an eternity. Finally, we stopped, tipped to the right, and the overhead hatches popped automatically. I looked over my unit, some furry, some scaly, all anxious.

I bellowed, "Up and out!" and everyone moved like lightning . . .

SPEC OPS SQUAD

HOLDING THE LINE

RICK SHELLEY

ACE BOOKS, NEW YORK

SPEC OPS SQUAD: HOLDING THE LINE

An Ace Book / published by arrangement with
the author

PRINTING HISTORY
Ace mass-market edition / August 2001

Visit our website at
www.penguinputnam.com

Check out the ACE Science Fiction & Fantasy newsletter
and much more on the Internet at Club PPI!

ISBN: 0-441-00834-8

ACE®
Ace Books are published by The Berkley Publishing Group,
a division of Penguin Putnam Inc.,
375 Hudson Street, New York, New York 10014.
ACE and the "A" design
are trademarks belonging to Penguin Putnam Inc.

PRINTED IN THE UNITED STATES OF AMERICA

10 9 8 7 6 5 4 3 2 1

If you want to know about the war between the Alliance of Light and the Ilion Federation, I'll tell you—straight and true, to the best of my ability. You won't get all the pious posturing and the high falutin philosophy and moralizing you've been hearing from the politicians and generals. I've got a different perspective, and I see the war up close and personal—which none of the politicians and damned few of the generals can honestly say. My name is Bart Drak. Friends call me Dragon to my face. Others sometimes use that nickname behind my back. That's okay with me. I'm a buck sergeant leading a Special Operations Squad in Ranger Battalion of the 1st Combined Regiment. *Spec Ops*—we get the dirtiest, most dangerous jobs. If the mission is something no sane individual would attempt, the big shots dump it on us, Spec Ops—the SOS.

CHAPTER 1

IT WAS MAJOR WELLMAN WHO INFORMED ME
that I had volunteered for a new unit called the 1st Combined Regiment.

We were in the middle of a training operation. I had
been assigned as an instructor in Advanced Infantry
Training at Fort Campbell for the past six months—ever
since I finished my medical leave following the debacle
on Dintsen. My ranger battalion had been there for a
joint training mission with a divotect battalion. The war
had caught us all by surprise, and Dintsen just happened
to be the first target the Ilion Federation hit. And brother,
they hit us hard. Of the twelve hundred humans on the
planet, only three hundred survived the attack, and two-
thirds of us were wounded. It was a miracle that any of
us got off Dintsen alive. The divotect battalion we had
been training with got hurt worse, and they had nowhere
to go. It was their world.

So now I had this platoon of trainee infantrymen
drawn from just about every corner of the western hemi-
sphere. My job was to make sure they absorbed enough
knowledge—and discipline—to give them a chance to

survive combat when their turn came. As a full member of the Alliance of Light, Earth was committed to the war with the Ilion Federation.

We were out in the field, as usual. The tactical problem at the moment was to infiltrate positions held by a superior aggressor force—regular troops who were out to show the rookies how much they had left to learn. Maybe in another month my trainees would know enough to give a good accounting of themselves. Right now, they were making more mistakes than I could have counted with both boots off.

The radio call from the battalion sergeant major was a surprise. "Hey, Dragon. Turn your men over to your corporal and haul your ass over to the fire road north of you. On the double. I've got a crawler on the way to pick you up. Major Wellman wants to see you like ten minutes ago."

From the tone in Fritz's voice, I didn't think that the major was going to pin another medal on my chest. "What the hell did I do wrong this time?" I asked.

"Nobody tells me nothing," Fritz said, and I didn't bother calling him a liar. He knew more about what went on in the regiment than any of the officers. "Just get your ass in gear. The major doesn't like to be kept waiting."

I got my sigh over before I keyed my transmitter again. "Okay, Fritz. On my way."

It took me thirty seconds to give Corporal Hernandez the unwelcome news that he was in charge until I got back—and twenty of those seconds were wasted telling him I didn't know when that would be. Then I lit out, at the double, through the woods to the fire road. Whatever it was that Major Wellman wanted me for, I didn't want to give him any more time to steam than I had to.

He and I did not get along under the best of circumstances.

JOSIAH WELLMAN WAS A CAREER OFFICER, AN Academy man who couldn't forget that he had come out of the "trade school"—and who never let anyone else forget it either. Normally, a battalion would rate a lieutenant colonel as commanding officer, even in a training unit. Wellman had arrived two months earlier, without the promotion he had evidently expected. The rumor in the NCO club was that he had been passed over, that there was some black mark on his record that would keep him from ever making light colonel—until he was forced out of the service for being passed over for promotion too many times. With a war on, the brass might not be in any hurry about dumping him, but they weren't going to promote him if they could avoid it.

I needed twenty-three minutes to reach the battalion orderly room on main base. Fritz looked apprehensive as he got up from his desk and moved toward the door to Major Wellman's office.

"He's waiting for you. I'm to usher you right in."

"Level with me, Fritz. What's up?"

Fritz shook his head. "Honest, I don't have any idea." Then he knocked on the old man's door, opened it far enough to stick his head in, and said, "Sergeant Drak is here, Major."

Wellman's "Send him in" was muffled but didn't sound happy. Fritz swung the door open all the way and gestured me through. He closed the door behind me.

"Sergeant Drak reporting as ordered." I braced to attention and saluted. Since I didn't know what was up, and figured I was in trouble for *something,* I made it all as crisp and proper as I could, acting like I loved all the routine bullshit.

Major Wellman looked up slowly and returned my salute as if he were trapped in gelatin. Then he stared with his watery blue eyes. Staring was one thing the major was excellent at. He had made it nearly an art form. Wellman looked me up and down, then back up again. There was no steam coming out of his ears, but I didn't need much imagination to picture it. I remained stiffly at attention. Maybe I don't look much like a recruiting poster soldier—I'm too short and stocky for that—but I do know my job; I'm damned good at it, if I do say so myself. I can handle any weapon in the inventory, and I can take care of myself without any weapons but those I had when I entered the world.

"At ease, Sergeant," he said after what felt like two or three minutes—but was probably less than thirty seconds. I moved my feet apart and put my hands behind my back.

"I have good news for you, Sergeant," Wellman said. He leaned back so he could stare with less discomfort. "You have volunteered to be part of a new unit, the 1st Combined Regiment."

"Sir?"

Wellman scowled. That was the other thing he was good at. If there were more than those two, I hadn't seen them.

"The Combined General Staff of the Grand Alliance has decided—in its infinite wisdom—to attempt to integrate the armed forces of all the species in the Alliance down to the battalion level. And *our* chief of staff has decided that we need to contribute the, ah, most capable soldiers available, especially combat veterans, and *most* especially decorated heroes." At this point his scowl got so deep and convoluted I thought he was about to puke. "Personally, I don't see how a soldier deserves a medal for somehow surviving when damned near his entire platoon was killed around him."

"Sir, maybe you'll see how if you ever manage to get in combat yourself. And survive. Sir." Okay, I was way out of line, even though his jibe was a dig at me, but I couldn't stop myself. It wasn't the first time I had sounded off out of turn, and I wouldn't make book on it being the last.

Wellman got to his feet slowly, leaning on his desk with his long, pickpocket fingers until he was nearly all the way up. He didn't have to get all the way up to be taller than me, but he stretched out to his full six feet four inches—eight inches taller than me. I could see his face go from its usual pasty white to a brilliant crimson. "You've got three hours to report to the flitter port for transportation to West Memphis. You are not to discuss your orders with anyone while in transit. Have fun playing with the lizards and monkeys. Now get out of here before I have your orders rewritten to send you out as a corporal."

I got out, without bothering to salute. As soon as Wellman's door was closed behind me, I let out a long breath . . . and realized I was sweating like a pig. Fritz got up from his desk and picked up several sheets of paper.

"These were delivered right after you went in," he said, handing the papers to me. "The 1st Combined Regiment—what's that?"

I shrugged. "Some bright idea the brass came up with, putting soldiers from all the Alliance peoples together, down to the battalion level, from what *he* said." I jerked my head toward Wellman's door. "I get to be one of the guinea pigs to see if it works. I've got three hours." No, I hadn't forgotten the major's warning not to discuss my orders with anyone, but if Fritz wasn't safe, no one was. In any case, Wellman had merely said that I wasn't to discuss my orders with anyone *in transit,* and I hadn't left yet. I can split hairs with the best latrine lawyer ever born.

"Just remember to keep your head and your butt down," Fritz said, sticking out a hand. I nodded and we shook hands.

MY ORDERS JUST SAID THAT I WAS TO REPORT to the troop movements office at the spaceport outside West Memphis that evening for transport to the space station at Over-Galapagos for further transport to someplace with the code name Dancer. I went to the armory to turn in my weapons and electronic gear, dropped by the personnel section to pick up the data chip with my personnel and medical records, then hitched a ride back to the barracks. Packing didn't take long. I was a bachelor living on base, and six months hadn't been long enough to accumulate much excess baggage. I filled my duffel bag and one suitcase—all I was permitted, according to the orders—and set them next to the door of my room. I had time for a meal before I signed out. If you've got the chance, always eat before you leave. You never know when you'll get an opportunity in transit, and the food might be even worse than what you're used to.

Fritz found me in the mess hall. "I've got a crawler lined up to take you to the flitter strip," he said, sitting across from me. "I asked around, trying to find out about this unit you're going to." He shook his head. "I didn't have much luck. Everything about it is classified. The most I could come up with is that all of the armies are sending their soldiers to some frontier world to train together. After this training period is complete, the big shots will evaluate the results and decide whether the unit is fit for combat."

"Or something only useful to show civilians how well the alliance works," I said.

"No doubt. Just take care of yourself."

"Yeah. You too. The way this war is going, they're going to get all of us out somewhere with our butts hanging out."

EARTH AND MOST OF THE WORLDS HUMANS have settled belong to the Alliance of Light. We had been colonizing worlds for more than a hundred years before we ran into another sentient species. That must be some sort of record for stumbling around in a crowd and not bumping into anyone. Then we learned that there are at least another ten sentient, spacefaring peoples in our stretch of the Galaxy. We joined the Alliance so fast it could have made your head spin. Since we weren't "alone" any longer, we didn't want to be the odd people on the outside. We had to be part of the group. It was only after joining that we learned the Alliance of Light didn't speak for all the settled worlds and all the sentient species. There was another group, the Ilion Federation, and the two alliances did not get along at all well. For myself, I figure we joined the right alliance, but that was pure luck—happenstance. Over the years, a few human worlds did switch sides, mostly because of political beefs.

The political and social situations get confusing. The

Alliance of Light and the Ilion Federation had both started out as trading associations, and neither has a really powerful central government yet—though the Ilion Federation comes a lot closer, since it is dominated by one species, the tonatin. And since the tonatin majority doesn't want any competition the rest of the Ilion Federation has little choice but to go along with the tonatin's plans to wipe out the Alliance. I don't think any of the sentient species are all members of one group or the other, except the divotect—their six worlds were all in the Alliance of Light . . . and three of those worlds had been captured by the Ilion Federation. That was what had precipitated the war, and cost me more friends than any man can stand to lose. I'm not completely certain why the Ilion Federation struck the divotect worlds first. Maybe the propaganda we get is right, that the tonatin were on a genocidal tear against the divotect—the only lizardlike sentient species. Or maybe they attacked the divotect first simply to weaken the Alliance of Light, thinking (rightly or wrongly) that the other species would be less likely to risk their own people for the divotect than any of the other species in the Alliance.

Both the Alliance and the Federation are political conglomerations, originally established to foster trade among the worlds rather than being based on race or species. That isn't to say that there is no bigotry among species. There is, in just about every direction. That's what I got to thinking about during the short flitter ride to West Memphis. They were going to put all of the species together in one unit, where humans, divotect, porracci, abarand, biraunta, ghuroh—and who knew how many other species—would have to work together, back each other up, try to keep each other alive. It looked like a disaster just waiting to happen.

I had a headache before we landed at the spaceport.

UNTIL THAT DAY I HAD NEVER PUT MUCH STOCK in the medals they had given me after the slaughter on Dintsen. Counselors had helped me through what they say is a fairly normal feeling of grief and guilt at surviving when many of those around you didn't. That still hasn't stopped the nightmares, but now I can deal with it when they wake me in a cold sweat, shaking with worse fear than I felt when it was really happening. It wasn't guilt that made me indifferent to the medals, maybe just a feeling that I hadn't done anything special. In addition to the automatic awards—the Battle Star for being in combat and the Purple Heart for being wounded—most of the dozen surviving noncoms and all three surviving officers were awarded the Star of Gallantry, the second-highest decoration the human armies award. We fought as if the Devil were biting us on the ass because the alternative was waiting for the tonatin regiment that hit us to kill us at their leisure. That is what they did with those humans and divotect they captured alive. Every last one.

Hearing Major Wellman voice what I had thought more than once changed my mind. Maybe it was pure obstinacy, but I figured that Wellman was wrong so often that if he said I didn't deserve the medals, it was odds-on that I *did*, one way or another. On the short flitter flight across the Mississippi I found myself wishing I had taken time to put the bar with the ribbons on my uniform for the trip. I promised myself that I'd get them out of my suitcase at the spaceport—if I had time.

The way it worked out, I didn't. I reported where I

was supposed to and got hurried off to a boarding gate and had to check my duffel and suitcase immediately. Half a dozen other soldiers had already arrived—a couple had been there six hours—and we were herded out to a bus five minutes after I checked in. Only one man arrived after me. We were put under the temporary command of the senior man—a Captain Johnstone—and warned not to discuss what we were doing or where we were going, even among ourselves. We boarded the shuttle through one hatch while our luggage was pushed through another, got our seats, strapped in, and sat there—all pretty much in silence.

The shuttle was a standard transport model that could hold sixty men and ten or twelve tons of cargo, not an assault craft. The fact that it was sealed up for takeoff with only eight passengers seemed unusual. The military is usually too cheap to waste money like that. A shuttle burns almost as much fuel empty as full.

I looked around at my fellow passengers. A couple of them I knew slightly from previous postings, but most were strangers. The only one I knew well was Antonio Xeres, a platoon sergeant. He looked as if he had just stepped out of a recruiting poster—the image of the adventure-vid soldier: tall, strong, and handsome, with a chin that looked as if it had been carved from granite; the kind of man mamas would trust their sons to. Tonio was an old friend. He had been on Dintsen as well, one of only three men in his platoon who had survived. If it hadn't been for those three men, probably no one would have made it off Dintsen. Each of them had earned the Order of the Golden Galaxy, the top military medal for heroism in the Alliance.

Tonio and I stared at each other. We were too far apart for comfortable conversation, but I could read a lot in his eyes, and I'm sure he saw as much in mine. We had both been to the edge of hell and—by the grace of God or a kind Fate—made it back when a lot of others didn't. That kind of tie is thicker than blood. Blood spills.

The mutual stare ended when the shuttle pilot announced that we would take off in thirty seconds. She told us to make certain our safety harnesses were fastened, and to stay put until we docked. "If you didn't do what you had to do before, it's too late now," she said. Well, I hadn't thought of that before, and there hadn't been time anyway. I wished she had kept her mouth shut, because once she put the idea in my head . . . It would have been one thing had we only been heading for a ship in low orbit. That kind of trip takes little more than a half hour usually, but we were going all the way to geostationary orbit, more than 22,000 miles out, and that meant at least ninety minutes, perhaps two hours, if we made a standard, economical once-around-the-world ascent to Over-Galapagos.

A ride in a military transport shuttle is not the same as a ride in a civilian shuttle. Civilians pay their way and expect a certain degree of comfort. We were grunts whose expectations and desires didn't count. The shuttle taxied to the end of the runway, hesitated for ten seconds while the pilot ran the jets to full throttle, then we got shoved into our seat padding as she released the brakes and we hurtled forward. Five seconds later, the nose of the shuttle lifted to about fifty degrees. Another ten seconds and the pilot cut in the main rockets and I felt all the blood running to my back.

The intense acceleration lasted for three minutes, then eased until I only felt twice my normal weight and could think of things other than being squashed to a pancake while my blood squirted out from under my toenails. I guessed that we were going to make a direct burn for Over-Galapagos and not the fuel-conserving full-orbit route. Someone sure felt a sense of urgency about getting us wherever we were going. It's not just that we were burning fuel like it grew on trees. Taking a shot like that, direct from the spaceport just outside West Memphis to the big habitat at Over-Galapagos meant rerouting any other air and space vehicles out of the way—including *civilian* vehicles.

At least it meant that we could count on a relatively short ride, fifty minutes or so, allowing for the usual back and fill of docking at the end. I closed my eyes and practiced taking normal breaths. I didn't expect to get any sleep, but I could rest. Maybe once we got to O-G we'd learn where we were going.

OVER-GALAPAGOS IS THE LARGEST SPACE HAB-itat in our Solar System and the oldest continually inhabited. The first section was built years before we figured out the hyperspace drive that let us get out of the system. Initially O-G was designed to be a scientific and industrial complex, as well as a way station for travel to the Moon, Mars, and the asteroids, with workers and their families living on-station for no more than a year at a time. As the habitat grew, O-G developed a more or less permanent population. The complex was kept spinning enough to simulate Earth gravity on the outer levels, so people could come and go, and not get so used to low-gee that they would be permanent exiles from the ground. Once we became interstellar-capable, O-G became Earth's major transportation hub, connecting us to the rest of the Galaxy. The military established a more open presence, especially after we joined the Alliance of Light. By the start of the war with the Ilion Federation two hundred years later, the permanent population of O-G was thirty thousand, and there were usually several thousand transients, many of them military.

I had passed through O-G several times before but had never seen much more than the launching hub and the military ring on the far end of the complex. This time wasn't any different. As soon as we docked, we were shunted through to the military barracks and assigned rooms. Tonio and I paired up. I hoped that he knew more about what we were in for than I did.

"I never heard about it before this morning," Tonio said once we were alone. Neither of us unpacked more than what we needed for the night and a change of clothes for morning. We didn't worry about disobeying the order not to discuss our travel orders, not in private, between us. Trust Tonio with my life?—hell, the man had *saved* my life. How much closer a bond can two people share? "The old man told me they needed veterans for a special unit and wanted combat veterans, and he asked me to volunteer." He shrugged. "I figured maybe it would give me a chance to get a little payback."

I was in the middle of telling him how I came to be there when the comm unit told us that supper was being served and showed us a map to guide us to the mess hall. We had both been in the army long enough to know better than to miss a meal, so the conversation was tabled. We would obey orders where there was any chance of someone else hearing.

MESS CALL WAS A BIT OF A DODGE. WE DID GET fed—and the food was better than what I was used to—

but we also had to sit through a five-minute spiel from a light colonel whose face was the same color as the tasteless mashed potatoes that had been plopped on our trays. The first thing we were told—again—was not to discuss our orders with anyone, even among ourselves, until we got where we were going, and we weren't to speculate on where that might be. Blah, blah, blah. The informative part was that we had only a short night ahead of us in O-G; reveille would be at 0400 hours and we would board ship at 0515 hours. "Eat, get what sleep you can, and be ready to move in the morning," the light colonel said.

Tonio and I looked at each other and shrugged. Well, we did know more than we had before. It wasn't much of a surprise that we were going out so quickly. Everything so far had been done at the rush. For once it looked as if the army—and the space navy—had forgotten the ancient axiom of "Hurry up and wait."

"Fine with me," I said. "The sooner we get wherever we're going, the sooner the minny-moe crap stops." Somebody at the table snorted what I took to be agreement, but that was it.

It wasn't until we were moved to the out-bound docks in the morning that we learned that the eight of us who had come up from West Memphis weren't the only passengers going out. *That* would have been too extreme, even for our military. Altogether there were sixty officers and men going as passengers on the ship. Some of them had been at O-G as long as twenty hours. The last shuttleload arrived an hour before we were mustered to board the ship. The ship—it only had a number, not a name—also carried cargo, but we didn't learn that until we got to Dancer and everything was unloaded. Still, with only sixty passengers in a ship that could have carried a thousand, we had a lot of room—not that the trip was long enough to make that important.

It's almost faster to travel between star systems a hundred light-years apart than it is to get from downtown New York to downtown Memphis. The ship makes its first transit of hyperspace within an hour after leaving the dock. There can be two to six hyperspace transits during a trip, and each of those takes no more than ten or fifteen seconds of subjective time, separated by five or ten minutes in normal space while the computers confirm the ship's current location and calculate the next jump. Then you come out of hyperspace after the last transit within an hour or two of your destination—or a lot closer if you're heading in for a combat assault.

I STILL DON'T KNOW THE LISTED NAME OF THE world that was waiting when we came out of hyperspace the last time, or where it is. Dancer is the only name we were ever given. From the brief glance I had on a monitor while we were moving toward the shuttle bays, there didn't seem to be anything extraordinary about Dancer. It was a lot like Earth—which stood to reason, since we had to be able to survive on it. Land, liquid water, clouds. There was more water than land, and the temperature ranges were not much different from what they are on Earth. The air was a lot cleaner than Earth's, and it smelled better.

That is pretty much the limit of nice things I can say about the place. As soon as the ship reached a low parking orbit we were transferred to a shuttle with our bags and a couple of tons of other cargo and were sent on our way.

WE LANDED SOMEWHERE IN THE NORTHERN subtropical zone of Dancer's largest continent, at what appeared to be an hour or two past noon. It was summer: hot—well above ninety degrees Fahrenheit—and humid. By the time I got down the short ramp from the shuttle to the springy turf of an open field I was drenched in sweat. The air was heavy, almost junglelike.

No one seemed to know what the hell to do with us. We were rushed off the shuttle as if it were in a hurry to take off again. The passenger hatch was sealed. We were told to grab our bags and move away from the craft. The crew chief merely gestured vaguely off to the side and mumbled that someone was supposed to be there to collect us. Several air cushion trucks pulled up to receive the heavy cargo the shuttle was carrying. I looked up and saw another shuttle on its way in—one of the big cargo carriers.

Looking up was less discouraging than looking at what was on the ground. There were a lot of temporary buildings, starting fifty yards from the unimproved landing strip. The nearest buildings were large, inflatable jobs—about forty feet by eighty—that turned out to be warehouses. Past them were a dozen inflatable buildings about half as large—offices and quarters for senior officers. Beyond those were the tents—mess halls, field offices, and squad tents.

"I don't see our four-star hotel," Tonio said. "I do believe we've been dumped beyond the edge of nowhere."

"No porters or buses either," I replied. "Not even a pretty girl to tell us where to go."

"I've got a sneaking suspicion there isn't a pretty girl anywhere on this world," Tonio said. "I think the brass found a world with no local sentients, a place where they can lose us proper. Want to bet against me?"

"Not even a penny." I gave him a theatrical sigh. "Good thing we've got officers with us. We don't have to worry about how long we stand here with our thumbs up our butts before we go looking for someone to tell us what to do. Let them do the worrying. That's what they get the big bucks for."

Tonio ignored that. He kept looking around, the same way I did. "I don't see anyone but humans" he said after a minute.

"I always hate to be early for a party." I nodded toward the buildings. "I think I see our welcoming committee." Two men were coming toward us, walking fast but awkwardly, as if they didn't want to dirty their nicely shined boots. There was a lot of mud around. "Maybe we'll find out what the hell's going on."

THE TWO MEN REACHED US. ONE, A MAJOR, took the officers aside for introductions and handshakes. The other man, a mere JL, junior lieutenant, came to a halt twenty feet from the largest grouping of enlisted personnel, as if he didn't want to contaminate himself by getting *too* close. "Listen up!" he said—not *quite* in a shout. We moved in his direction, coming closer together. "I've got your unit assignments. Sound off when I call your name."

The list was alphabetical by rank. I was about in the middle. Company B, Ranger Battalion. By whatever stroke of luck or chance, Tonio had drawn the same company. We were the only two. The JL went through the entire list before he told any of us where our companies might be located . . . emphasis on the *might*. Tonio and I picked up our bags and started walking. Our company was—supposedly—located off to the right and near the far end of the rows of tents, about half a mile away.

I wasn't surprised to learn that the JL didn't know his right from his left. Tonio and I made almost a full tour of the camp before we found Company B, Ranger Battalion, 1st Combined Regiment. It *was* at the far end, but on the left, not the right. We had to ask where the orderly room was, and the first two soldiers we talked to didn't know. They spent a couple of minutes arguing it between themselves. We found it, eventually, and reported to the officer holding down the desk.

"Welcome to the boondocks," the officer, Senior Lieutenant George Fusik, said as he returned our salutes. "We're nowhere near full complement yet. We don't have all the humans assigned to the company here, and none of the other species has landed."

"Sir?" Tonio said, interrupting. He apologized for that before he continued. "I was told that the integration was going to be at the battalion level, and I assumed that meant that we would all be humans in the company."

Fusik gave us what I guess you'd call a wry smile and shook his head gently. "That's what I was told, too, before I got here. Most of the regiment will be integrated at the company level; each company will be homogeneous, except for liaison personnel, with each battalion consisting of companies from different species. But they decided to carry the experiment to the extreme in Ranger Battalion. The integration will run all the way to the

squad level, four to six different races in each squad.
Our basic organization will be as special operations
squads, emphasis on small unit tactics. I know you've
both done SOS duty before, and you've both seen combat. It's in your records. Xeres, you'll be first platoon's
platoon sergeant. Drak, you'll lead that platoon's first
squad. My clerk should be back in a minute or two. I'll
have him give you the nickel tour, show you where to
bunk and where to draw your weapons and other gear.
Get settled in and take the rest of the afternoon to find
your way around. By tomorrow morning maybe we'll
have enough people in to start doing something more
constructive."

Tonio and I saluted and left the tent. I turned through
a slow circle. Next to me, Tonio did pretty much the
same thing. When we came back face to face, I shook
my head. Tonio grinned. "Really homey, huh?" he
asked.

I made a face. "This looks like a major disaster just
waiting to happen. All we need is a big foot to come
down out of the sky and squish us all into the mud."

CHAPTER 2

OH, YES, THE MUD. UNDER THAT NICE, springy carpet of curly grass the ground was saturated. Your feet sank into it and squished, and anywhere that got any real traffic, the thin, wiry grass was quickly beaten into a garnish on mud soup. It wasn't that bad—comparatively—when we first landed on Dancer, but as more men came in, it got worse in a hurry. It started raining before Tonio and I got our gear and moved into our tents, across the "street" from each other. I don't mean a gentle shower, either; we got four inches of rain in an hour. By the time I was done with the necessary running around, I was muddy halfway up to my knees. My impulse was to change into a clean uniform, but I was going to have to go out again shortly—for supper—so I hesitated. Laundry facilities were likely to be primitive, if they existed at all, and I didn't have all that many uniforms.

"Try to make a good impression," I told myself. No one else from my squad had arrived—only twenty of the thirty-nine humans assigned to the company had reached Dancer—so I had a ten-man tent to myself. "This is your first day and the CO seems like a decent sort." I didn't know Lieutenant Fusik, but the name was trying to kick a memory loose. I couldn't force the memory out of whatever recess of my mind it was hiding in, though. I put it aside, telling myself to ask Tonio when I got a chance. Then I changed clothes. As it worked out, it was a couple of weeks before I asked Tonio about Fusik.

There were no lockers to store anything in, so I didn't have any real unpacking. I made my bed—a folding cot with an air mattress. The pillow was only a little thicker than two pieces of cloth sewn together, but it would give me something to wrap around my head at night. I glanced at my watch, which I had reset after the company clerk gave me the correct local time. Supper was two hours off. The rain had stopped, at least, and the sun was steaming everything. It felt hotter than ever.

I had been in the army ten years and a few odd months. I knew what to do with spare time. I sacked out . . . and even managed to get a little sleep, despite the heat and humidity.

BY THE TIME I WOKE FROM MY NAP NINETY minutes later, four more ships had arrived and started unloading personnel and materiel. The big ships never touch ground, never enter atmosphere; they're not built for that. Dozens of shuttles were going between ships and the landing strip. On the ground, everyone below the rank of sergeant had been dragooned into working parties to get crates unloaded and moved into the warehouses—or stacked in the open with huge, supposedly waterproof tarps to cover them—with the occasional sergeant to boss a work detail. Somehow I got missed. I hadn't seen much in the way of power-moving gear before, just a few motorized wagons, so most of the energy expended was human.

I learned later that there had been nothing at all on the site of our camp four days earlier, and the world had only been visited by exploration patrols three times before. Engineers had come in and drilled wells, laid plumbing, and so forth. The camp had been surveyed and the first buildings and tents erected. Weapons ranges had been laid out. There were still engineers on site, but a lot of the rest of the work was going to be left to us. Conditions were just barely short of spinning into chaos. Snafu.

The other human assigned to my squad arrived. Lance Corporal Fred Wilkins had been in the army a little over two years and was twenty years old. He had never seen combat. That wasn't particularly surprising. The war was only eight months old, and the only humans who had seen action in it were those of us who had been caught on Dintsen. The only combat any humans had seen during the previous two decades had been small-scale counter insurgency operations, like the so-called Paul Bunyan Rebellion in the Pacific Northwest, and that had faded out six years back. Wilkins was three inches taller than me, thin, with black hair and eyes that were such a dark brown they were almost black. After we introduced ourselves, I pointed him to the bunk next to mine.

"Welcome to Bedlam," I said as he tossed his duffel bag on the cot. "Don't bother asking what's going on because nobody knows."

He sat on the cot. "I got that impression." He shook his head. "The shuttle I was in damn near collided with another boat. I swear, we came within two feet of each other. I could hear our pilot screaming at the other one."

"Doesn't surprise me. Everything else is fouled up here. Lieutenant Fusik brief you?"

Wilkins shook his head. "Just told me I was assigned to you, and the clerk showed me where to go."

"For the record, this is first squad, first platoon, B Company, Ranger Battalion, 1st Combined Regiment," I said. "Spec ops. I'm the squad leader, and you're the only other member of the squad who's arrived. The way I understand it, you and I will be the only humans in the squad."

"You've got to be kidding!" Wilkins said.

"I'm not. The organization is SOS, and we'll have one or two soldiers from each of the other participating species in the squad. The whole battalion is going to be like that. That's why they gave us translator plugs when we got our gear." I tapped my right ear. The plug sits just outside the ear canal and is supposed to give you instantaneous interpretation of any language programmed into it. "By the way, put yours in now before you forget." I waited until he had attached the buttonlike device before I continued.

"You'll be assistant leader of the squad's first fire team—unless I get orders to do it differently. I don't know when the rest of the squad is going to show up, but the lieutenant seemed to think that most of the regiment will be here in the next three days and the soldiers for this battalion were supposed to arrive first to get in a little extra training."

"Just tell me one thing, Sarge. Is this setup as crazy as I think it is?"

I shrugged. "Probably, but we're still going to have to do our damnedest to make it work."

THE COMPANY'S MESS TENT WAS FAIRLY close, and since most of the company hadn't reported, there was no real line. All of the humans, at least, had arrived. I didn't get a chance to talk to Tonio. He ate with Lieutenant Fusik and a porracci junior lieutenant, Krau'vi Taivana, who was to be the company's executive officer, second in command. That was the first time I had ever seen a porracci up close.

Back home, media reports always say that porracci look like orangutans, but the resemblance is really vague. The arms aren't as long nor the legs as short as orangutans'. Krau'vi Taivana had pale golden fur, clipped to about an inch in length. The skin on his face and the palms of his hands was a very light ocher, almost ivory in color. He stood 5 feet, 2 inches tall and weighed about 350 pounds. His fingers looked to be about twice as long as mine, but I've got relatively short fingers, even for a human.

The two officers ate quickly, even though one or the other of them appeared to be talking constantly. Having officers in the room cramped the style of most of the enlisted men. We kept our conversations soft. We ate, and we watched the officers for any clue. I wasn't close enough to hear anything they said, but I figured I'd get anything important soon enough. If nothing else, Tonio would keep me filled in. Apart from our friendship, as first squad leader I was his *de facto* assistant as platoon sergeant, supposed to be kept in the loop enough to take over his job if anything happened to him.

The food was better than it might have been, but nothing to write home about. It was edible, plentiful, and the coffee was hot and strong. That's about all a soldier can ask of his victuals. There seemed to be no rush about eating, so I took my time. Even so, I was nearly finished when Tonio and the two officers got up and moved toward the back of the tent—where the serving line was.

"May I have your attention," Lieutenant Fusik said. Everyone turned to look at him. The porracci stood at Fusik's right, Tonio at his left. "I know you've got a lot of questions." *That* was certainly a Galaxy-class under-statement. "New personnel, new unit, new camp, new world." Fusik gave us a weak smile. "Things appear rather chaotic." Very brief pause for effect. "All right, they *are* chaotic." That earned him a few polite chuckles. "I can't answer all your questions, mostly because I haven't been given the answers yet, but I expect I can give you a little more information than you have so far." As if *that* would be some accomplishment.

"I anticipate that the situation will remain hectic, con-fused, for at least the next several days—by the way, the day here is twenty-eight hours long, give or take a few minutes—but we'll get organized and on some sort of rational schedule as quickly as we can. Reveille will be at oh-seven-hundred hours tomorrow, which—if the information I have is correct—will be twenty minutes before sunrise. The bulk of the personnel for the battal-ion should be here within the next thirty hours, and we will start training operations the day after tomorrow. We will have at least four months of training before the higher-ups come in to evaluate our performance and de-cide how to employ the regiment." The smile left his face. "I'm certain the war will still be waiting for us when we finish training." He paused so long that I started to think he was done.

"This is a new situation for all of us. The decision to integrate the Alliance species so closely is going to add problems none of us have ever had to face before. Each sentient species has its own history, customs . . . pecca-dilloes. We're going to need a lot of mutual tolerance and understanding while we learn about each other. Our job will be that much harder if we start bickering and fighting within the unit. It will be up to the officers and noncoms to make sure we don't have that sort of problem. Part of the solution is open and continuous communication, or as close to that as we can come. Lieutenant Taivana and I, and the rest of our officers once they arrive, will be available as much as possible. For the time being I'll do my best to address the company regularly, and I'll share as much information as I can. I expect my officers and noncoms to do their part. We'll have specialists to help us learn about the other species and to help deal with any difficulties. We have to make this unit combat-ready in four months, gentlemen, and that is not going to leave time for unnecessary distractions."

I felt like crying in my beer, except I didn't have any beer, or anything alcoholic, to drink or to cry in. I hoped they had whoever dreamed up this scheme safely tucked away in a room with padded walls and floor so he couldn't hurt himself.

A TWENTY-EIGHT-HOUR DAY—FOURTEEN HOURS OF daylight, fourteen hours of night. I wasn't too worried about the length of the day. It was longer than the day on any of the worlds I had been on, but humans are adaptable, and soldiers learn to sleep whenever they can. With a big rush to get us ready for combat in four months, we might still end up short on sleep. Regularly.

Dancer had two moons. The first was a little smaller than Earth's Moon, but it was enough closer that it looked larger, and it completed an orbit in twenty hours. The second moon was a rock fifteen miles in diameter, and it managed a little more than two orbits in a day.

The word we had from regimental headquarters was that the orbits were stable so we didn't have to worry about a moon falling on us. Not being a rocket scientist, I had to take their word for it. I was going to have enough other things to worry about.

After supper, Fred Wilkins and I spent a little time cleaning our weapons, getting rid of the packing grease they had carried, and making certain the actions worked. Human armies use three separate infantry rifles, the mix differing from regiment to regiment. The battalion armorer had all three available. Wilkins and I both chose 4.8mm slug throwers. The bullet is depleted uranium, and the liquid propellant gives it a muzzle velocity about twice the speed of sound, so your target is dead long before he has a chance to hear the "bang" . . . if your aim is good. The double-drum magazine gives you a hundred bangs before you have to reload, and if you hold the trigger down you can pop those hundred rounds out in eight seconds. The other two rifle types are a needle gun and a beamer, an energy weapon. As a non-com, I was also entitled to a sidearm. There is only one standard pistol in the human armies, a needle gun, and it's just what the name says. It fires half-inch-long needles, also of depleted uranium, in small batches, like a shotgun. The effective range is about sixty yards, but within that range it can turn a target into hamburger.

Each species was going to bring its own weapons. With the physical differences, that stood to reason. We weren't even going to have identical uniforms—even allowing for anatomical variations among species. Everyone would use what they had, what they were used to. Eventually, the armorer told me, we would get some sort of uniformity in weapons and uniforms, providing the experiment worked and the regiment was actually employed. He expressed considerable doubts on that score. "I figure we've got four months to waste, maybe less, before they throw up their hands and send us back to our own people. Then we can get on with the real work of winning this war" was the way he put it.

IT WAS ABOUT 2130 HOURS WHEN THE COMpany clerk came into the squad tent and told Wilkins that he had the duty as Charge of Quarters for the night and led him off to the orderly room. An hour later I was in the sack, ready for sleep. Maybe I hadn't done a heck of a lot, but tropical heat and humidity can sap energy out of you faster than work. I wasn't looking forward to morning. My guess was that the confusion would really get intense then. I was wrong. It started sooner. I was wakened just after 2700 hours. Two more members of my squad had arrived.

"There are about three dozen porracci on their way to the company from the landing strip," Fred Wilkins said once he had shaken me awake. He was carrying a small lantern that gave out a ghostly light. "Two of them are for our squad. The SL's orders are to rouse you for anyone coming into our squad. Sergeant Xeres will get the others settled."

"You mean draw their gear and everything?" I asked after fighting my way past a yawn. I sat up slowly, feeling absolutely cruddy with sweat and the remnants of sleep.

"Bedding and so forth. The porracci are carrying their weapons and everything else."

"How long do I have?"

"Not more than two or three minutes."

"Crap." I closed my eyes for an instant and tried to

yawn myself awake. "Okay. I'll be out there as fast as I can."

As Wilkins left the tent, I reached for the fresh fatigue uniform I had laid out before going to bed and got into it, then pulled my boots on and sealed the tongue flaps. I was still yawning as I put on my cap and headed for the door of the tent.

I was surprised at how bright it was outside. It wasn't just that Dancer's larger moon was nearly full, though that contributed to the effect. The engineers had strung a lot of outdoor lighting, and it was all on. I won't say that the camp was as light as broad daylight, but I could have read by it without straining my eyes. I stood in front of the squad tent and went through a few seconds of vigorous stretching, as much to get my mind alert as to work the kinks out of my joints. There had been no nighttime cooling to speak of. The temperature still had to be above eighty, and there was virtually no breeze. The air was heavy and damp, oppressive. I told myself that I had better get used to it. Conditions weren't likely to get any easier over the next four months.

The porracci members of the company came trotting down the muddy lane toward the orderly room tent in formation. They carried rifles, field gear, and baggage— maybe 150 pounds per man, twice what a human soldier would be expected to carry—and none of them seemed to notice the load. Well, I had been told that they were much stronger than humans, the way the great apes of Earth were before the last of them went extinct. When the porracci got to where Tonio and Lieutenant Taivana were waiting, they fell into formation without orders. None of them set down any of the baggage they were carrying.

Impressive show, I thought; *what do you do for an encore?*

Lieutenant Taivana talked to them for several minutes, sort of a pep talk with frequent graphic threats of extreme bodily harm for failure or disobedience. Taivana reminded them that they were to obey the orders of all superiors regardless of race, again with threats that he would personally do great physical damage to anyone who failed to do what they were supposed to do. Within porracci culture, dominance is still a physical thing, part of everything they do. The pecking order gets established on the line of who's the meanest SOB in the group. It was a few days later before I realized that the porracci who end up in their army do so because they were not the dominant males in their own extended families. The alpha male always remains behind, in charge of all the rest, the only one who gets to enjoy the sexual favors of the breeding females. Maybe porracci soldiers have the reputation of being among the best in the galaxy because of that combination of sexual frustration and some hope that they might get good enough in the army to go home and become number one in their family troop.

Taivana ended his harangue with a roll call, giving each porracci his assignment. The names all sounded alike to me then, even with the translator button, but two of the porracci were named to my squad, then turned and trotted over toward me. They stood at attention again, still without setting anything down.

"Corporal Ying'vi Souvana reporting for duty, Sergeant," the larger of the two said, his voice a belligerent growl that lost nothing in translation. Souvana was just barely over 5 feet tall and appeared to weigh about 320 pounds. Where Lieutenant Taivana's fur was a very pale gold, almost a washed-out tan, Souvana's was a brilliant

gold, except where patches were missing—scars of dominance challenges in his past, I later learned. Souvana
did not give in easily.

"Lance Corporal Trau'vi Kiervauna," the other porracci said. Kiervauna sounded almost meek compared to
Souvana and bore no visible scars. From one of the ori-
entation lectures I sat through, I learned that was probably because Kiervauna had always accepted the fact
that he was not going to be dominant and had never
challenged anyone. His fur was almost a chocolate
brown, and he weighed perhaps 290 pounds and was
about an inch shorter than Souvana.

"I'm Sergeant Bart Drak," I said. "Good to have you
both here. Corporal Souvana, you'll lead the squad's
second fire team and be my second in command. Lance
Corporal Kiervauna, you'll be assistant leader of the second fire team." Souvana growled and made a clucking
noise with his tongue against his teeth—a porracci af-
firmative.

"Yes, Sergeant," Kiervauna said, carefully waiting until Souvana had finished before he spoke.

I took them into the squad tent and told them to put
their gear on the first two bunks on the left. Souvana
hesitated—for about half a second, just enough to be
noticeable—before he complied. Kiervauna obeyed so
quickly he almost anticipated what I said. Then I took
them to draw bedding. While we did that, I told them
what little I knew about the situation. They listened but
asked no questions.

The two porracci made me feel . . . uneasy. I guess
that's the word. I was considerably taller than either of
them—though I'm a bit below average height for a human—but both of them outweighed me by a considerable margin. Barehanded, I doubted that I could take

either of them in a fair fight—not that I would let myself be restricted by notions of what was or wasn't "fair" if it ever came to that. Size isn't everything in unarmed combat. I don't think it was xenophobia that made me uneasy. While I had never been around porracci before, I *had* been around aliens, especially divotect, and *their* ancestry is lizardlike, the only known sentients to evolve from reptiles rather than mammals. The divotect are really different, and I was able to work with them without qualms once I got used to being around them. Porracci were much closer to humans on the comparative evolutionary charts; maybe that was why they seemed more of a threat.

I had trouble getting to sleep after the porracci bedded down. It wasn't that I feared one of them might slit my throat while I slept. My mind simply needed time to turn itself off. I did get back to sleep eventually, though it was not as easy a sleep as before; I tossed and turned, and woke several times.

IT WAS JUST AFTER 0400 HOURS WHEN WIL-kins woke me again. The two porracci were awake before Fred got me to open my eyes. "We've got more . . . people coming in, Sarge," he whispered. "Biraunta this time, monkey men."

"None of that crap," I said, sitting up. "I don't ever want to hear biraunta called that in this squad again. No slurs against *any* of the species. Understand?"

Wilkins went stiff before he said, "I understand."

"This is going to be tough enough without that," I said, softening my voice a little. "I know it's just a habit, but it's a bad habit, and we've all got to make sure we don't fall into the trap." I guess I was reminding myself as well as Wilkins.

"It's been a long night, Sarge," Wilkins said.

I got up and dressed again. I could understand Wilkins using the slur "monkey men." Heaven knows I had thought about biraunta that way myself often enough. I had never met one, but of course I had seen videos and holos. To a Terran, the comparison is almost inescapable. Think five-foot-tall spider monkeys, complete with prehensile tails. Those tails are functional, though they complicate life for biraunta tailors—okay, that's a bad pun. Biraunta remain partly arboreal; they're as comfortable in the trees as on the ground. There is very little variation in size among adult biraunta—about five feet tall and seventy-five pounds. Their fur runs from dark brown to black, often with white or beige faces and palms. The eyes are either blue or green and look almost feline.

Tonio Xeres handled the briefing this time. Although the biraunta, twelve of them assigned to the company, were supposed to be at attention, they fidgeted endlessly, tails coiling and uncoiling, moving from one foot to the other, looking around almost constantly. I found it distracting. I eventually had to look away before they started me fidgeting as well.

Two biraunta were assigned to my squad, and the general difficulty of telling biraunta apart was multiplied in this case. Privates Iyi Col Hihi and Oyo Col Hihi were identical twins. Both had emerald green eyes and a rim of white facial fur between bare skin and their black body and scalp fur.

The biraunta had carried little in the way of clothing or gear. They're so light that they can't carry as much as porracci can. They could carry nearly as much as a human, despite the fact that they weighed less than half what the average human soldier weighs, but not for as long. The rest of their things had been delivered. I had to get them equipped after we deposited what they did have with them in the squad tent.

I started learning about biraunta very quickly. When I opened the tent flap, both Iyi and Oyo screamed—loud, high-pitched, and penetrating. I think at least one of them had an accident as well. The smell was there.

"What is it?" I demanded, more than a little scared by the way they had both screamed, then cowered in obvious terror.

One of them pointed. Corporal Souvana was sitting on the edge of his bunk, just inside the tent.

"The porracci?" I asked, looking from Souvana back to the biraunta. "They're part of the squad. There are porracci in every squad." I thought, *Oh, great! Biraunta are terrified of porracci. Somebody should have thought of that before.* I squeezed my eyes shut for an instant. Biraunta make excellent scouts, especially in forested areas since they can move about faster in the trees than most folks can on the ground. I had intended to put one biraunta in each fire team. That obviously wasn't going to work, at least not immediately. I was going to have to put both of them in my fire team, and I wasn't certain *that* would work. I wasn't confident that we could ever get to the point where they could function well close to the porracci.

It took five minutes just to get the biraunta brothers into the tent, and they stayed as far from the porracci as possible. I put Iyi and Oyo in the bunks closest to those Wilkins and I had; then we went to get the rest of their gear and their weapons.

I didn't get back to sleep this time, even after the two

biraunta managed to whimper themselves to sleep, or at least to silence.

SOMEDAY, SOMEWHERE, SOME ARMY IS GOING to go through an operation in which everything happens according to plan, right on schedule. When that occurs, time itself will stop for a moment while the entire universe gasps in amazement. That perfect operation was definitely *not* the establishment of the combined regiment's training facility on Dancer. We provided a textbook example of all the things that could go wrong. I'll concede it could have been worse, though I'm not certain how.

The major problem in those first few days was the general reaction of biraunta to porracci. Absolute terror. Apparently the biraunta soldiers had not been told that they would be serving with porracci. The scene I had witnessed was repeated throughout the battalion. In some cases it was much worse. There was one fatality— not because a porracci had *done* anything, but because one biraunta apparently scared himself to death. A medical officer gave the cause of death as heart failure, without any official guess as to what had caused it. I don't know of a single case where any porracci offered so much as a veiled hint of a possible threat to a biraunta. The porracci attitude toward their much smaller cousins seemed to range between total indifference and silent contempt, but they were well disciplined and offered no resistance to serving with them. Finding a solution to the problem was pretty much up to the humans, and I'm sure we did more than our share of fumbling around in the process.

The second problem was scheduling. All of the humans, porracci, and biraunta had arrived—pretty much within a span of thirty hours. The rest of the troops—divotect, abarand, and especially ghuroh—were supposed to arrive that second day, along with a few liaison personnel from other species who weren't furnishing major armed contingents to the 1st Combined Regiment. Somehow timetables had been fouled up, and only the liaison people and a few specialists showed up in the three days following the arrival of the biraunta.

There was little point in beginning combat training with only half our personnel, so we didn't try. We spent the time trying to find some accommodation between the porracci and biraunta and pulling work details. When the rest of the troops did start arriving, I still wasn't sure that we could function. The biraunta remained scared half out of their wits around porracci, though they were—of necessity—getting used to the situation.

"We've got four months of training," Tonio reminded me as we ate breakfast together the third morning after the arrival of the biraunta. "That gives us plenty of time to get everyone working as a team." He didn't sound as if he really believed it, more as if he was just repeating the official line.

I looked around the mess hall. All of the porracci were on one side, the biraunta on the other, with the humans in the middle. "Does the phrase 'When pigs fly' come to mind?" I asked, very softly so that no one else would hear.

"Really, Bart," he said, and he sounded almost sincere. "Once all the contingents are here and we start training, the difficulties should pass in short order. There are some things porracci are good at, and other things biraunta can do that porracci can't. Once everyone sees that we're stronger as a team with the individual talents of each species exploited to best advantage, and the bir-aunta see that the porracci aren't going to do anything to them, the other stuff will fade."

I grunted. "I'll bet you've got your toes crossed."

"I'm serious," he insisted. "We get the mix complete and get our full stretch of training in, we'll have the best special ops squads any army has ever fielded. I've sat in on a few more briefing sessions than you have since we got here. There was some solid thinking behind the creation of this unit. It *can* work if we give it a chance."

EVEN OUR ROUTINE MORNING PHYSICAL TRAIN-ing got complicated with three species. Our requirements and abilities were too different for us to do the same routines and get as much out of them as we needed. Biraunta were extremely agile and fast, but they could not lift as much as humans—let alone porracci. Humans and porracci had almost the same running ability, and when it came to using overhead bars, we were better than porracci . . . but couldn't *begin* to compete with bir-aunta. Biraunta could use hands, feet, and tails, and when we put it to the test in one of the forested tracts near camp, we found that they could travel faster in the trees than humans or porracci could on the ground.

I think that was when I finally decided that *maybe* we could work together, though I still wouldn't have risked serious money on a wager. Once the biraunta saw that there was something they could regularly best porracci in, they lost some of the edge of their fear. And they turned out to be the stealthiest soldiers in the battalion. One thing we all turned out to be fairly even in was marksmanship—not just the first three species to make it to Dancer, but all of us. The weapons were different, obviously. The standard biraunta rifle was about as light as a toy plastic rifle for a human child and fired an extremely high-velocity 3.5mm slug. The porracci infantry rifle, on the other hand, fired a 15mm bullet, slower than the ammunition any of the other races fired but massively lethal. The porracci rifle weighed twice what my rifle did. Porracci and biraunta also used beamers, but not in the same numbers that human armies did. In each case the design of the beamer was similar to the design of the standard slug-thrower.

We did get a little serious training in other than physical conditioning during those first few days, but not much, mostly time on the firing ranges.

I HAD BEEN ON DANCER NEARLY FIVE FULL twenty-eight-hour days before the next two members of my squad reported. Their shuttles touched down a few minutes apart, and both reached the company area in the same group.

Private Jaibie was an abarand. The abarand derive from flying mammals but retain only rudimentary wings, suitable for no more than short glides. Abarand developed flying and spaceflight relatively early in their history. Except for the fact that abarand are exclusively bipedal and have no tails, they rather closely resemble Terran cheetahs, except that their heads look more canine than feline. They are almost totally hairless, their skin color tawny with dark brown spots. The hands and feet have only four digits. Jaibie was slightly over 6 feet tall and weighed about 130 pounds. He went into the squad's second fire team. Porracci did not fluster him. Nothing flustered Jaibie.

The other new arrival that day was Private Ooyonoa

Nuyi, a divotect. The description "a lizard standing on two feet" would be only moderately accurate, but it gives a good starting point. Divotect have heads something like Terran iguanas, loose folds of skin below the chin, and a rudimentary tail—normally encased in clothing rather than allowed to poke out the way biraunta tails are. Divotect are primarily bipedal, but they *can* get down and run on all fours. Nuyi's skin was almost purple, and he was about average in size for a divotect, 6 feet tall and 165 pounds. I took Nuyi into my fire team.

I had anticipated difficulties once the divotect arrived. They are the odd species out in the Alliance, the only reptilian sentients. They are also the least numerous sentient species, not particularly fertile, and they had spread to fewer worlds than the rest of us, even though they had been traveling in interstellar space longer than most species. I had worked through my own prejudiced ideas about divotect while I was training with them on Dintsen. I understood their drive for vengeance; to a certain extent, I shared it because I had been on Dintsen when the tonatin attack came, and I had lost a lot of good friends. But getting the rest of the members of my squad to accept Nuyi might prove as difficult as getting the biraunta to work with the porracci.

Well, I had all but two members of my squad, but even before we got Jaibie and Nuyi settled into the tent, Tonio sent me word that the final two—the ghuroh— would not arrive anytime soon. The entire ghuroh contribution to the regiment had been delayed for some reason that had not been passed along to Tonio or Lieutenant Fusik. They had no idea how long it would be before the ghurohs would show up, so we got ready to start serious training the next day—with Ranger Battalion short 20 percent of its personnel.

CHAPTER 3

EVEN THOUGH WE WERE SERIOUSLY SHORT-
handed, we finally looked like a unit when the battalion
stood at formation the morning following the arrival of
the abarand and divotect contingents. Work formation
was at 0830 hours. Reveille, morning PT—physical
training—and breakfast were over. There would be only
a few work details this day, just what was absolutely
necessary. We were going to start a full training schedule.

I stood at the right end of my squad in formation.
Tonio was in front of the platoon. Three lieutenants were
out in front of the company; besides Fusik and Taivana,
we also had a biraunta JL, Eso Vel Hohi. We had two
more lieutenants scheduled to join the company, but they
were ghuroh. For the time being, Taivana doubled as
platoon leader for first and second platoons, and Hohi
was handling third and fourth platoons.

The integration of the battalion was planned to extend
to every level. The battalion commander was human,
and his executive officer ghuroh, although the exec
hadn't arrived yet. The four companies were set up so

that a human, a porracci, a biraunta, and a ghuroh would each command one. We were the four species committed to providing the bulk of the soldiers to the combined regiment. There were far fewer abarand and divotect, and most of their officers would hold staff positions. The regimental commander was also human, Brigadier General Wallace Ransom. The line battalions would be commanded by officers of different species. In the line battalions, the integration of the species would not be as complete. Each company would be homogeneous, except for liaison and specialists. Only the heavy-weapons battalion would be exempt from integration. Earth was supplying all of the remote-controlled artillery and armor, and all of the crews, maintenance men, and their normal escorting teams were human. Yes, remote-controlled. The crew-served rocket launchers and big guns are just too inviting as targets—and too vulnerable—to risk soldiers inside them. They're all guided from a distance by specialists with portable consoles.

WE WERE CALLED TO ATTENTION. LIEUTENANT Colonel Hank Hansen, the battalion commander, started to give us a pep talk. I had served under Hansen when he was a captain and I was a corporal. He was an okay officer, but he did have a tendency to ramble on. This morning he had scarcely started before there was a bit of a commotion in Company C—an extraordinary breach of military protocol. Hansen stopped, then turned to one of his staff officers, who moved closer to the C Company commander to find out what was going on.

The problem turned out to be that the translator buttons of some of the porracci were not functioning—not translating what the colonel said. He posted a porracci whose translator *was* working to repeat what he said, then went on with his spiel.

There was nothing particularly important in what the colonel said. The talk might almost have been copied out of a book, from some speech given hundreds of times over the centuries, modified to cover current circumstances. Do your best; work hard; be the best you can be—that kind of jazz. Who needed a translation of that? Anyway, the colonel didn't talk long. He turned things over to the company commanders and retreated to his office with his staff officers. On a day-to-day basis, we didn't see much of the colonel during training, and there was nothing wrong with that. Having the brass looking over your shoulder is usually more trouble than it's worth.

"Okay, everyone move in closer so I don't have to shout," Lieutenant Fusik said once the colonel had left. "We've got a lot of work to do."

TRAINING. WE WERE ALL TRAINED INFANTRY- men before we came to Dancer. Whatever species, whatever world we had come from, every soldier in the battalion had been through basic training, advanced infantry training, and—in nearly every case—the equivalent of ranger or special operations training. About 20 percent were combat veterans, especially among the other species. We knew how to march, how to fire our weapons, how to maneuver. That did not mean that we wouldn't do that kind of training on Dancer. Practice makes perfect; armies always subscribe wholeheartedly to that. We would spend hours marching and hiking cross-country. We would spend days on the firing range. And so forth.

Our problem was that we had to learn to operate with soldiers of different species, learn to *trust* each other when our lives might soon depend on that trust, despite the bigotry and fear that existed among the species—the way biraunta feared porracci. Yes, it was—and remains—a problem. But the whole purpose of the 1st Combined Regiment was to demonstrate that it was a problem that can be overcome. We had to take the old "book" of tactical operations and rewrite it for mixed units.

That first day of serious training, we hiked out into the wilderness, each company by itself. . . .

WE HIKED EIGHT MILES ON A HEADING OF SIXTY degrees—east-northeast—in full combat gear, taking more than two and a half hours. When we left camp, the temperature was a hair under eighty, and by the time we reached the end of our hike it was over ninety. That was thanks to a heavy layer of clouds. Without them it would have been even hotter. But the clouds were a mixed blessing. It looked certain to rain, and rain heavily, before we got back to camp. There had been at least a little rain every day since I had arrived on Dancer.

Hiking cross-country, especially through forested country, is not like marching on a parade field. There are no close formations, and no attempt is made to keep in step. With soldiers of five different species, anatomical differences precluded it. We moved in an open formation. There was distance between the platoons, and distance between squads within each platoon. Altogether the company stretched out over about three-quarters of a mile while we were moving.

Lieutenant Fusik gave the order to halt. He passed the

word on the radio circuit that connected him to all of the noncoms in the company that we would take a fifteen-minute break. Our previous breaks had been more on the line of ten minutes.

"Okay, sit and rest," I told my people. "Fifteen minutes." I was the last man down in the squad, but the break was welcome. I wasn't in the best shape I had ever been in. My months as a drill instructor had meant that I hadn't gotten as much exercise as I needed.

My biraunta were the first to plop down, as they had been on both of our previous rest stops. The eight miles had taken more out of them than any of the others. They were careful to make sure that they were as far away from the porracci as possible, and sat facing them, but they were too tired to show any fear. They were even too tired for the usual nervous agitation they showed almost all the time.

The porracci showed no sign that they had felt any exertion at all, which was no surprise. They sat back to back, as if remaining alert for any threat, a little apart from any of the others. Private Nuyi, the divotect, squatted and lowered his head until his chin was on his chest. Divotect aren't the most active of species, except by necessity. Private Jaibie sat and flapped his arms—wings— idly, cooling himself. Fred Wilkins had flopped on his back after sliding his pack off.

There was noticeable distance between all the species. It was a visible reminder of the difficulties that faced us. I sighed and went to Nuyi. I squatted facing him, no more than two feet between us; anything closer would have made a divotect feel uneasy. Nuyi looked up as I squatted.

"I am not in such good shape as I would like, Sergeant," he said. He did not sound as if he were trying to make excuses. He was simply making an observation, an honest evaluation of his performance. "My condition will improve in days to come."

"I know it will," I said. "None of us are in top condition yet." I glanced over my shoulder. "Except, perhaps, the porracci. This hike doesn't seem to have affected them at all."

Nuyi glanced their way. "One cannot tell about them. Porracci will endure anything stoically until their bodies fail them. I do not like porracci myself, but for the sake of my people, I wish all porracci were on our side in this fight."

"I wish there were no need to fight, that the tonatin and their allies in the Ilion Federation had not attacked your people to start with. But perhaps it is better that there are worlds of several species on each side in this war. There are many who realize that genocide is evil and must be fought no matter who is threatened. Perhaps the tonatin will be somewhat restrained by the need to placate the other species in their federation."

Nuyi blinked, with just his inner eyelids, and nodded. "I have heard that you were on Dintsen when the tonatin invaded. Is that true, Sergeant?"

I nodded. "So was Platoon Sergeant Xeres. I think that there may be twenty humans in the battalion who were on Dintsen. Perhaps more. I haven't had a chance to see all of the humans in the battalion yet. Our army wanted combat veterans for this job."

"The tonatin want to totally destroy my people," Nuyi said. "And what the tonatin want, the rest of the Ilion Federation must go along with, no matter what they themselves may want. I pray we are in time to stop them before the only divotect alive are those of us in this regiment."

Despite the heat, I felt a cold shiver. I had never thought of the war in quite those terms, or consciously realized just how much the divotect had to lose. I knew about the exterminations on Dintsen, and I had heard that similar campaigns were being waged on the other divotect worlds that had been captured by the Ilion Federation in the first sweep of the war, but. . . .

"You have my prayers as well, Ooyonoa Nuyi," I said before I got up and went over to where the biraunta were sitting.

At that point I couldn't tell Iyi and Oyo apart. Oyo's fringe of facial fur was just slightly darker than his brother's, but the distinction was minuscule. I hadn't picked it out yet. Both of them looked up as I sat facing them.

"This has been a hard march for you," I said.

"Any march must be long with porracci behind us," one of them said without looking up.

"Why are biraunta so terrified of porracci?" It was not the first time I had asked them that question, but I had not received much of an answer before. The first time, they had teetered on the brink of total incoherency.

"They look like our nightmares," the other biraunta said.

His twin took over then, without missing a beat. "In the far past, on our first world, there were creatures that looked like porracci. They hunted us, ate us. It was a miracle of the gods that we survived and learned to hunt them instead. And when we could, we killed all of them we could find."

The other twin took over speaking again, so smoothly that the transition would not have been noticeable if I hadn't been looking at them. "But even when we had weapons, it was a close fight. There was always the fear that some of them would survive and come back to finish the job of killing all biraunta."

"It is a story every mother tells her young, to make certain that we never lose our vigilance."

It was during this time, while they were switching back and forth—almost as if they could read each other's minds—that I first noticed the slight difference in their faces. So I stopped their narrative, such as it was, and asked which was which. A squad leader has to know his men. Oyo was the one with the slightly darker facial fur.

"The porracci are not the creatures from your past," I said, though both of them had to know that—intellectually, at least. "These porracci fight on the same side you do. They are your allies, not predators out to hurt you."

Iyi glanced at our two porracci, briefly, as if he were afraid of being noticed. But neither biraunta spoke. I moved over to Private Jaibie. He had stopped fanning himself and was lying on his back now, staring into the sky.

"How are you making out?" I asked.

Jaibie started to sit up, but I waved for him to stay as he was. "My people are not made for walking so much," he said. "The sky is where we belong." He hesitated, then, in a dreamy sort of voice, said, "Perhaps losing the ability to fly was too high a price to pay for intelligence."

I turned my head so Jaibie would not see my smile. "I don't think any of our peoples had any choice in how they developed. You did develop intelligence, and learned how to fly with machines, much earlier in your history than the rest of us."

"It cannot be the same," Jaibie said.

The fifteen minutes Lieutenant Fusik had offered were over, but no orders had come through for us to do anything, and I wasn't about to remind the lieutenant that time was up. I went to the porracci and sat facing them. "Any problems, Corporal?" I asked Souvana.

"There has been no challenge to cause problems, Sergeant," he said in a matter-of-fact way.

"True." I hesitated. "Do you know why the biraunta fear you so much?"

"We remind them of some prehistoric creature of their home world, or some myth from their earliest memories," Souvana said in the same tone. "This has been known since before the founding of the Alliance of Light. It almost kept the biraunta from joining, but they feared others more than they feared us."

I found that difficult to believe, but I had to accept it—at least until I learned better. "If we are going to function as a unit and do what our leaders expect of us, we have to find a way to get around that fear," I said. "I am counting on the two of you to help me dispel it."

"What would you have us do?" Souvana asked.

"That's part of the problem. I still don't know how we're going to manage this. I only know that we have to."

"A leader should have no uncertainty," Souvana said. "I will give this problem my full attention."

I looked closely at Souvana. There was something about his tone that I . . . didn't quite like, but I couldn't pin down what it was. It was the first indication I had that the senior porracci might not be fully satisfied serving as my assistant. The porracci had been founding members of the Alliance of Light. They had been traveling between the stars since the Montgolfier brothers were making their first hot-air balloon flights on Earth, nearly a thousand years ago, and they had been fighting one war or another for most of those years. They make humans look downright peaceable.

I WAS ON MY WAY OVER TO WHERE FRED WIL-
kins was sprawled when Tonio came on the radio to tell me that our break was over. It was time to get up and moving. "The lieutenant is sending each platoon out in a separate direction," Tonio said. "We're to get as far as we can in thirty minutes, then take up defensive positions and wait for further instructions."

"You mean orders for half the platoons to try infiltrating the other half," I said. It was a fairly common exercise in special ops.

"Don't anticipate the command," Tonio warned, a phrase every drill instructor in any army would be familiar with, but he sounded as if he were struggling to suppress a laugh.

I switched to my squad frequency. Human battle helmets have considerable communications channels built in. Most of the other races had similar gear, but not all of it was compatible. That was something the engineers were still working on. We did have enough common channels that we *could* communicate, but it was sometimes voice only. We couldn't share maps or targeting data among systems yet across all the species—not reliably enough to depend on.

"On your feet. It's time to move out," I said. The porracci were up so fast they might have had springs under them. The biraunta were up almost as quickly, but I suppose that was as much an instinctive fear response to the porracci as anything else. Nuyi and Wilkins were the last to get up.

Fred came over to me and lifted the faceplate of his helmet so what he said wouldn't be transmitted over our squad frequency. "You get peace made among the races?" he asked softly.

"I hope I've helped the cause," I replied, also whispering. Then I told him how to distinguish between the biraunta. "It's not easy to pick out, but we have to learn. Take your position. We've got to get started." Then I passed along the orders I had been given, first to Fred and then to Corporal Souvana.

As soon as we were moving—our platoon was given a heading of 340 degrees, just a little west of north—I called Tonio on the noncoms' channel. "Can I offer a suggestion?" I asked.

"Go ahead."

"How about letting our biraunta work up in the trees, at least a little. Give them a change of pace. My two are a little footsore. Put them out as high scouts, maybe?"

Tonio hesitated for about five seconds before he said, "Good idea—so good somebody should have thought of it sooner. Okay, your squad has the point, so use your biraunta out in front. I'll put the others out on the flanks and behind."

Iyi and Oyo were clearly delighted at the chance to get up in the trees, and not just because that allowed them to get farther from our porracci.

THIRD PLATOON HAD A BIRAUNTA SERGEANT, so I was confident that third would think of letting the ones who were adapted to brachiating get up in the trees. There was a chance that neither of the other platoons would think of it, though, so first and third platoons could be expected to move the farthest during the thirty minutes. Whether that would make a difference remained to be seen. If we needed to defend and try to keep one of the other platoons from infiltrating our position, we might be that much harder to find. If we were to be the aggressor, it was something we would have to take into consideration when we started looking for our target. Second platoon had been sent west, third northeast, fourth east-southeast. Half an hour should put approximately a mile between neighboring platoons.

Tonio pushed the platoon hard during those thirty minutes. Where there was fairly open ground under the forest canopy, we even moved at a jog from time to time, using changes in pace to keep us from tiring too quickly. Since we were wearing full field gear, including live ammunition for our weapons, we couldn't flat-out run for thirty minutes.

Yes, live ammunition. Although it might present a safety problem if things went really wrong between any of the species, I was relieved that we had it, even though the ammo was not *in* our weapons. We had exercise lasers and marking tags instead so we could *simulate* gunfire. Sure, Dancer was supposed to be a top-secret training base, but there was a chance that a ship from the Ilion Federation might find us and have troops to put ashore. Or maybe the secret had gotten out at some other point. With most of the species split between the two alliances, there was always a chance of information leaking. That might lead to a full-scale assault on Dancer. Maybe we wouldn't be able to do a top-notch job of holding off an invasion, but we would be able to put up a fight if we were discovered. Maybe even enough of a fight to let the Alliance reinforce us before we were destroyed.

*   *   *

THIRTY MINUTES. TONIO CHEATED US AN EXTRA ninety seconds, so that we could reach better ground to set up a defensive perimeter before we halted. "Take your positions. Make what improvements you can quickly. I want concealment more than hard positions. No digging, no moving large rocks. If they can't see us, they can't touch us."

We were near a small stream, camouflaged in the thick underbrush that flourished by its banks. Vines, brambles, wild growing bushes, man-high grass and reeds. Infested with a lot of bugs. My squad drew the quadrant of the perimeter facing the stream, with the ground sloping gently down in front of us. I put Oyo and Iyi in the trees, higher—I hoped—than anyone would look for them.

Understand, we might make ourselves virtually invisible to unaided eyes, but we could not make ourselves invisible to all forms of surveillance. The fatigues, boots, and helmets that the human soldiers wore were supposed to provide good thermal camouflage, especially in a setting where the ambient temperature was close to body temperature, but that camouflage is never quite perfect. And I wasn't certain how good the thermal qualities were in the uniforms of the other species. The porracci and biraunta left a lot of skin and fur exposed on arms and legs, and our abarand left considerably more skin open—a necessity because of the rudimentary wings that joined arms and chests. Jaibie's uniform looked more like *Lederhosen* from Europe than proper combat gear. Most battle helmets included infrared capabilities in their faceplates. The one member of the squad I didn't have to worry about was Nuyi, the divotect. His body naturally adjusted to the ambient temperature, part of the species' reptilian nature.

The other way in which an army unit is vulnerable to detection is through electronic emissions—radio traffic and so forth. Most of that comes through our battle helmets. Those are shielded, but—again—the shielding is rarely perfect. Sound discipline is still vital, using the radio as little as possible in a combat situation. We *were* simulating a combat situation.

"Get down and stay still," I warned my men on the ground. "The lieutenant might send one of the other platoons to try to breach our perimeter without letting us know they're coming. Keep your eyes open for anything." That's what I would have done, changed the orders for two of the platoons early on, redirected them to try to infiltrate the others. You try to catch your people off-guard to find out how good they really are. It's not a fair test when everyone knows who's coming and how many there are.

Every minute that passed without word from Lieutenant Fusik for us to get up and do something made it feel that much more likely that he had ordered an "attack" on us by one of the other platoons. If we were going to be hit, I assumed the aggressor force would be second platoon, coming in from somewhere to our left. That would leave third and fourth platoons to play with each other on the right.

Waiting is one of the first things any soldier learns, and one of the first things he discovers to complain about. Even later, when he knows *why,* he'll still complain. But lying motionless is one of the best ways to make certain that any enemy doesn't see you too soon. Once I was certain that my squad was deployed properly, the only thing I moved was my head, looking around, and I kept that to a minimum, and slow. I worked at keeping my breathing slow and regular as well. To keep from cramping up or getting stiff if the waiting lasted more than a few minutes, I did simple isometric exercises, tensing and relaxing muscles.

I did not tell my squad to concentrate on the area to our left, though I gave that side slightly more of my own attention. Even if my guess was right and second platoon was moving to infiltrate us, nothing said they had to come in a straight line. If their platoon sergeant was smart, they wouldn't. Instead they would try to find the best angle of attack, preferably one we might not expect.

Ten minutes. Fifteen. By then I was convinced that I had guessed right, that one of the other platoons had been sent to try to infiltrate our position. If not, there would have been other orders for us, and Tonio remained silent. I didn't call him to ask. Neither did any of the other squad leaders. That would have been poor sound discipline, and given any enemy a chance to mark our location.

Twenty minutes. *Maybe they're having trouble finding us,* I thought, though it was premature to think that. If we couldn't be found, we won—assuming I had diagnosed the exercise correctly. The other way to win was to spot the incoming platoon before they spotted us, and start tagging them with our laser simulators first.

Twenty-five minutes. *What's the time limit on this?* I asked myself. *How much time did the lieutenant give the other platoon?* It wasn't that I was getting impatient myself; I'd wait as long as I had to. But time would start working against us before long. It would be more difficult to keep everyone motionless as the waiting dragged on and the men grew impatient. I worried most about the biraunta. They always seemed agitated.

I squeezed my eyes shut for an instant. I didn't know my people well enough. I couldn't be sure how any of them would react to anything out of the ordinary. That was one of the things that training was supposed to correct, and we had barely started.

Thirty minutes. *Don't get lost in thought,* I told myself. *Keep your eyes open and your mind on the job.* I forced a yawn to get adrenaline pumping. It wouldn't do much good for my men to stay on their toes if I sloughed off. I did a careful scan of as much of the forest as I could along the squad's side of the perimeter, letting my eyes move back and forth slowly, one level at a time from the ground up, looking for any movement that was out of harmony with the natural motion of leaves and branches, for anything breaking the pattern.

It was one of the biraunta who spotted second platoon. He sounded so excited that I couldn't tell if it was Iyi or Oyo. I relayed the sighting to Tonio. "Three men moving toward us, compass bearing three-five-two," I reported. "I can't see anything from my position, but they're visible from above."

"Tag them," Tonio said.

I passed the word to my squad. "Look for them and tag anyone you spot. But stay low, don't make targets of yourself."

That kind of gunplay, with laser simulators, is totally silent, not the noisy hell of a real firefight. It's the major flaw in the system, though silent firefights can be more than a little eerie. The head-up display on my faceplate showed me the points of fire and when the marking tags on the other side were hit. At least the hits were all on the other side at first. Iyi and Oyo tagged all three of the visible targets before second platoon started returning fire.

That gave us more targets, though Iyi was tagged in the first volley and Oyo was tagged seconds later, putting them out of the exercise as simulated casualties. Once we had more targets, the rest of my squad, and half the rest of the platoon, were able to get in on the "firefight." That went on for about eight minutes before Tonio gave the order to cease firing.

"WE WOULD HAVE DONE BETTER HAD YOU GIVEN the order to move forward and engage the enemy at close range once we had them located," Corporal Souvana said after Tonio released us from exercise conditions. Souvana stood too close, right in my face, his sour breath almost enough to gag me, but I wasn't going to back off—in any sense.

"Those weren't our orders," I replied, leaning toward him.

"Once combat was joined, the duty of a soldier is to destroy the enemy. The time for lying in wait had passed. The battle was there. We could have done more. We *should* have done more."

"We did what we were supposed to do."

"Had I been in command of the squad, we would have done better," Souvana said.

"Then perhaps it's better that you are not in command," I said, "because you would have disobeyed orders."

"In *our* army, the better soldier is always in command. It is the duty of each soldier to compete until the rankings reflect the ability of the porracci in each unit."

I knew that. It had been stressed in the briefings we had been given about the other species. If a porracci felt he was more qualified to command than his immediate superior, he challenged him and they fought, hand-to-hand, with the winner taking the higher ranking. Fatalities were rare but not unknown.

"It is the duty of each porracci to obey the orders of those who have proven themselves superior to him, is it not?" I asked.

"Naturally."

"And the porracci who outrank you in your own army gave orders that you were to obey all superiors, regardless of species, in the combined regiment. They informed you that organization in this combined unit is not to be determined by challenge. Are these not true?"

I could see the fur bristle on Souvana's neck. He withheld an answer for as long as he could. "I obey my orders," he said then. My translator button could not disguise the turmoil in his voice. "It is also my duty to give my best advice to superiors, regardless of species," he added after another pause.

"Well-considered advice is always welcome, and invaluable," I said. "Any commander would be a fool not to consider such advice, but the commander must make the final decisions. For an army to operate otherwise would bring disaster."

I was not surprised by Souvana's hesitation. Then he drew his shoulders back and nodded before he turned and strode over to Kiervauna. Once Souvana's back was turned, I turned the other way and allowed myself a brief smile. Two victories in one day. That felt good. But I didn't assume that it would be the last time my assistant squad leader would edge toward a confrontation.

CHAPTER 4

Two biraunta from fourth platoon did not respond to the recall order at the end of the exercise. The rest of the company assembled near where fourth platoon had been. No one else was missing. Attempts were made to contact the missing biraunta by radio. There was no sign of their helmet electronics on the scanners, no locator blips. The next move was to set the company to search for the missing soldiers. Flitters were brought in to search from the air, while the rest of us searched on the ground and in the trees.

The remaining biraunta in the company went up into the trees to search their way. The abarand used their gliding abilities where those could help, climbing trees and diving off, covering the edges of clearings and the openings over the many little creeks in the area. The rest of us hoofed it, dividing the terrain into grids and searching each one closely, paying as much attention to the trees as to the ground. Meals and drinks were airlifted to us. Another company of rangers was moved in to help us cover more ground faster.

"They took a powder," Fred Wilkins said over our

private radio circuit an hour after we had started searching. "They got spooked and took off as fast as they could."

I grunted. "That's my guess, too, but we can't assume it. Hell, they've got no place to go. There's no one on this whole damned planet but us, and they can't think they can get off."

"Fourth platoon has a porracci sergeant. They were probably so damned terrified by him that they didn't think it through."

"Just keep your eyes open. We'll find them."

Eventually, I warned myself. And: *maybe.* Two biraunta running in panic, on a continent 70 percent covered by trees, where they could move faster than any grunt could on the ground—they might run for days or weeks before they called for help or started back. That's assuming that they didn't fall prey to one of Dancer's native predators. The biraunta were armed, but guns aren't always enough, especially if you're not thinking straight. Or they might run into trouble some other way—fall out of a tree or something like that. There weren't enough soldiers on the planet to do a thorough search, so there was a chance they would never be found.

We searched our grids, covering each twice, quartering every bit of territory. I had been on searches like that a couple of times before, on Earth, but in each of those cases it had been soldiers helping civilian authorities look for missing children who—we had hoped—wanted to be found. One time we had succeeded, locating two small, very frightened children and returning them to their frantic parents. The other time . . . well, I don't like to think about what we found that time, let alone talk about it.

Wilkins went through the motions, but he had made it clear that he didn't expect to find anything. Several times I talked to him about it, and he made the proper noises and put on a show of greater intensity for a time. Private Jaibie put everything he had into the search, climbing and gliding, never asking for a rest, and going on until I had to order him to stay down for a time. Nuyi was slow and methodical, traits I had noticed in all the divotect I had known; he appeared ready to continue the hunt for the rest of his life if necessary. Souvana and Kiervauna were diligent but showed no enthusiasm for the task.

If a porracci had spooked the two biraunta into running—whether or not it was intentional—being found by one of them might not help the situation. If those biraunta were running in panic, it wasn't out of the question that they might *shoot* any porracci who happened to be the first to spot them. But we couldn't very well tell the porracci—20 percent of the company—to sit on their butts while the rest of us searched. That would make it that much harder to get the mixed unit to *ever* function. It could screw the combined regiment so far into the ground it might never get out.

We had fourteen hours of daylight each day. There had been nearly eight hours left when the search started. By the time the sun got near the horizon and long shadows made it difficult to see in the forest without night-vision gear, we still had not located the missing biraunta. The search continued. We moved more slowly in the dark. There is *some* loss of visual resolution with night-vision gear. You can't see *quite* as far or as well.

We took a break as dusk was resolving itself into dark, time to eat and get off our feet for thirty minutes.

We needed time to rest or we wouldn't be able to operate efficiently.

"How long are we going to keep searching?" I asked Tonio. I had my food and sat next to him, a little apart from everyone else in the platoon. "Those biraunta didn't get lost, they took off. They could be twenty miles away by now, maybe farther."

Tonio had just put food in his mouth and took his time chewing and swallowing, then took a drink of coffee. "I know they took off," he said very softly. "They turned off their helmet electronics—or disabled them—and lit out as fast as they could swing from one branch to the next. Whether their platoon sergeant said or did something in particular to spook them, or worse . . . we won't know until we find them and one of the biraunta officers questions them."

"So why do we put so much into the search?" I asked. "Why not head back to camp and wait for them to realize they don't have anywhere to go and they call for somebody to pick them up?"

"I could give you half a dozen reasons and they'd all be valid," Tonio said.

I shrugged. "I've come up with a few myself, but I've about given up trying to second-guess what the brass-asses are thinking. I just wondered what the official line is."

He snorted. "Colonel Hansen laid it out for the officers and top noncoms. We search because we don't abandon any of our people while there's any chance they're alive. We search because it will help build unit cohesion, like no training drill could. We search because it gives us a solid practical exercise. Finally, we search because everyone has to know they can't escape their problems by running away. And on and on." He snorted again.

"It sounds as if you don't fully agree," I ventured.

"Oh, I can understand the reasons, all right," he said. "Intellectually, at least. We search for all the reasons the colonel gave and for one even more important reason—we search because we've been ordered to."

"There is that. But how long do *we* keep at it tonight? When do we knock off to let the men sleep? Half an hour here, ten minutes there won't keep everyone going indefinitely. We'd get so groggy we could trip over our AWOLs and not see them. Is the colonel going to bring in the other half of the battalion to take over for a few hours?"

"You'll find out as soon as I do," Tonio said.

"There's one other thing I've been meaning to ask, almost since we got here," I said after a brief hesitation. "Lieutenant Fusik. I've got an itch in my head that tells me there's some reason why I should recall the name, but I can't place it."

"The Bunyan Rebellion," Tonio said. "Vancouver Island. He lost half a platoon, dead and wounded. It wasn't his fault—the board of inquiry cleared him—but a whole string of officers up the line tried to make him the scapegoat. It's why he's still a lieutenant and not a captain. Don't give him any grief you can avoid, Dragon. The way I hear it, he volunteered for this outfit the same way you did."

I nodded. Once he had mentioned the rebellion and Vancouver Island, the rest had trickled out of my memory as he talked. "Yeah, now I remember," I said. "Stuck the shaft in him and broke it off."

* * *

THE COMPANY WAS FINALLY ALLOWED TO SACK
out for what remained of the night a little after 0100
hours—after being up and active for twenty-three hours.
But we did not go back to camp. We unrolled our waterproof bedrolls and made do where we were, in a slow
but steady rain that had started three hours earlier. Two
platoons from Delta—D Company—continued the
search.

It was Delta that found our missing biraunta—fourteen miles from where they had dropped out—about an
hour before sunrise. Both of them were dead, apparent
suicides. Junior Lieutenant Krau'vi Taivana and fourth
platoon were flown back to camp just before dawn. The
rest of us were wakened, fed, and marched back. It was
mostly a silent hike, and the pace was slow. We knew
that the two biraunta were dead. The noncoms and officers knew *how* they had died, but we had been told not
to spread that news, that the colonel would make an
official announcement later.

By the time we got back to camp—and I had never
expected that makeshift collection of tents floating in
mud to look so homey—Lieutenant Taivana had ques-
tioned each soldier in fourth platoon individually, apparently at some length. An hour later there was a
meeting for all officers and sergeants in the company.
We learned that the porracci platoon sergeant had been
relieved of his duties and would be transferred to one of
the line battalions in the regiment, to a company manned
entirely by porracci. We were not told why or exactly
what Lieutenant Taivana had learned about the relationship between the sergeant and the dead biraunta.

As far as that goes, we were *never* given any additional information about the circumstances that had led
to the biraunta running off and killing themselves. Their

platoon was given strict orders—enforced by threats of severe discipline—not to discuss it. If any of them disobeyed those orders, the details still haven't reached me.

The colonel made the official announcement concerning the deaths of the two biraunta. Training resumed the next morning.

THERE IS A LONG-STANDING POPULAR MISCON-ception that "military intelligence" is a contradiction in terms. Even many soldiers fall victim to the notion that most of the mind-numbing routine is a sign of poor organization or a lack of anyone in command knowing the difference between where the food goes in and where it comes out. To be sure, there are officers and noncoms who get caught up in the minutiae of ritual without being able to see the rationale. But there is finely honed logic, developed mostly through trial and error, behind the routines of training and discipline—and behind nearly everything else that an army does when it is not actually facing a hostile foe.

An army has to overcome one of the deepest instincts in almost any living creature—the instinct to survive. By its very nature, combat is a lethal occupation. You can't ask a bunch of civilians or untrained soldiers to willingly go into a situation where there is a strong chance of getting killed or maimed and to do it by the numbers, do what their superiors tell them to do, without their thinking about the danger, without saying, "The hell with *this* nonsense" and running for their lives.

It takes time to "make" a soldier. You have to train him to obey orders—*any* orders—without question, without hesitation. You train him, and you drill him over and over. You make him hurry up and wait. You make him pull fatigue duties that would make a civilian revolt. You expose him to miserable conditions in the field. You give him opportunities to feel mild fear and teach him to work through that fear. You don't want to rob him of his brain, the ability to reason and react, but he has to be ready to act on orders, without taking time to reason it out for himself, without time to realize the odds against him.

The days of infantry being mere "cannon fodder" ended centuries ago. Any army today needs soldiers with enough intelligence to use modern weapons and gear, and training those men takes time and money, so you try not to *waste* soldiers. Good soldiers are harder to replace than rifles or battle helmets—or any of the thousands of other pieces of gear an army uses. The army's most important weapon is always the soldier who wields the other equipment. A weapon that costs too much to risk in combat is as worthless as a weapon that doesn't work.

Still, there are going to be casualties in combat. There are times when a leader has to order his men forward even when he knows some of them will not come back. But you have to handle your men as economically as possible, the way you budget your personal finances. And some leaders are better at that than others.

A WEEK OR SO AFTER THE SUICIDES, WE WERE actually given an entire day off—our first since the start of training. There was nowhere to go and not much to do, but the luxury of having a full day to do nothing felt like a three-day pass in the wildest town in the Galaxy.

Like just about everyone else in the battalion, I slept late that morning, nearly two hours past sunrise. It felt wicked, but all the sweeter for that. I wasted time in the shower, then strolled over to the mess tent for a late breakfast. I wasn't the last to arrive by a long shot. The cooks had gone out of their way to prepare special meals for all the species, and there was as much as anyone wanted. I took large helpings of everything that looked good and ate slowly.

I had only been at it for a few minutes when Tonio came in, got himself a cup of coffee, and came over to sit across the table from me. He didn't look properly cheerful for our first day off, so after we exchanged greetings, I asked him why he was wearing such a sour puss. He shook his head, screwing up his face even worse. I waited him out. He looked like he had something to say. He needed a bit longer to start, though.

"Have you noticed what happens whenever we get a little time off?" he asked.

"Like what?" I didn't have any idea where he was headed.

"We go off with others of our own species, away from the others, each race its own little clique."

"So?"

"So nobody fraternizes with any of the other species, doesn't have anything to do with them except when duty requires it."

"As long as we can work together while we *are* on duty, what's the problem?" I asked.

"The problem is that the integration isn't working. We're not meshing. Look, any unit I've been in before, the guys in each squad pretty much hung around together all the time—played games—sports—together, went on pass together, got drunk together, screwed the same whores, whatever. Guys in a squad get closer than most people are with their own family."

"Hey, don't rush things. It's a big climb for all of us. Not many of our men have ever had experience with any of the other species. We've still got time. Besides, there isn't a whore on Dancer. Not *that* kind."

"We've got to push. And it's got to start with the noncoms. This comes all the way from Colonel Hansen. We've got to encourage more mingling off duty, and the colonel thinks the way to start is for sergeants and corporals to start making a point of crashing these exclusive cliques."

"And I suppose it's to start today, on what was supposed to be a day off for all of us."

Tonio shrugged. "We're always on duty, one way or another, Dragon."

Tonio had completely taken the pleasure out of breakfast and my alleged day off.

CORPORAL SOUVANA'S REACTION TO THE NEWS was about the same as mine had been, except that he didn't bother to suppress a growl. "It comes straight from the colonel," I told him. "We don't have much choice but to obey."

"One does not have to agree with an order to obey it," he said.

For once I had no argument with him.

ALL THE SAME, I WASN'T CERTAIN JUST HOW I was to go about obeying the order without screwing up one way or another. After breakfast, I hung around outside for a time, watching where people were going. It didn't take long for the pattern to become obvious. Men from each species had gotten into habits—going off to the same location to be with others of their kind. Although the areas were not marked in any way, they seemed fairly well delineated. Humans went to one area, biraunta to another, and so forth. I guess I had realized what was going on before, subconsciously, but I hadn't given it any real thought. Hell, I had been guilty of it myself, going over to chat with men I knew from other postings—other *humans*.

For a minute I was tempted to follow the other human soldiers I saw meandering off to our usual gathering place on the north side of camp. The crazy idea that tried to make itself sound reasonable was for me to tell the others to go mingle with the other groups. That wasn't what Tonio had said the colonel wanted, though.

I stalled as long as I could. After all, I didn't expect to be welcomed very warmly when I strolled into a gathering of porracci—or any of the other species. There were reasons why they were gathering separately, after all, even if those reasons weren't sufficient for the colonel.

It wasn't until I saw Nuyi walking off to the east that I quit stalling. I was almost comfortable among divotect. I knew enough about their culture to keep from feeling totally alien with them. And I shared the loss of Dintsen with them. Maybe they didn't all know that I had been there when the IFers—soldiers of the Ilion Federation—invaded, but some did.

There weren't as many divotect in the battalion as there were porracci, biraunta, or humans. The gathering I crashed consisted of only about a dozen divotect. As I approached the group—most of them lying on their backs in the sun—the conversations stopped as they became aware of me. Nuyi sat up and said something, undoubtedly telling the others who I was.

"Do you require me for something, Sergeant?" Nuyi said, getting to his feet as I got close.

"Nothing special, Nuyi," I said. A few of the others had stood, and most of them at least sat up. "This is informal. May I sit and talk with you all?"

"This is Sergeant Bart Drak, my squad leader," Nuyi said, looking around the group. "He was one of the human soldiers who fought at our side on Dintsen."

One of the other divotect stood. "I am Sergeant Hiorayma Keisi, second squad leader in third platoon, Company B, Sergeant Drak. I was born on Dintsen. My family was there when the tonatin invaded. I am glad to welcome you."

I nodded. "Thank you, Sergeant Keisi. May the sun always warm you." That was a standard divotect greeting I had picked up on Dintsen.

"May you never be cold," he replied. "Please, sit with us."

"Has your platoon sergeant spoken with you today?" I asked after we were all on the ground and as comfortable as we could get. Keisi shook his head.

I told them what Tonio had told me. "I came here first because I am more comfortable with divotect than any of the others." I may have grinned a little self-consciously. "This does affect all of us. We have a lot to work through, everyone in the regiment, if we are to function properly."

"We are well aware of the prejudices against us, Sergeant," Nuyi said. "Our people have always experienced this, since we first came in contact with those who are not like us."

"I know, Nuyi, as I know of the fear biraunta feel for porracci, and the ... contempt some humans feel for both of them. I know how divotect have suffered. But have you divotect considered your own prejudices against the other sentients?"

We certainly weren't going to solve all of the prejudices and distrust in one day, or one week, but that first encounter went better than I had expected. It was a start. It made it a little easier for me to brave a couple of gatherings of porracci—that afternoon and several days later. Not that I could see that I accomplished anything substantial. The segregated cliques continued to meet, rarely integrated by more than the occasional noncom doing it because we had been ordered to.

SIX WEEKS INTO TRAINING, THE REGIMENT WAS still missing its ghuroh contingent, now more than 20 percent of our total manpower. Only a handful of ghuroh had arrived, mostly liaison officers and specialists. We finally learned why the more than nine hundred ghuroh soldiers supposed to be assigned to the regiment had not reached Dancer. The main ghuroh army had been in a major battle, with heavy casualties, and was doing some much-needed reorganization and training of replacements on several of their worlds. Our ghurohs were expected to arrive, we were told, within the next two weeks.

A soldier learns to take information like that with many grains of salt. We continued training, improvising to handle our jobs with more than 20 percent of our people missing. Whenever the ghuroh did show up, we'd do our best to integrate them into the unit and bring them up to speed as quickly as possible.

On the other hand, the report of a ghuroh army being involved in a major battle was the first war news we had heard since coming to Dancer.

*   *   *

THERE WAS ONE VERY IMPORTANT ELEMENT OF
our training that we had not yet started on six weeks
into the program. It *had* been on the schedule, early on,
but had been pushed off repeatedly after the suicide of
the two biraunta. That was unarmed combat.

Humans knew about fighting hand-to-hand with other
humans. Biraunta knew about fighting other biraunta . . .
and so forth. The problem was that we all needed to be
able to fight other species than our own, nearly all of
them. Most of the sentient species have worlds in both
the Alliance of Light and the Ilion Federation. The divotect were only in the Alliance, but they were the least
numerous sentient race in any case. The tonatin were
almost exclusively in the Federation. A few tonatin
worlds were independent or members of the Alliance,
but there were no tonatin soldiers in the Grand Alliance
(the highfalutin official name of the combined armies of
the Alliance of Light).

The brass on Dancer was afraid of what might happen
when we tried to pair biraunta and porracci as opponents
in unarmed combat drills. They were afraid that we
might have a lot more biraunta falling apart in panic.
Maybe they were afraid that the entire biraunta contingent would withdraw from the combined regiment and
go home. Maybe they were right to worry. But it left a
big hole in our training, one most of the men recognized.
It was too glaring to miss. Maybe the brass was waiting
for enough of the biraunta to come out and *ask* for the
training.

We worked around it as best we could. There were
lectures on how to attempt to best an opponent of each
species, but—out of deference to the biraunta fear of

porracci—those lectures were broken down by species. It was one of the few occasions when we were segregated, especially after we started trying to minimize the separation off duty. Biraunta were lectured to by their own officers, and so forth. Without hands-on training, over and over, the lectures wouldn't be much good. You need to train reflexes so the body does what it has to when there isn't time to remember a lecture and try to implement it.

Okay, some of the possible matchups were never going to offer much hope. There is simply too much variation in size and strength. A human would be hard pressed to defeat a porracci, and biraunta and abarand are even more outclassed by anatomical reality. Speed and agility are fine, but they can only carry you so far. There are limits to what even the ancient martial arts can do. I thought that maybe divotect would fare well against porracci, and from what I'd heard about ghuroh, they might give the porracci an even match.

"When it comes down to the crunch," I told my squad, "let's just try to make sure that no one in the squad has to go one-on-one against a larger and stronger opponent. Teamwork. We all have to work together." Yeah, I can spout that kind of stuff by the yard when I have to.

─── CHAPTER 5

OUR TRAINING GOT MORE INVOLVED AS THE weeks went on and we got used to working together. We were beginning to break down *some* of the barriers among the species, but we still had a long way to go, even though all of the officers and noncoms continued visiting the one-species groups that still came together off duty. Maybe the groups were smaller, and the visits less ... intrusive than they had been at the start, but I still had the feeling of being an outsider, even among the divotect.

The tactical exercises became more complex, larger, longer. I think some of the tasks we were given were assigned simply to find our limits, discover what we could and could not do. There is one that really sticks out in my mind, at the end of our seventh week on Dancer. It was the first time we practiced a combat landing.

There was no advance warning. We were simply wakened about forty minutes before midnight—after three hours of sleep—and told to fall out in full combat gear. It was twenty minutes later before the rumor that the

Ilion Federation was about to invade Dancer was
squelched officially. The way we were dragged out of
sleep had lit the candle of fear in a lot of minds, and
rumors always seem to spread at something approaching
the speed of light in a military unit.

Officers and sergeants were called to a briefing held
in the open, with a dim screen serving in place of our
electronic maps—the little folding charts, specialized
computer terminals, that noncoms and officers carry in
combat.

"Today's exercise will involve all of B Company,"
Lieutenant Fusik told us. "We are going to simulate
spearheading the invasion of a hostile planet, engaging
specific targets to open the way for line troops. We will
be broken down into squad and platoon assignments,
each group operating independently." That was SOP for
spec ops. We're trained to handle different objectives
than line companies are—infiltrating enemy lines or operating behind them to take out specific targets and make
it easier for the rest of the army to move in. "You will
be given individual orders and objectives. The company
will board shuttles and we will make our insertions on
airsleds, the way we would if real combat lay at the end
of the flight."

We were shown holographic maps of the objective
area, but it was difficult to see much on a single screen
set off too far from most of us, and the information had
not been distributed to our personal map computers yet.
Fusik turned the briefing over to the platoon sergeants,
who had been wakened a little earlier than the rest of us
to get their instructions.

"First platoon has drawn four one-squad assignments," Tonio started when he had the four squad leaders together. "I'll be going in with fourth squad, running

that operation personally." That was the squad that would have a ghuroh squad leader eventually—assuming they ever showed up. "So I'll save that briefing for later." That was directed mostly at fourth's acting squad leader, Corporal Don Klewn. Don was a big, hulking human, one of the few I would give an even chance in unarmed combat against a porracci. He was six feet, six inches tall and weighed close to three hundred pounds. He was fast and strong. He also held black belts in three separate martial arts specialties. Don just nodded, unconcerned with being relegated to a subordinate position.

Tonio needed only a couple of minutes to lay out my squad's assignment. I listened intently and repeated the essentials of it back to him when he was finished.

He nodded. "Okay, get to your men. Head over to the landing strip. There'll be someone there to head you to the right shuttle."

I HAD NEVER BEEN ON AN ACTUAL COMBAT drop, but over the years I had done more than a hundred practice landings, so I knew what was coming, what to do. This was, after all, just another practice drop, with a team I had been training with for more than six weeks—long enough to give me a pretty good idea what each of them was capable of . . . and for each of them to have a damned good idea what I expected of them and what they could expect from the others in the squad. I briefed my men while we jogged toward the landing strip at the edge of the main camp.

It was no surprise that none of the combat shuttles had landed yet. We would have heard shuttles coming in. The first one was on its final approach as we got to the little operations shack by the warehouses. There was no one waiting to tell us what shuttle to get on yet, either.

"Might as well sit and get comfortable," I told the squad. "I don't think we'll have long to wait, not if they want to get this operation launched before dawn." We were in full combat kit. For Fred Wilkins and me, that meant about seventy pounds each, including weapons and ammunition. I slipped my pack off and set it next to where Fred sat. Much as I would have liked to sit as well, I stayed on my feet, looking for whoever was supposed to direct us. I saw several other groups of soldiers coming; most of the rest of the company was already in sight.

The first shuttle landed, coming in almost as fast and as heavy as it would on a combat landing—assuming it came in all the way. Sometimes they do, but more when they're handling line companies than spec ops teams. With us, it's more likely to be airsleds dropped from a shuttle at anything between five hundred and eight thousand feet. After the first shuttle landed, the rest came in quickly, with no more than twenty seconds between them, six birds in all. While they were coming in, it was too noisy to talk—almost too noisy to think—at the edge of the strip.

I had turned to watch the landings, partially because I worried that one of those pilots might get just far enough off course to pose a hazard to my favorite body. I didn't notice the abarand JL who came to tell us which shuttle to board until he was almost directly in front of me. When I did see him, I came to attention and snapped off a proper salute—more proper than I might have had I had more warning. Fred got the rest of the squad to their feet and at something approaching attention.

The lieutenant asked what squad we were and, after I

told him, he consulted a notepad, then pointed off to his right. "You will be on the first shuttle that landed," he said. "Forward starboard hatch. The shuttle's crew chief will show you which assault sleds to board."

"Yes, sir," I replied, giving the JL another salute. I'm not quite sure just what it is, but there is something about abarand that commands respect. My guess is that it must be something chemical—pheromones, or something like that—because abarand officers get me more military in bearing than any of the others do, and without the confrontational quality of porracci. Fred handed me my pack and helped me get it slung. The JL was already gone, heading for the next squad.

"Let's not waste any time," I said, speaking over my squad channel. That was the only way anyone was going to hear what I had to say over the din of the shuttle engines. "On the double."

I GUESS THERE'S ONLY BEEN ONE OFFICER I'VE served under who I not only unreservedly respected professionally but actually liked and counted as a friend. Tim Budgie had just made senior lieutenant when I was transferred into the company he was executive officer of, and he was a captain, almost due for promotion to major, the last time we served together. He was the one who explained our assault shuttles to me.

"They can't make them strong enough to survive the weapons that might be fired at them without making them too big, too slow, and too hard to maneuver to be any practical use. Since they don't like to spend too much money on something that might only get used once before it's destroyed, they go in the opposite direction. They build something that's cheap but fast enough to get the basic job done, which is to get combat soldiers on the ground in a hurry. That way, if they are destroyed the first time in a combat situation, the budget doesn't take as big a hit. Comfort isn't even on the list of things to consider."

You've only got to peek inside one to know that what he said about comfort is true. An assault shuttle is basically a pressurized shoebox, and shoes have more elbow room in a box than soldiers do in an assault shuttle. The ones our army uses will hold fifty-six passengers—a little more than one full-strength infantry platoon—with their weapons and the gear they normally pack on their backs. The human worlds were supplying more than half of the shuttles and transports for the combined regiment, more than half of a lot of the equipment other than personal weapons, uniforms, and so forth. I can stand upright in a shuttle, but I'm a bit below the average height for human soldiers. Anyone over six feet tall has to keep his head down, one way or another. Packed into web-sling seats, you're literally elbow to elbow with the men on either side of you.

It gets worse when the web seats are pulled and replaced with airsleds. The sleds stick up through the bottom of the shuttle after the seats are removed. Once the sleds are dropped, hatches close over the openings, and the passenger compartment can be pressurized again. The airsleds are little more than tubes twenty-four feet long and five feet, seven inches in diameter inside, with a couple of small engines and just enough lifting surface to keep them from falling like rocks. They have just enough life-support gear and air to keep their passengers alive during the few minutes of flight time they are expected to have after being dropped from a low-flying shuttle. Each airsled will hold six men, barely, crammed together like bobsled teams, crouching with knees pulled up and heads low. With our mixed squads, I wasn't certain if even five soldiers would fit. Porracci take up a lot of room.

I don't like airsleds at all, and I'm not all that much more fond of the shuttles, but nobody asked my opinion. Captain Budgie? He didn't make it home from the debacle on Dintsen.

BEING SHORT TWO MEMBERS OF THE SQUAD helped. We had a little breathing room after we were sealed into the airsleds. I warned the men against any grousing over their radio. "We wait, so get as comfortable as these contraptions allow." The low growl I heard on the squad channel could only have come from Fred Wilkins, but I didn't say anything. It would be easier to get comfortable in one of those medieval torture devices than in an airsled. Even the air that was being pumped through from the shuttle tasted foul. We would draw air and power from the shuttle until we were dropped.

I could feel tiny movements and hear feet moving and voices grumbling as other squads came aboard and got packed into their sleds. Then, after ten minutes, there was silence inside—as close to silence as possible in that tin box. There was only the low rumble of the shuttle's engines idling. I told myself that the engine noise was encouraging. If the wait were going to be very long, they would have shut down the engines to save fuel. Still, I was surprised at how quickly the shuttle started moving.

We had been in the airsled less than twenty minutes when the engines cycled up a couple of notches and we started taxiing through a tight left turn. Then the movement stopped, but the engine noises increased radically.

"We're about set to go," I whispered over the squad channel. "Hang on." I hardly had time to get the last words out before we were pressed backward when the pilot released the brakes, and the shuttle rushed forward.

Seconds later, the nose of the shuttle came up, quickly reaching a sixty-degree angle of climb. The engine noises peaked about two decibels short of causing semi-ipermanent hearing loss, uncomfortable even through the insulation of helmets. The gee load increased dramatically. For a second I wondered if we were going to burn for orbit instead of hitting a suborbital trajectory to take us to our drop point. But the maximum power burn did not last long enough for that. The engines eased off considerably, and we nosed forward a little.

"Everyone run a quick systems check," I instructed on the squad channel, and I started the diagnostic routine on my own electronics. That takes fifteen seconds, and I started getting reports from the others as quickly as I got my own. All of the gear appeared to be in working order. That was a pleasant surprise. Failures in human gear because of a shuttle takeoff are rare, but they do happen, and I didn't know how good the gear of the other species was.

It gets steamy quickly inside an airsled, even if you don't start out with hot temperatures—and we had. We were hot, sweaty, and rank by the time we got off the ground. The mixture of odors from different species doesn't make all that much difference to the overall smell. You learn to breathe through your mouth. That helps. It's one more thing to make a guy thankful that rides inside an airsled usually don't last long. This one was about average for a suborbital shot, ground to ground, about nine minutes. I had frequent updates from the copilot, telling me how long it would be before the sled was launched. Those updates started out a minute apart, then went to thirty seconds. During the final minute, they came every five seconds, with a final countdown of the last fifteen.

The shuttle blew us out the bottom and we dropped while our guidance system caught up and took over directing us toward our landing zone. It's all automatic. There are no controls inside the airsled, and nothing to let the passengers see where they're going. You have to trust that the autopilot is functioning and has the right information in its memory. The shuttle crew can override or correct, but the slight time lag that involves could be critical if things were going wrong. An out-of-control airsled landing is about as survivable as riding a bomb. Even when they're not out of control—which is, thankfully, the vast majority of the time—airsleds scare the crap out of me. The first time I had ridden one in, that had been literally true. For some soldiers, it's true every time.

I held on to the rails at my sides so fiercely that no one, not even a porracci, could have pried my fingers loose. The air buffeted us from side to side. We dropped on an extremely steep glide path. That's normal. The idea is to get the sled on the ground as quickly as possible, to give an enemy minimal time to target you with a shoulder-fired missile or a crew-served heavy weapon. It doesn't take much to do lethal damage to an airsled.

We hit the ground, but not hard enough to burrow in. The sled skidded along the turf, using only compressed gas jets to slow us down. The terrain provided more braking. We could hear underbrush, maybe even small trees, snapping and hitting the sides of the tube. That final part of the ride always seems just shy of eternal, but according to the people who are supposed to know, it's never more than twenty seconds and usually significantly less. The sled came to a halt, tipped ten degrees to the right, and the overhead hatches popped open automatically. I meant every word of the brief prayer of thanksgiving I offered before I said, "Up and out!" over the squad channel. It was time to be infantrymen again and not sardines in a can.

MY SQUAD'S TWO SLEDS HAD COME TO A STOP within fifty yards of each other. With my helmet's night-vision system I could see the tracks the cans had followed plowing their way to a halt. There was a noticeable temperature difference to the terrain where friction from the sleds had heated the ground and greenery. Not that I spent more than about half a second contemplating the scenery. The first thing you do when you get out of the sled is put distance between you and it, in case an enemy is targeting it. Those trails the sleds leave are awfully large markers.

My people all knew the drill even though this was the first time we had done the maneuver out of a real sled together. Our rendezvous point was sixty yards in front of the sleds and halfway between their tracks. We needed no more than twenty seconds after the hatches popped to gather. Adrenaline will do that. Since I didn't have full telemetry from all of my people, I had to do the head count visually. Everyone had made it.

"Our compass bearing is eighty-five degrees," I said after a quick look at my folding electronic map. "We've got three hundred yards of this high grass and brush before we get to forest. Iyi and Oyo, I want the two of you on point, thirty yards in front of the rest of us. Once we hit trees, you'll go high and out to either side. Fred, you're next in line, then me, then Nuyi. Souvana, I want you next, then Jaibie and Kiervauna."

"Kiervauna and I should exchange places," Souvana said. "I should be the rear guard. I am more capable of handling that."

"We do it my way," I said, annoyed that my assistant squad leader would question my orders. Besides, the number two man should not be at the back end except under the most extraordinary circumstances. "Now, let's get moving. We've got a lot of ground to cover." I stared at Souvana, silently daring him to continue the argument. But he didn't.

The two biraunta started out. The rest of us fell in behind, in the order I had chosen.

THE AREA WE HAD BEEN DROPPED INTO WAS closer to Dancer's equator than the regiment's main camp. It was 0020 hours when we popped out of the sleds. Even in the middle of the night the temperature was close to ninety and humid, without a breath of wind to make it less uncomfortable. Beyond the verge of savanna the terrain turned to rain forest, so humid that there was a layer of ground mist that came nearly to our waists. Forest, not jungle. That meant that ground level was mostly clear of bushes, grass, or any other low flora. Everything fought for sunlight, and so all the vegetation grew as high as possible. You only find "jungle" conditions where there are breaks in the forest canopy, at treefall sites and along watercourses, where sunlight penetrates to ground level and new growth has a chance for its share of the light.

We ran into our share of watercourses. I think we crossed half a dozen creeks in two hours. Some of the

underbrush along those streams was so thick that we had
to cut our way through. Of course, Iyi and Oyo were
able to go over the tangle some of the time, where the
crowns of trees came close to touching over the water;
and even when they had to come down to ground level,
they were so thin and agile that often they could slink
through where the rest of us could not. Other than at
those brief times, they remained generally thirty feet or
more above the heads of the rest of us, breaking radio
silence only rarely, when one or the other had something
important to say. The biraunta were excellent on sound
discipline.

There were no opportunities for long rests. We were
on a tight schedule. Up ahead was the escarpment at the
edge of a rift valley. We were in the valley, and we were
to climb the cliff before sunrise. I had to push the squad
as hard as it could go. Our speed was limited by Nuyi's
pace. Divotect are not made for great speed, though they
can keep going far longer than some of the rest of us
can.

Of the nonhumans in the squad, I think I knew Nuyi
best. That might sound strange, since divotect are the
most alien of the species we've met. Maybe that was
part of the reason why I put more effort into getting to
know him. The other part was the fact that I was more
familiar with divotect from my time on Dintsen. We had
fought alongside one another as long as fighting was
possible. While we had not lost as many humans as divotect in the battle, the proportion was about equal. But
the divotect kept losing people after the surviving humans had been evacuated. It had been nearly nine
months since the humans had been lifted off that world.
There was a chance that there weren't many divotect left
alive there.

Before war reached Dintsen, I had opportunities to see how the divotect lived there. Life was slow-paced, and that is not a slur based on their reptilian ancestry. The divotect on Dintsen had an agrarian lifestyle for the most part, and that only requires intense effort during a couple of short periods during the growing cycle—and much of that work was automated. Dintsen was a colony world, small and not as industrial as the older divotect worlds. In their earliest stages, most colony worlds are agrarian. It's only later that industry and commerce become important.

Divotect are strictly monogamous, mating for life, with both parents caring for their eggs and young. The period of dependency for their young is nearly as long as it is among humans. The concepts of divorce and remarriage are so alien to divotect thinking that they had difficulty dealing with the fact that not all sentient species bond as strongly as they do. I'm not sure they understand it yet, though they do accept it, out of necessity if nothing else.

It is difficult to read emotion, or anything else, in the face of a divotect. Their leathery skin is not very expressive. I've heard people say that divotect go through life with a constant "hangdog" look. But you *can* read emotion and mood in their faces once you get used to trying, in the eyes and the small folds of skin around them.

Nuyi was several inches taller than me, but we weighed about the same. I could outrun him at any distance up to a mile. Beyond that, my pace slowed a lot sooner than his did, and at any distance over five miles he was likely to beat me. In unarmed combat we would be about equal, whenever we finally got around to doing that.

I put Nuyi directly behind me in the line of march for one reason. I trusted him absolutely.

THIS WAS A TRAINING EXERCISE, SO I KEPT MY eyes open for items to critique after it was over. But there were few of those. None of the soldiers in my squad was a raw recruit. They knew what they were supposed to do and—mostly—they did it. And we had worked together long enough to get the awkwardness of new comrades behind us. We were all learning about our squadmates, what each was likely to do in any given situation. That process would go on for as long as we served together, but we were already getting to a point where I was less concerned about someone doing anything completely unexpected. It was rarely necessary for me to make any of the routine noises about minding the spacing between men, and no one had developed the bad habit of chattering with others in the squad. Of course, that was largely due to the fact that we came from so many different species. In a way, it would have been comforting had the squad started doing some of that unnecessary chatter. To be our best as a *team,* we would have to get a lot closer in ways most of us had still not managed.

We moved single file, doing what we could to step in the footprints of the soldier in front of us. That makes it more difficult for an enemy—even the hypothetical sort in a training drill—to count your numbers, and it cuts down the chances of tripping a mine or a booby trap. The point man takes that risk. But it isn't easy when everyone is built for different-size steps.

"Move as if you expect an aggressor force to pounce on us any second," I warned my men before we entered the forest. "Nobody said there won't be opposition out here, and the odds are we'll run into *some*thing."

I was pleased that no one was goofing off. A long hike at night, with only a *possibility* that there might actually be simulated trouble along the way, makes the tendency to slack off all the greater. I started feeling optimistic about the whole deal—the combined regiment and sticking all of the species together. We still had a long way to go, but maybe, just *maybe,* the experiment would succeed.

By my calculation we had two hours and fifteen minutes until first light when we reached the edge of the rift valley and saw how much climbing we had to do—a rock wall more than a hundred feet high. Then we had a couple of miles of ground to traverse as well. Before sunrise. The forest ended fifteen to twenty yards from the base of the cliff, held back by the piles of loose rock—scree—that had fallen over the ages. I told the men to rest for a few minutes while I used binoculars to survey a stretch of the cliff, looking for the easiest route up. After I had done my part, and everyone had a chance to catch their breath and take a few sips of water, I took Oyo and Iyi aside and had them look as well.

"I want the two of you to take ropes up and secure them so the rest of us can make the climb," I said, lifting my faceplate and whispering just to the biraunta. "That's the only way we're going to make it on schedule." The twins nodded in unison.

"It should not be difficult for us," Oyo said. "I see a clear path." The biraunta could climb rock almost as handily as they could traverse a forest canopy. "We can start there and move toward the right about a third of the way up."

"Whatever works best," I said. We had plenty of rope.

Fred and I each carried two hundred feet of a quarter-inch-diameter cord that was stronger than steel wire of the same dimension but weighed only about twenty ounces per hundred feet. The ropes the porracci carried were about as strong, but bulkier and heavier. Jaibie and Nuyi carried shorter lengths of rope. The biraunta did not carry rope as a normal part of their gear. Since the human rope weighed less, that's what they would take.

While the biraunta climbed, I put the rest of the squad in a defensive perimeter, facing away from the rock wall. I kept my eyes on the two men climbing, and also watched the top of the cliff in case there was an "enemy" waiting for us there. I was amazed by how quickly the biraunta were able to scramble up the rock, especially since they climbed freehand, without using the ropes or any of the "technical" mountain climbing gear the rest of us would have required. They needed less than fifteen minutes. I doubt that I could have done it in under an hour.

Iyi and Oyo secured the ropes at the top and let the coils fall. It was then that I decided to take the gamble. "Souvana, you go up first on the left rope. Jaibie, you lead on the right." I knew how big a chance I was taking, setting one of the porracci first on one of the ropes behind the biraunta, but . . . well, I thought it was a chance I had to take. We all had to be able to work together, in whatever combination circumstances dictated. I hoped that Jaibie's presence up top would be enough to prevent any extreme reaction from Iyi and Oyo, and if it didn't . . . well, that was something I had to *know*. I went up in the next pair with Nuyi, taking care to stay level with him. Kiervauna and Fred brought up the rear.

Until I got to the top of the cliff, I had no idea what I would find. I half expected to find that Oyo and Iyi had put as much distance as possible between themselves and Souvana—maybe just taken off running the way that one pair of biraunta had early in our training. But no, they had stood their ground, beginning the new defensive perimeter on top of the escarpment.

Score a big one for us, I thought. *We're making progress.*

FIFTEEN MINUTES FOR THE BIRAUNTA TO GET TO the top and secure the ropes. Twenty minutes to get the rest of us up. The terrain was a lot different above than below. The plateau was arid, rocky, and appeared almost devoid of vegetation, almost as monotonously bleak as the landscape of Mars. I had the impression of being able to see almost forever when I looked east of the escarpment, but that was deceptive. The ground was uneven, rolling, and littered with rocks up to the size of a large house. Thousands of soldiers could hide in a square mile of that terrain.

Looking west, I could see the forest canopy below us. We wouldn't have to walk very far east before we would lose sight of that completely. The tallest trees in the forest topped out at least twenty feet below the level of the plateau.

"We'll take fifteen minutes to rest," I said, "but I want to move two hundred yards from where we came up first." I pointed north. The terrain there appeared marginally more convoluted than the terrain to the south, and I was thinking about concealment . . . in case there were aspects to this exercise we hadn't been warned about. And I would have been surprised if there weren't.

If nothing else, I figured we were running at least fifteen minutes ahead of what anyone would expect.

Dawn was an hour away. Using the biraunta to get us up the cliff fast might have bought us enough time to get into position before any aggressor force would look for us.

We moved quickly but cautiously toward the area I had chosen for our rest. When we got there, I had the squad take defensive positions and inspect the area inside our perimeter to make certain we were alone.

"Stay low, under the rock overhangs as much as you can," I said. "You all know what to do: Put sensors out and then move around as little as possible. If you hear air traffic or anything else, freeze." If we were being tracked from space, we were going to be visible unless we all crawled under rocks, but there was nothing we could do to prevent that sort of surveillance. If it was there, it would see us. We had to do what we could about the things we *could* affect.

We had two miles to traverse before reaching our final goal, a cluster of large rocks below a gentle slope that put the top of those rocks thirty feet or more below our current positions. My orders were simply to transmit a radio signal once we reached the goal. We were to remain unobserved, if possible, until then. That goes almost without saying in spec ops. Don't let the enemy know you're around until you strike, then disappear again and get out before he can hurt you.

I took a long, slow drink of water, holding it in my mouth and allowing it to trickle back into my throat a little at a time. For a few seconds I allowed myself the luxury of closing my eyes. The aches in my legs and arms weren't too bad, just a dull throbbing that I noticed only because we were resting. Once we started moving again, the aches would fade; now they were like a metronome, as regular as my heartbeat, almost hypnotic in their effect. It helped me ignore the rivers of sweat caught between my skin and outer clothing.

I blinked myself alert, worried that I had come close to letting myself fall asleep. I looked around, to where I knew each of my men were. Then I checked the time. We had three minutes left of the fifteen I had promised.

I moved my arms and legs a little, trying to work out the kinks. That's more of a worry for me now than when I first joined the army. I was younger then. Another sip of water. Several measured breaths, taking in as much air as my lungs would hold, then expelling it all. *We're getting close to the end,* I told myself. In time, you pick up all kinds of little tricks for getting through the day, no matter what it brings. And we still didn't know what *this* day was holding for us.

"Okay, let's get going," I said, exactly at the end of fifteen minutes. I got to my feet slowly, conserving energy. The others got to their feet as well, without so much as an audible groan. Even two weeks earlier, I was sure the result would have been different. We were making progress.

"Assume there's an aggressor force waiting somewhere between here and our objective," I reminded everyone. "Concealment and silence. We've got plenty of time, so there's no need to rush."

Though sunrise was nearly an hour off, we could see a slightly brighter area rimming the horizon in front of us. We moved into field order. I kept our biraunta out as scouts, off to either side and fifty yards ahead of the next man. I put Jaibie there. His vision was perhaps sharper than anyone else's in the squad. I followed him, with Nuyi still behind me, then Souvana, Wilkins, and Kiervauna.

Our camouflage wasn't appropriate for these surroundings. In the forests, where most of our training had been done, the patterns—slightly different from species to species—were almost perfect, but against the red rock and orange sand of this plateau, they were completely out of place. That provided good reason not to linger. The farther we got before daylight, the longer we could remain undetected visually.

We did not attempt to follow a straight line toward our objective. Instead, we picked our route to take advantage of the terrain, making certain we were never silhouetted on high ground, going around rocks and along the lowest paths through them. We moved silently. Our progress was slow, but perhaps not as slow as a civilian might expect. Although I kept the external microphones on my helmet up near the maximum gain, I never once heard a boot scrape on rock, or any other noise from our passage.

We had been traveling for not quite twenty minutes when Jaibie stopped abruptly, ten yards in front of me, and held up his right arm with his fist clenched—*halt*. I stopped and repeated the gesture for the soldiers behind me, then waited while Jaibie conveyed a more complicated series of hand gestures. One of the biraunta had spotted something, or someone, in front of us. I gestured for everyone to get down and remain motionless while our scouts investigated.

It was fourteen minutes later when Iyi worked his way back to me. He got right up close, lifted his faceplate, and made his report, whispering, scarcely vocalizing at all. That was more secure than reporting over the radio. Electronic emissions might be detected. Iyi had spotted three soldiers between us and our objective, and thought he had seen movement indicating at least two others— about four hundred yards in front of us. His guess was that this force had our objective completely surrounded. "It is not a *tight* perimeter," he added. "There seem to be ten yards between soldiers, maybe more. I know my brother and I can sneak through without being observed."

"Okay. The rest of us will move in as close as we can without being seen, and get in position to cover you and your brother. The two of you will infiltrate. Leave all of your gear but your weapons. Get to the objective and send the signal."

Iyi nodded, then took off his field pack and web belt before crawling off to find Oyo. I used the next couple of minutes to pass the word to the others, then gave the biraunta another three minutes before I started moving the squad. We crawled, literally, the last hundred yards, faceplates sliding along the rock, ending up no more than fifty yards from where Iyi had said the "enemy" perimeter was located. There was no alarm given.

Then we waited. I set my radio to monitor the channel we were to use to report success. The sky was showing definite signs of the approach of dawn, a gradual lightening that had already hidden all but the brightest stars in the eastern third of the sky. Iyi and Oyo did not have many minutes left if they hoped to reach the objective unseen, and that pile of rocks was a good quarter mile inside the perimeter of the defending force.

Ten minutes. The edges of the rocks east of us were clearly defined now, even when I switched off my night-vision gear for a few seconds. We were running out of time. I had to remind myself not to hold my breath. That's a bad habit I have when tension starts to build. I was staring at the seconds ticking by on the timeline on my head-up display. Any second now Iyi or Oyo might be spotted, an alarm given.

Then I heard the arranged signal that we had reached our objective. Fifteen seconds later I had a call from Lieutenant Fusik. "Good work, Dragon. Your squad is the first to complete its mission. There was no sighting report from the aggressor force. Gather your men. We'll have air transport for you in . . . thirty minutes."

"Right, sir," I said. "Has the aggressor force been told we're here yet?"

"I believe they're being told right now. One of the line companies."

Well, they had received eight days less training than we had. It would have been more satisfying had we infiltrated part of Ranger Battalion. But it still felt good. And it felt even better a few hours later, when I learned that we were the only squad to make it in all the way, on schedule, without being observed.

CHAPTER 6

GOOD IN WEEK SEVEN IS NOT THE SAME AS good in week eleven. The longer our training went on, the more General Ransom and Colonel Hansen expected of us . . . and the more I expected from the men in my squad. We were all in peak physical condition by the start of week eleven. For the past two weeks we had been working an average of eighteen hours a day, from before sunrise until after sunset. Twice we had been out on exercises that lasted a day and a half to two full days— twenty-eight-hour Dancer days—with little or no chance for sleep. The second of those exercises had involved another simulated combat landing in airsleds, with more complex missions once we were on the ground.

Our ghuroh contingent had still not arrived, but that Monday morning, the first day of week eleven, the colonel announced that he had definite word that they would arrive before the end of the week, which would give us at least six weeks to train with everyone who was supposed to be part of the combined regiment before the big shots who were going to evaluate our performance for the general staff came in to see what we could do.

Main camp looked a little less ragged than it had when we first arrived. Apparently the worst of the rainy season had ended. Sometimes we went two or three days without noticeable precipitation, so the ground had time to dry out a little. The engineers had been turning big rocks into little ones with a couple of large stone-crushing mills, so there were gravel streets between the rows of tents and temporary buildings, and a better landing strip for the shuttles.

WEEK ELEVEN. WE WERE FINALLY GOING TO AT-tempt to start the cross-species unarmed combat training. There had been no end of lectures and conferences, in addition to the "visits" of junior officers and noncoms to the various groups. General Ransom had bucked the decision up the chain of command and off-planet weeks before. Specialists from every species in the regiment had been consulted, brought in to ask questions, observe, and make interested humming noises before they left. Some of them were almost comical, not far from the "let's cross our fingers and pray it works" variety.

All along, I had been doing what I could to get my biraunta more accustomed to porracci. I was fairly sure that Oyo and Iyi wouldn't go berserk when the time came for them to go hand-to-hand against Souvana or Kiervauna. At least I *hoped* they wouldn't. I suspect that every squad leader and platoon sergeant was doing the same sort of thing, with extra emphasis in the squads that were led by porracci.

It was crunch time. Reveille, morning exercises, and breakfast had come and gone. The battalion mustered for work call, then had separated into companies and platoons for unarmed combat training. I'm certain there were plenty of people standing around with crossed fingers, including General Ransom. He was out to observe, along with his entire staff, roaming from group to group. It was one of the very few times he had been visible watching any of our training.

Tonio Xeres formed first platoon in a circle around the "arena" we would be using—an area with a few inches of sand spread over the grass and dirt to cushion falls. None of us was wearing anything but fatigue uniforms—no weapons, field packs, or web belts. "Okay, you all know what this is about," Tonio said, standing in the center and turning to look at each squad. "This is a vital part of our training. When we get into the war, we have to know how to deal with the enemy. The enemy is any soldier who wears the uniform of the Ilion Federation. That is the only distinction that counts.

"Look around the circle," Tonio ordered. "We're human, biraunta, porracci, divotect, abarand. By the end of the week we'll also be ghuroh. We're different, like members of no army in any of our histories have been. But we are the same." He spaced each word of that sentence, emphasizing. "We are all part of the same army, serving the Alliance of Light. Despite the differences, we are comrades, brothers. When we go into combat, each one of us will depend on every other one, for our very lives and for the success of our mission. How well we work together, how far we trust and respect each other, could spell the difference between life and death, could even determine whether we can ever win this war."

Man, Tonio was good spouting that stuff. I knew he meant every word he said, but still . . . it almost made you want to stand at attention and salute. We did not have a common anthem, but if a band had broken out playing "The Green Hills," the human anthem, I might have teared up, even though a look around that circle showed that—as far as possible—we were still segregating ourselves within each squad.

"Our unarmed combat training may well save your life. Everyone has been lectured on how to approach hand-to-hand combat with opponents of each species. Once each pairing is announced, you'll be given a moment to review the essentials before the match starts. This is not going to be a free-for-all. The purpose of this is training, nothing more. We are here to learn, not to attempt to prove who is better than whom. Each match will be closely refereed to make certain no one is seriously injured. You will immediately obey any order by your referee. *Immediately!*" The repeat of that word was shouted.

I was not at all surprised when the first pairing Tonio called pitted him against the porracci leader of second squad, because I had told him that when my squad got into the act, the first pairing should match me with Souvana, my porracci assistant. We had to face up against the porracci first—even if we got our butts kicked flat in five seconds—before we could think of biraunta-porracci pairings.

Sergeant Chouvana, the porracci squad leader, was about the same size as my assistant, Souvana, and a few years older. His fur was a dark ocher, and showed a considerable number of scars through bare patches from his past dominance challenges. He moved out into the center of the ring as soon as the pairing was announced. The biraunta leader of third squad, Sergeant Aytah Vul Nemmi, was to referee. That was something I hadn't thought of in advance, but putting one biraunta in control early on ought to give the rest of his people a little more confidence later, when they came face to face with porracci.

Aytah gave the order to begin. The match takes longer

to describe than it took to happen. Tonio took a step forward, feinting left, then his right foot struck out in a low, sweeping kick that connected with the back of Chouvana's left knee. As the knee started to buckle, the porracci went into a backward roll, and he was back on his feet almost before Tonio could get set again. Tonio appeared to start the same sequence of moves, but when Chouvana adjusted to meet the same attack, Tonio tackled him head-high, putting his feet into Chouvana's middle, then fell backward to flip the porracci over his head. Chouvana landed on his back, hard. Ten feet away, I could hear the air forced from his lungs. A drop like that would have left me unable to do anything long enough for an opponent to tattoo *the end* on me, but Chouvana recovered a lot faster, and the third time Tonio came at him, Chouvana pinned his arms to his sides and lifted him off the ground in a bear hug.

Aytah immediately called an end to the match, and Chouvana set Tonio down—not *quite* gently. Tonio took a couple of cautious breaths, then nodded at Chouvana, who nodded back—more abruptly.

Souvana and I were the next pairing. I'll spare you the gory details. I tried to get to Souvana's side for a hip throw and ended up standing on my head in short order, with Souvana dangling me by my ankles. At least I learned not to attempt *that* particular move against a porracci in the future.

After the first two, we moved to running two pairings at once, getting the whole platoon involved faster. Once all of the squad leaders and their assistants had their first matches, it got more general. I concentrated on the matches in my own squad, of course, apart from facing off against each of my men, except Wilkins, during the course of the morning. The biraunta versus porracci pairings were put off as long as possible, to give the biraunta as much time to get used to the idea as we could, to let them see that they weren't the only ones who were not a direct match one-on-one against the porracci . . . and to let them see that the porracci were not necessarily invincible.

There were surprises. It took Jaibie less than a minute to defeat Kiervauna, and he fought Souvana even-on for more than two minutes before I stopped that match. Jaibie weighed about the same as I did, but was a lot faster than the porracci, and not that much weaker than either of them. But the real surprise was Nuyi. He showed quicker reactions than I had ever seen from him. He was still slower than most of us, but he was also stronger, and able to bear more pressure—if not real pain. It took him less than thirty seconds to put Kiervauna down, and only about twice as long to put Souvana in a hold that caused the referee to stop that match. Souvana requested a rematch, and Nuyi agreed. This time the fight went on for three minutes, even, before I stopped it, with compliments to both of them.

Neither of our biraunta could stop a porracci, but Iyi and Oyo went into it without visible hesitation. For about two seconds, I thought Iyi might actually stop Kiervauna. Iyi leaped onto the porracci's shoulders and got his tail wrapped tightly around Kiervauna's neck, in a stranglehold. If he had managed to hold that grip for another ten seconds, the referee would have been forced to end the match, but Kiervauna got both hands on the biraunta and simply peeled him off, then dropped him.

We all put on a good show that morning. In the entire battalion, no biraunta panicked, and only two refused to attempt to go into unarmed combat drill with porracci—and one of those was eventually coaxed into it. The other . . . was transferred to one of the line companies before the day was out, and replaced by a bir-aunta who was not quite so terrified.

AFTER MONDAY MORNING, THE UNARMED COM-bat training continued, but not with the entire battalion doing it at once. We went into a rotation of training segments again, but usually with two companies dedicated to hand-to-hand at any given time. We were so many weeks behind in that aspect of our training that extra time *had* to be devoted to it. Something like that is a learning process on many levels. We learned what did not work against each variety of opponent, and—slowly—we started to learn tricks that might work, and countermeasures, and so forth.

Still, there is a limit. You have to include other training to give time for the inevitable bruises and aches to ease, to strain other muscles, to flex the mind in different ways. There were hikes, often at a forced pace; map problems; infiltration techniques, day and night; hours spent on the firing range; and so forth. We kept busy all day, every day, with night exercises every other evening—the same demanding sort of schedule we had been following all along, only longer, more intense.

Besides the great relief that almost everyone in the regiment shared at the success of our unarmed training combat, I found one other benefit. Corporal Souvana was much less contentious that week. I can't say that his initial defeat at the hands of Nuyi *humbled* him, but his ego had taken a blow, and he remained relatively subdued for several days. It was Thursday before he had recovered enough to remind me how handily he had defeated me.

* * *

THURSDAY WAS ALSO THE DAY THAT THE GHU-
roh contingent for the regiment finally arrived. The first
three ships popped out of hyperspace all at once, coming
in on different courses, as if they were worried that they
might find Dancer held by the enemy. Once they were
reassured, their troops started coming in by shuttle. Additional ships followed, about fifty minutes apart. There
were eight ships altogether.

In many ways, I found the appearance of ghuroh more
intimidating than porracci. They were rather canine in
appearance, with pronounced muzzles and jowls, and
pointed ears set on top of their heads. But they were
exclusively bipedal, and the hips were more like those
of humans than dogs. The facial features reminded me
of mastiffs on Earth. I had a feeling of *The Hound of
the Baskervilles* from them. Tailless and almost totally
hairless, the ghuroh soldiers varied from just over six
feet to about seven feet tall, broad across the shoulders,
and thin at the hips, weighing from 180 to 260 pounds.
Their hands had four digits, but the stubby thumbs were
just barely opposable. Biraunta and divotect were the
only species in the regiment with tails.

The two ghuroh assigned to my squad reported, carrying their weapons and gear, after the fourth ship unloaded. They were both privates, Kworamitamikayen
and Kwayimminiwelyan. Since the names were even
harder to pronounce than they are to spell, they were
quickly discarded and the two new privates, both placed
in the squad's second fire team, quickly became Fang
and Claw, respectively. They suggested those names
themselves, and seemed to find them more than a little
humorous. Fang was a little taller than Claw, weighed
fifteen pounds more, and his skin color was light enough
to make it easy to distinguish between them.

We started integrating the ghuroh into our training the next morning, Friday. We were given two priorities by the colonel: Work on squad tactics, and get the ghuroh involved in the hand-to-hand training as quickly as possible. The hand-to-hand matches were something, especially those between ghuroh and porracci. When Fang and Souvana went at it, I had to get help to stop the fight before they injured each other. We had to pry them apart. Ghuroh society was formed in matriarchal clans. Adult males were isolated from family life, being tolerated by the females only when they were in estrus. Between that and the fact that they had a pack-hunting ancestry, they were perhaps the species most suited to military life. Dominance was as important to ghuroh as it was to porracci. Neither wanted to quit before the other, neither wanted to admit that their opponent was at least equal in ability. Even after we pulled Fang and Souvana apart, they moved around, facing each other, posturing, ready to resume the contest. I had to keep a close eye on them the rest of the day to make certain they didn't set at each other again.

And I had both ghuroh assigned to the same fire team as the porracci. I thought hard, all weekend, about rearranging the fire teams.

All in all, we managed four days of training with our complement complete before Colonel Hansen dropped a load of bricks on our heads. We weren't going to get the full four months of training we had been promised. In two days the regiment would be shipping out, headed for combat.

The war wouldn't wait on our convenience. And I had to keep my fire teams the way they were, no matter what problems that might cause. There wasn't time to switch people around and get them functioning properly.

CHAPTER 7

FOUR DAYS SIMPLY WEREN'T LONG ENOUGH.
You can't add more than 20 percent to your numbers
and expect anything to run smoothly that soon, even
without the antagonism between ghuroh and porracci,
and the lingering "We're better than you are" that just
about everyone felt. New soldiers disrupted the rhythms
the rest of us had fallen into, and a team has to have
that rhythm, the timing that comes from knowing what
your comrades will do.

The fifth day, the one between the colonel's announcement and our departure, didn't add a lot to the
integration of the ghuroh. Actually, we only had half a
day for actual training. We were given the morning to
work on whatever we thought we needed most in each
squad. That afternoon—and well into the evening—we
had lectures, briefings, and a draw of replacement gear
for anything that might have been damaged in training.

The first bombshell was where we were going. Colonel Hansen broke it to the officers and sergeants of
Ranger Battalion, bringing us together near his head-

quarters. He was staring at Tonio and me when he mentioned the name of the planet.

"We're going to Dintsen." He said it in what was almost a conversational voice—considering how many people he was talking to. My stomach knotted up. I felt as if the blood were starting to drain from my head. *Back to Dintsen.* It was all in my head, but I imagined that I felt twinges from the wounds I had received there. That was impossible. I was fully healed, and there weren't even any visible scars from the holes that two bullets and several dozen pieces of shrapnel had put in my body.

"We're going to take Dintsen back from the Ilion Federation, stop the genocide that the tonatin have started there. This is the first step on the long road to victory over this mindless aggression and crimes so horrible that sane people can scarcely countenance the possibility," Hansen continued. "We will hold our faith with our divotect allies. They have borne the brunt of this war's horrors. We must liberate the occupied worlds before it is too late." It sounded like a prepared speech, something he might have been reading, something the politicians back home might have scripted, but he didn't have any copy to read from.

"We had hoped to have more time to get the 1st Combined Regiment prepared for action, but that time has been stolen from us. Alliance intelligence has information that suggests that the Ilion Federation will strike at the core worlds of the divotect as soon as they consolidate their victories on Dintsen and the other divotect colony worlds they invaded to start this war. We have to start taking back the worlds they have invaded and prevent them from invading any others."

He went on for another twenty minutes, laying on the

soap with both hands—how we had progressed so well in the time we had, and so forth—but long before he finished, I had read all the way between the lines. Other than the goal of halting the genocide, and the possibility that the remaining divotect worlds might switch sides to try to protect their people, the Alliance was simply trying to buy time to get more troops trained. We were going to be thrown to the wolves to slow down the timetables of the Ilion Federation. Colonel Hansen never said it straight out, but the 1st Combined Regiment was expendable.

IN ADDITION TO BEING THE COMPANY'S EXEC-utive officer, Junior Lieutenant Krau'vi Taivana was also the nominal platoon leader of first platoon. I had found the porracci JL fairly easy to work with. That wasn't simply because he left the platoon sergeant and squad leaders to do their jobs without unnecessary interference. I was human, so I wasn't competition, the way he might view others of his own race. His attitude was "Do whatever you have to do to get the job done." He was only interested in results, not the minny-moe stuff. That was just dandy with me.

Actually, we hadn't had much direct contact with Taivana. Until the two ghuroh JLs arrived, the company was short on officers, and the three we had were bogged down trying to carry all the red tape while getting in their own training. Taivana and Hohi had each tried to look after two platoons, and that didn't give them much time for anything but essentials.

I don't know if the company commander found his assistant as contentious as I found mine. If Taivana was giving Lieutenant Fusik any lip, it was never in front of the enlisted men.

Lieutenant Taivana made the announcement of our destination to the platoon without the sugarcoating Colonel Hansen had felt necessary. "We go to Dintsen to throw the Ilion Federation off and keep them from attacking any more divotect worlds," he said. "Assume that our battalion will go in first. That is our job. We will complete whatever missions we are given to the best of our ability. We will not fail. Failure is not acceptable."

The look he spread around might have added a little stiffness to a few backbones. *Fail to do your job and you'll have to answer to me* seems to be a pretty fair translation of that look. Porracci weren't renowned for accepting excuses for failure. I knew the other porracci in the platoon would rather face anything else in the galaxy than a dominant porracci who was pissed off at them.

FANG AND CLAW HAD BOTH SEEN COMBAT FAR more recently than anyone else in the squad. Their unit had been part of the action that had caused such a delay in the arrival of all our ghuroh. We had heard some of their stories. The battalion their unit had faced directly had been tonatin, so we were all interested in the tactics the enemy had used. The tonatin provided the bulk of the army of the Ilion Federation—more than half the troops and two-thirds of the command structure, according to the intelligence briefings we had received—and the overall conduct of the war was according to their strategic plan. We had received a series of lectures on the tonatin—history, politics, and everything else that might help us fight them successfully.

Human army units had been receiving briefings about the tonatin since the start of the war. Our general staff had made a point of issuing and reinforcing one caution right from the beginning: "Just because they look almost human, don't make the mistake of believing that they will act human."

If you didn't look too closely at a holo of a tonatin, you might think the picture was of a Neanderthal from Earth's prehistoric period. Tonatin have the same brow ridge, the forward-thrusting jaw, the same slightly hunched-forward posture. Some people on Earth think of them as "long-lost cousins," suggesting that we might have common ancestors. A couple of political fringe groups had long suggested that we had joined the wrong interstellar alliance, that we should not be opposing tonatin. But tonatin have no genetic relationship with humans or Neanderthals.

Tonatin average slightly larger than humans. The figures we were given were six feet, three inches and three hundred pounds for the average height and weight of adult males. Their brains are also slightly larger, and equally developed; the briefing officers always stopped short of saying that that made tonatin more intelligent than us. The primary visible physical difference is in the hands, I suppose, since I can recall seeing a few humans who bore some resemblance to Neanderthals. Tonatin have four fingers, two opposite two, making the hands look like mechanical claws.

AFTER SUPPER THAT EVENING I GATHERED THE squad in our tent. The day had been less hot than most we had spent on Dancer, with heavy cloud cover but no rain, and a nice stiff breeze. We had the flaps up at either end of the tent to take advantage of it. Everyone was sitting on their cots except me. I paced up and down the aisle between the rows while I talked. I'm more comfortable that way.

"Okay, you know what's going on as much as I do. The brass-asses are dumping us in the middle of all the crap a lot sooner than we expected. We haven't had all the training we need. Fang and Claw haven't had time to get used to working with us, and we haven't had time to get used to working with them. We'll have to take that one step at a time, think through our actions a little more than we might otherwise, but it's something we can overcome. Once the bullets start flying, we'll all learn about each other in a hurry.

"I don't know anything about the coming operation. I'm not sure anyone on Dancer does. The Alliance has ships scouting the situation on Dancer, according to what Lieutenant Fusik told the company sergeants. As soon as the latest intel comes in, the regimental staff will put the final touches on how we're going to be deployed. As soon as they tell me anything, I'll pass the pertinent information on to the rest of you.

"Remember, we are a team, the ten of us. We take care of each other. We do our jobs. If every squad functions the way it should, the platoon will function. And right up the line. The brass will take credit for the good we do, and they'll be the ones who are faulted if we don't, but *we* will know." There was a knot in my stomach as I looked around and talked about the teamwork we needed. The porracci and ghuroh were staring at each other as if waiting to start fighting again. The biraunta were still not comfortable around porracci. Fred Wilkins was bigoted against all of the other species. And just about everyone gave Nuyi as wide a berth as they could. Some team.

"They are sacrificing us to buy time for more troops to be trained," Souvana said, just loud enough to make certain that the rest of the squad would hear.

"If it comes to that," I said. Hell, I wasn't going to lie to my men. "We are soldiers and we'll go where they tell us, do what we're ordered to do. Maybe we won't do anything but buy that time, but maybe we'll end up proving that we're better than the big shots think we are. Fang, Claw, you've been in combat against the enemy recently. That will make up for some of the time we haven't had together."

I'm sure I wasn't the only one thinking, *But will it be enough?*

I HAD GIVEN MY PEP TALK. IT DIDN'T SEEM TO pep anyone up. After I finished, the others continued to sit around, looking as though they could already read their obituaries. Oyo moved from his bunk to sit next to his brother. Both their tails were coiling and uncoiling, but slowly, as if they lacked the energy to be as fidgety as they normally were. I stood in the center of the tent for a moment and looked around. No one wanted to meet my gaze, so I shrugged and left.

I wasn't feeling all that peppy myself. Maybe my squad *was* in good enough shape to pull its weight, but I had my doubts that the regiment as a whole was ready for combat. And I find it hard to conceive that anyone who has experienced battle once could ever look forward to a return engagement. But no one had forced me to join the army, and I could have left after recovering from the wounds I received the first time I went to Dintsen. I had known that we were in for a real war, that it was almost certain that I would find myself in combat again if I stayed in the service, but I had not taken a discharge when I could have. Maybe I'm just not too bright. Enough people have told me that over the years.

When I walked out of the tent that evening, I had no place special to go. Dancer had no recreation facilities to speak of, no bars or shows. I wasn't even certain if there was a chaplain for the human soldiers; and if there was, he was going to be up to his collar in people that evening. About the only place I *could* go was the mess tent for coffee and a sandwich or doughnuts. I didn't want to get too far away, so I sort of stooged around the company area, not getting out of sight of our tent for more than a few minutes at a time. I expected that some of the others would want to talk to me. And I wasn't at all surprised that the first one to come out and look for me was Nuyi.

He stopped just outside the tent, looked around until he spotted me, then shuffled in my direction. With only the artificial lights over the main camp, his leathery skin looked more purple than ever. By the way he moved, with his head down, feet scarcely leaving the ground, I could tell he wasn't happy.

"Nuyi," I said when he got close.

"Sergeant." He seemed reluctant to meet my eyes, even out alone the way we were. He slowly shifted his weight from one foot to the other. I started to prompt him, then changed my mind and closed my mouth to wait him out.

"I am afraid," he said after more than a minute of silence.

"So am I," I replied. "It's normal. We just can't let it get the better of us."

"It is not simply the fear of what might happen to me, Sergeant," Nuyi said, finally meeting my gaze. "I understand that fear. I accept it. More than that, I fear what we might find when we get to Dintsen, what we might learn, what the tonatin have done. I fear how I might react when I see evidence of the atrocities the tonatin have committed against my people."

I hesitated before I said, "None of us can say how we will react to something like that, but we will deal with whatever we find. If there is pain, or anger, we will have to hold it inside until we have leisure to let the feeling out. But we will *act* with discipline, as soldiers. We can't let ourselves become beasts, no matter the provocation." That did not come out quickly, and I was not trying to pass off his worries with glib lines. I was simply giving him the best answer I could. Some of it came out barely more coherent than a stutter. I could see how much concern Nuyi felt. I would not make light of that.

"If what we find is as terrible as what my fears paint in my mind, I do not know if I will be able to act with discipline, as a soldier," Nuyi said, returning my words. "I fear that I might not be able to control my actions, that I might disgrace myself and my comrades."

"We will help one another through whatever we face," I said. "We are all brothers in arms." Nuyi lowered his head again. I found myself looking at the top of his head, noticing the lack of external ears. All divotect have are slight depressions to focus—no holes or anything else—and there are times when those depressions are not easy to spot.

"I will do my best," he said before he turned and

started walking—very slowly—back toward the squad tent.

I shook my head. How *would* the divotect in the regiment react if we found evidence of wholesale slaughter of their people on Dintsen? How many of our divotect *came* from Dintsen? How many might be going home to find their families murdered? It wasn't just Nuyi. There were several dozen divotect in Ranger Battalion, and more in the rest of the regiment. "I hope somebody's thought about that," I mumbled.

It was several minutes later when Fang and Claw came out of the tent. They moved off to the side together and seemed to be intent on some topic between them. I saw a lot of gesturing, as if they were debating something, but they spoke too softly for me to hear anything. After a couple of minutes Claw made a gesture with both hands, and Fang returned it. Then they came toward me, walking with their arms almost touching.

"Sergeant Drak," Fang said when they reached me. "We do not know a lot about humans and, as you said, we have not served with you as long as the others have. It is unfortunate that we will not have more time before we go into battle, but we will do our best. We have indeed already faced the tonatin and their allies. We have both lost friends, comrades. I understand that you, too, have been in battle with tonatin and lost friends and comrades. And that you yourself were grievously wounded."

"Yes," I said very quietly.

"The divotect in our squad, his people have faced the worst of the tonatin barbarism." I don't know what word Fang used in his own language, but *barbarism* was how my translator button rendered it. The translators seem to give a somewhat stilted interpretation, making people sound more formal than they are.

"Yes," I said again, not certain where Fang was going.

"We have many close bonds through this," he said next. "We will fight as if we were pack brothers."

That was a term that had not been covered in our briefings about ghuroh, but I sensed that it was something they considered important. "Thank you," I said. "That is how a squad must function, especially in a unit such as ours, as if we were all pack brothers. Each of us must stand with all of the others—*all*. Stand or fall."

"You can count on us to the last drop of blood," Fang said, and Claw nodded, awkwardly, a gesture he was not used to.

"I will do my best not to let any of the soldiers in the squad down," I said. It was almost as if we had just gone through some sort of ritual, some ghuroh bonding ceremony.

"We will be ready to go in the morning, prepared for whatever we might smell out on Dintsen," Fang said. Then he and Claw turned to head back toward the tent.

"You might mention that I'll be in the mess tent for the next fifteen or twenty minutes," I said before they got too far away. I decided that it was time for that cup of coffee.

I WAS JUST FILLING A COFFEE CUP FROM ONE of the machines at the end of the serving line in the mess tent when Tonio came in. He looked the way I felt—totally spent, ready to melt into sleep at the slightest provocation. I took my first sip of coffee while I waited for him to get a cup and join me.

"I wish you'd tell me that this has all been somebody's idea of a bad joke, that we're not really heading for Dintsen and combat tomorrow," I said while he was filling his cup.

He shook his head weakly. "I wish I could, but it's for real. I don't know how soon combat will come, but we leave here tomorrow. Don't tell me you've gotten to like this mud hole."

"It started taking on a certain charm when I heard the alternative," I said. We moved toward a table. I made sure I sat so I could see the entrance, in case anyone from my squad came looking for me. I told Tonio what Nuyi had said and how I wondered what kind of reaction we might get from other divotect.

"You're the second squad leader to mention that," he said. "I've already kicked the question up the chain." He shrugged. "Maybe it's a lucky thing that we don't have all that many divotect, and no squad has more than one. Keep one thing in mind: We take care of our people, no matter what. We do everything we can to keep them from going off half cocked if we get into that sort of situation. We do whatever we have to, regardless of what kind of nonsense the brass come up with."

"Yeah, I figured that. Do we have any idea yet what kind of opposition we're going to face when we hit Dintsen?"

"The last I heard, they were still at the guessing stage—planning on the basis of what we would commit to an operation like that if we were on the other end of it, then adding fifty percent to make sure the guess isn't too damned conservative."

"The tonatin used about three regiments in the initial assault," I reminded him. "That's twelve thousand soldiers or more, that we—you and I—know of the hard

way. They may have brought more in after we were out
of it."

He nodded.

"They didn't take all that many casualties during the
fight," I added. "They ran over us like we were toy soldiers, frozen in silly hero poses. And our general staff
is going to try to take Dintsen back with one under
trained mixed regiment?"

"Well, it's not going to be just the 1st Combined,"
Tonio said. "We'll also have an extra porracci battalion.
But most of the men in that unit are . . . not very experienced, less than ten percent combat veterans, barely
that many with six months in uniform. And we'll have
two batteries of mobile artillery from Earth to add to our
own complement, along with plenty of aerospace fighters and a dozen or more battleships to keep the Ilion
Federation from bringing in reinforcements."

"We might still be outnumbered by three to one or
more on the ground, against an enemy that's had the
better part of a year to set things up however they want,"
I said. "Any chance that there are any divotect units still
surviving on the ground?"

"I don't think so. It's been too long. We might run
across a few individual soldiers, but even that's doubt-
ful."

I finished my coffee and got up. "You really know
how to cheer a guy up," I told Tonio before I left the
mess tent.

FRED WILKINS WAS SITTING ON A ROCK BE-
tween our tent and second squad's. He was smoking a
cigar—not tobacco, one of the mild euphorics grown on
Franklin; I could tell that by the aroma. Fred gave no

notice that he saw me coming until my shadow moved over his face. Then he moved over to give me room to sit on the rock next to him. I sat.

"I think the others are all asleep, except for the bir-aunta," he said, his voice carrying a dreamy tone that suggested this wasn't his first cigar of the evening. "Oyo and Iyi didn't start to settle down until they were certain the porracci were sleeping."

In some ways I found Wilkins stranger, more alien, than any of the others in the squad. There was nothing lacking in his combat skills. He was smart, fast, and tough. He was also one of the best marksmen in the company. And after I warned him about it back at the beginning, he had been extremely careful not to say anything to or about the other species that was not proper. Not in my hearing or sight, at least. But I did not try to delude myself that he had banished his bigotry. Sometimes I could see it in the way he looked at one of the others, an expression of distaste on his face. He did not like being around the other species, was not willing to concede that they might be equal to humans—and he would certainly not consider the possibility that some of them might be superior to us in any way, even after he had been regularly defeated in unarmed combat training by both porracci and by Nuyi, and occasionally by Jai-bie, Fang, and Claw. "Drill isn't the real thing," he had told me after the first time a porracci had defeated him. "If it was for real, I wouldn't have to hold back." I'm not sure he even heard my reply: "But they wouldn't have to hold back either." I don't think he was *capable* of thinking that any other species might be equal to or better than humans. It was a blind spot I could not fathom.

"Oyo and Iyi aren't as nervous about porracci as they

were at the beginning," I said, half trying to hold my breath to keep from getting any of Wilkins's smoke. There are times, not often, but occasionally, when I like a little of the float you get from that weed, but not just then. I had too much on my mind, and the sweet aroma was almost annoying.

"I guess we'll find out who's got balls and who doesn't in the next few days," Wilkins said. I ignored the statement. It wasn't quite enough to call for any sort of reaction. "Supposing any of us survive this whorehouse gamble, what next?" he asked after staring through a fresh cloud of his smoke.

"We do whatever they tell us," I said. "Get more training in, fill any holes the campaign leaves, learn from our mistakes. If they decide to continue the experiment. If not, I imagine we'll get broken up, with everyone shipped to other units. Hard telling until we see what happens on Dintsen."

"Be a miracle if ten percent of us get off Dintsen. Trying to do anything with this . . . goulash regiment."

"This regiment will do okay if we can avoid having bigots like you screw things up for the rest."

"I know how many fingers and toes I've got, what I see in the mirror."

I stood up. I was never going to argue him out of his bigotry. "I know what you see in the mirror, too—an asshole. Just make damned sure you don't let your idiocy compromise the squad. You fuck up and you'll never see daylight again, except with bars across it."

CHAPTER 8

THEY LET US SLEEP LATE. IT WAS WELL PAST
dawn before reveille was broadcast across the camp. We
lined up along the company "streets" to go through the
regular morning routine, but there were gaps. There was
no physical training. Once the manning reports were
made, Colonel Hansen told us to take our time getting
cleaned up and fed and everything—the stuff we normally have to rush through.

"There will be no scheduled formations until we're
ready to embark," Hansen said. "We'll get word to you
on that as soon as possible." Which meant, of course,
that they didn't know yet exactly what they were going
to do with us.

Hansen didn't bother to give us a pep talk. I expected
that would come when we formed up to move to the
shuttles and up to the ships that had already started gathering. When the sky is clear you can see those ships
from the ground during the day, even though they don't
get much closer than two hundred miles from the surface. The transports are *big*—four to five miles long and
as much as seven-tenths of a mile in diameter. The car-

riers and battleships are even larger. There weren't as many ships as I would have liked, but there probably aren't that many ships altogether in the fleets of the Alliance of Light.

Ships had been furnished by the porracci, abarand, and ghuroh, in addition to the ships from the human worlds. Tonio told me that at breakfast. He also told me that all of the cartographic data on Dintsen had been downloaded to our maps, so after I finished eating I went off by myself to have a look.

DINTSEN. THERE'S NOTHING SPECIAL ABOUT IT. It's a little smaller than Earth, with a surface gravity 3 percent less—hardly enough to be noticeable. You can jump a little higher, run a little faster. The proportion of gases in the atmosphere is very close to Earth's—allowing for the fact that Dintsen's air doesn't carry all the pollution Earth's air has held for centuries. The ratio of sea to land is similar to Earth's, perhaps tilted a little toward more water. Virtually all of the land area is contained in a single continent, which straddles the north pole and reaches below the equator on either end, farther on the "fat" end. There are several active tectonic borders—earthquakes, volcanoes, and so forth. The polar zone effectively separates the two halves of the continent to all but air travel. No divotect lived above the forty-second parallel of north latitude. Most of the population centers are on the fat end of the continent, and the vast majority of the divotect live—or lived—in the tropical and subtropical regions. The smaller towns farther north were only planted there because that was where essential ores were located. The total population, prior to the invasion, had been slightly over six million.

The training area where my battalion had been stationed when the Ilion Federation invaded had been near
one of those mining areas. The single town nearby had
been razed during the initial fighting. Both sites were
referenced on the map. So were the locations of Ilion
Federation troops as of our escape from the planet. Nothing more recent had been added to the database yet.

I suspected that if I kept the electronic map open and
stared at it, I would be able to anticipate when the call
to formation would come—just after the latest intelligence data was added to the map. I had to force myself
to turn the map off and put it back in its pocket on the
leg of my trousers.

THAT DAY SEEMED TO STRETCH TOWARD INFIN-
ity. The waiting was murder. Either the general staff was
having a harder than anticipated time gathering the necessary intelligence, or the intel they *had* gathered was
so foreboding that they couldn't figure out how they
could go through with the assault without simply sending us all to immediate death.

The squad was packed, ready to go. Weapons had
been cleaned . . . and cleaned again. Electronic gear had
been double-checked; anything that didn't test perfectly
was replaced, and then the replacements were checked
twice. I had everyone spend a few minutes familiarizing
themselves with the map of Dintsen.

We made it through the morning and a long lunch.
The cooks weren't holding anything back for tomorrow.
There was plenty of everything—the menus varied for
the different species as much as possible. Anything one
species can eat the rest can eat as well, but most of us
stuck with what we were used to. All of the sentient

species are pretty much omnivorous. Maybe that goes hand-in-hand with sentience.

It was while we were at lunch that we started hearing shuttles coming in at the landing strip. That was mildly encouraging.

"We're going somewhere, at least," Fred Wilkins said.

"Somewhere," I agreed.

"The sooner we go, the sooner we can complete the mission," Souvana said. Normally I like to hear that kind of positive thinking from my people, but—coming from Souvana—this time it grated a little. I wondered if he ever had *any* doubts.

After lunch, I walked partway to the landing strip— far enough to see that there were only transport shuttles coming in so far. They were loading supplies from the warehouses onto the shuttles, not bringing in more stuff. "One way or another, we must be leaving Dancer," I whispered. There was a chance that we might be moved, but not into combat. I didn't figure that it was very likely, but it wasn't impossible if the brass decided that we weren't going to be enough to slow down the Ilion Federation on Dintsen or to keep them from attacking somewhere else.

I watched the loading operations for fifteen minutes. During that time, one loaded shuttle moved away from the warehouses, taxied to the end of the strip, and took off, burning for orbit. Then I told myself that it was time to get back to the company area. If the colonel called us out for formation, I didn't want to be late.

IT WAS THE MIDDLE OF THE AFTERNOON, NEAR 1700 hours, before word came from battalion headquarters. The move would start in two hours. Ranger Battalion would be the first shuttled up to its ship. The rest of the regiment would follow, as quickly as possible.

"That means we'll sit up there waiting for the rest," Wilkins said. He flopped on his cot and stared up at the ceiling. "As rotten as this place is, I'd rather do my waiting here than up in a bucket."

"Nobody asked us," I said. If your only images of interstellar ships are of the kind that convey civilians, your picture is as far from military transports as a limousine is from a pogo stick. As large as the transports are, they leave little room for creature comforts for their passengers. Since interstellar hops are a matter of hours, the grunts sit. There aren't bunks for all the passengers. The *crew* has bunks, private cabins, or small dormitories, but not the transients. Oh, there are *some* bunks for passengers, but when one of those ships is carrying a full battalion, there is one bed for four men. If a voyage should last longer than the minimum few hours, the grunts have to take turns sleeping, and the bunks never get a chance to cool off from one shift to the next. I figure we're lucky they even put artificial gravity generators in so we know which end is up while we're aboard.

Ten minutes later, the company's officers and sergeants were called to a briefing behind battalion headquarters. The officers were up front on either side. The rest of us ranged out in front of Colonel Hansen and his staff.

"When we finish here, the battalion will be ordered to fall out, ready to leave Dancer" was the first thing Colonel Hansen said after giving us the "at ease" order. He let those words hang while he looked around, making momentary eye contact with everyone who looked back. We could hear the shuttles starting to come in again, and

I knew without looking that this time they were personnel shuttles, not the transports—our rides up to the fleet.

"The latest intelligence we have on Dintsen is less than seven hours old," he continued. "You will receive full briefings once we're aboard ship. The best estimate intelligence can give us is that the Ilion Federation has cut back even farther on the number of troops on Dintsen than we had hoped. At most, they have six battalions of combat soldiers, and not as many fighting ships overhead as we're going to commit to the assault. We have chosen our beachheads and set up our initial plan of attack. It will be up to us to open the way and create enough chaos on the ground to keep the defenders from responding efficiently to the primary assault landings by the rest of the regiment and the extra battalion we'll have."

Well, that meant the assault force would only be outnumbered six to five, but defenders have another advantage—the chance to shoot down shuttles and sleds coming in, before the men aboard them can get into the fight. We couldn't even count on much surprise, except on an extremely local tactical level. The odds were close to certain that the Ilion Federation troops on Dintsen knew about the reconnaissance sorties, so they had to be expecting trouble, and once our ships popped out of hyperspace, the defenders would have an hour or more to get ready to meet us.

"I can say this much. We will be operating the way we've trained, mostly in one-and two-squad teams. The largest operational teams from the battalion will each be one platoon, and there will only be two of those."

There's both good and bad to that. It's what we train for, what we're best at. A single squad can move a lot faster, and with a lot better chance of escaping observation, than a company or a battalion. The bad is that when an op—operation—goes sour, it can be very difficult to escape.

"Our assault will be timed so we go in with as much night as possible left after we get on the ground," Colonel Hansen said. "There will be a number of deceptive feints to try to mislead the enemy about our intentions. Our battalion will be part of some of those feints, but most will be executed by the aerospace fighters and capital ships."

WHEN I GOT BACK TO THE SQUAD TENT, I ONLY had time to say, "No real surprises, we're going in," before the loudspeakers called us out for formation. We carried our weapons, gear, and bags. I warned everyone not to leave anything behind they wanted to see again.

Colonel Hansen did not take as much time with the entire battalion as he had with the officers and sergeants. There was more pep and less hard information; that would be left to lower management—captains, lieutenants, and sergeants. Hansen turned us over to company commanders, who got us formed up for the march to the landing strip. We could see some of the troops from the line companies watching us go . . . and knowing that they would not be far behind us.

Two more shuttles landed during the time it took us to march to the strip. There, we moved into another regular formation and went through manning reports again—apparently to make certain no one had taken a powder during the six or seven minutes since we had started moving. Then they started to load us on the shuttles. That was done in order, by company and platoon. Alpha Company boarded first. Then it was our turn.

Before I followed my men through the hatch, I turned to take one last look at the camp on Dancer. There was nothing wrong with my stomach, despite the huge knot that had settled there.

OUR SHIP WAS ALEXANDRIA , ONE OF THE OLD- est transports in Earth's fleet. She had been in service more than a hundred years, and although she had been renovated and rehabilitated several times, she wasn't wearing her age well. The ship felt old—it even *smelled* old, pervaded with a combination of odors that nothing could exorcise. This was not my first voyage on *Alexandria*. Tonio recalled her, too; she had carried us to Dintsen on our previous trip there. We got together for the operational briefings and had a couple of minutes before the business started.

"Looks like they're not wasting anything new for this mission," Tonio whispered to me. "I didn't get a good look at any of the other ships, but I'll bet it's the oldest collection of ships ever sent into battle."

"Old ships and a unit no one is certain can function in battle," I whispered back. "All expendable. Gives a guy no end of confidence. Tell me: Does the idea of going back to Dintsen give you the roaring heebie-jeebies? It sure does me."

"All things considered, I can think of places I'd rather go," Tonio said, "but we go where they tell us."

" 'Into the valley of death . . .'?" I suggested. Tonio had recited part of that poem to me once, a long time back. Afterward I had looked it up and followed links back to find out what it had been about—some idiot officer giving a moronic order and a lot of men dying to try to do the impossible.

"If that's what it is, we'll be in good company," he said, and that was all there was time for. Lieutenant Fusik came in and somebody called *attention*.

"Give me the map of our operational area," Fusik said, and somebody in a room next to the conference room keyed in the necessary commands to project a map on the bulkhead behind Fusik, a photographic mosaic of Dintsen. The portion of the chart we were shown didn't cover enough territory for me to recognize it right off. There were no place names shown.

"The center of our operational area is thirty-nine degrees, fifteen minutes north latitude, twenty-six degrees, thirty minutes east longitude." An arrow marked the spot on the map. The lieutenant's coordinates were enough to give me a decent idea of where we were going—less than three hundred miles from where my previous unit had made its *last stand* on Dintsen.

"The area is rough, rocky, hilly, and heavily forested, a mixture of evergreen and deciduous growth—good terrain for our line of work. There are, or were, three divotect towns at the edge of our area of operation—here, here, and here." The last was accompaniment to the arrows that blinked at each location.

"First platoon will go in at four separate locations." Once again there were blinking arrows as he pointed out the landing zones, LZs, for each squad. "Sergeant Xeres will be with first platoon's second squad, in immediate operational control of that squad and liase with first squad." I half tuned out the next part of the briefing, where the rest of the company would be, and which officers would be where. I absorbed the essentials, but I was busy staring at the map, noting as many landmarks around my squad's LZ as I could. I didn't really look at the lieutenant again until he mentioned my squad again.

"Sergeant Drak, your squad will go in here—by air-sled. We'll *all* be going in by sled." A marker moved on the map to show the LZ. "There is a company of IF soldiers, probably tonatin, but not first-rate assault troops, at this mining complex four miles from your LZ. Our suspicion is that the army unit is there to force local divotect to operate the copper mines along this stream." More markers on the map.

"Your mission is to provide harassment, keep those soldiers too occupied for the enemy commanders to consider moving them." That's right: Ten men to keep maybe two hundred of the enemy busy. In rough terrain like that, it wasn't as out of line as a civilian might think—not for a spec ops squad. Under the right conditions we could keep five times that number of hostiles occupied for weeks. "Sergeant Xeres will give you additional details after we finish here."

"Yes, sir," I said. "I recall a little about that area of Dintsen. We'll do our part."

The "additional details" Tonio had didn't add much. This was something we would have to improvise once we were on the ground and saw what we were up against. But it was a start. I headed back to my men. I wasn't eager for the fight, but I did feel more nervous anticipation than fear. The fear would come, but that's something you learn to use instead of letting it take over. If it takes over, you're not a soldier any longer.

I WAS BRIEFING MY SQUAD WHEN THE FLEET started its series of hyperspace jumps. I had everyone close so they could see my map, which I had unfolded and set on my lap. I told them what I remembered about that section of Dintsen, and answered questions. "We can't make definite plans much past the point of getting out of the sleds," I told them. "After that it depends on how quickly the enemy reacts." All we could do was concentrate on learning as much of the topography as we could, noting landmarks and so forth, so we could move with some certainty once we were on the ground. At the start I had the map set to show as broad an area as possible, then progressively changed the scale until we reached a point where we could see objects on the ground as small as two yards in diameter. We looked over the buildings of the mining camp and were able to identify which of those buildings were being used to house the divotect slave laborers, and which were being used as barracks for the tonatin guards.

We stayed with the map reading, with one short break, until the time the loudspeakers called for us to move to the shuttles, ready to head in.

"One last thing," I said before we headed toward the hangars. "This is the real thing. We leave all the bickering and bigotry behind. We do the job, not fight among ourselves. We're a team, and God help anyone who forgets that."

INSIDE ALEXANDRIA, AND IN THE SHUTTLES, WE had no way to see what was going on outside. And we couldn't *hear* anything out there either, not in space. It wasn't until later that I learned anything about the battle above Dintsen. Our fighting ships emerged from hyperspace several minutes before the transports and escorts. They moved to engage the few combat ships the Ilion Federation had left to protect their troops on the planet, to keep them from attacking our transports.

They were successful at that. We didn't lose any

transports going in. We did lose one battleship, with all hands, and a second battleship received serious damage, though only a few members of the crew were killed. A number of our aerospace fighters also were lost then and during the landing operations. But while that initial fighting was going on, we were already in our shuttles, sealed into our airsleds, waiting for *Alexandria* to launch us toward the ground.

The knot in my stomach got tighter.

CHAPTER 9

I DON'T KNOW MUCH ABOUT ALIEN RELIGIONS, except that all of the other sentient species combined haven't come up with as many different religions as we humans have—by a factor of at least ten. Every sentient race has at least one religion. Some of the others have as many as ten or twelve. I don't know if anybody has come up with an accurate count of how many religions, sects, and cults humans have, most claiming to be the only path to the Supreme Being or Beings. I've never been able to figure out which religion was right, if any, but a man going into combat can't afford to offend whichever god or gods might actually exist. Not knowing who to address when I prayed didn't make my prayers any less earnest while I was sitting in that airsled waiting to be dropped onto a planet full of hostile soldiers.

We had a long wait in the sleds before *Alexandria* launched us, more than forty minutes. The stench of sweat and fear was strong in the confined space. No one spoke, though we all had our radios on. I imagine we were all pretty much introspective, dealing with whatever tension or fear we felt. Making peace . . . or whatever.

Besides the squad frequency, I also monitored the battalion's command channel, but I only heard a couple of short reports on that, nothing that directly affected my squad—and nothing that gave me any *real* information about the assault or the preliminary fighting. There were times, especially after we had been confined to the sled for twenty minutes or so, when I wanted to scream, "What the hell is going on?" on the command channel, and get someone to say *something*—even if only to tell me to shut the hell up. Even cramped into that sled with four other soldiers, I was as *alone* as anyone can ever get.

Forty minutes. We had a warning one minute before launch, and a countdown through the last ten seconds. The shuttle was pushed out of the ship by jets of compressed gas. We went from feeling the artificial gravity of *Alexandria* to zero gee after we separated.

There was a pause after separation. The shuttle would not fire its rockets until it was a certain distance away from its mothership—standard operating procedures call for one hundred yards. Then the shuttle's rockets fired and we regained a sense of our own weight as we started to accelerate. But *down* was behind us now, not below, at least from the frame of acceleration. By that time the shuttle was *nose down,* with the ground in front of us.

The wait in the sled before launch was considerably longer than the 190-mile trip. The shuttle accelerated toward the ground, the intent being to give the enemy as little time as possible to target us en route or to get into position to meet us when we grounded. I've got no argument with that. A soldier can't defend himself until he gets out of the sled.

The ride in was rough and hot. As soon as we hit air we started to heat up, and the air buffeted the shuttle about enough to jar teeth out of their sockets. The pilot accelerated as long as he could, then reversed thrust—itself a bone-jarring maneuver—to brake, fighting to get the shuttle's airspeed low enough to allow it to jettison its airsleds.

The pilot kept me posted on the time left before the drop. I let the news flow through on my squad circuit so my men knew what was coming. It saved me the trouble of repeating everything or answering questions.

As bad as the shuttle ride was, the sled ride that followed was worse—rougher and hotter. But it did not last long, though it was long enough for two of the people in my sled to get violently ill . . . which did not improve the atmosphere we had to breathe. The sled yawed from side to side as its jets fought to slow us and get us to our designated landing zone. I kept a hand near the quick-release switch for my safety harness. When the sled came to a stop I didn't want to waste any time getting out.

We hit the ground too hard for comfort, but not hard enough to cause injury. The sled slid through grass and underbrush, rocking from side to side. Each time we snapped a sapling or scraped rock, the hull rang like a bell. The air inside got hotter yet—it had to be near 115 degrees before we stopped and popped the hatches.

"OUT!" I SHOUTED OVER THE SQUAD FRE-quency as I pulled myself through the open hatchway above my head. "Double time to the rendezvous point. Keep your eyes open. This is no damned drill. This is the real shit." I was out of that box by the fourth word, looking for any trace of hostiles or incoming fire, fixing my route by the arrow on my head-up display, and running as fast as I could toting eighty pounds of gear. "Safeties off!" It's doctrine—and common sense—to keep weapon safeties *on* during a sled drop. With all the bouncing around it would be far too easy for someone to let off a round, or half a magazine, without knowing it, and it wouldn't take many rounds ricocheting around the box to turn us all into ground meat—or to cut a control cable and send the sled hurtling out of control.

The squad's other sled had come in north of ours and eighty yards to our left, and had skidded a hundred yards farther than we had. That was more separation than there should have been, but we all made it out of the sleds whole and healthy, so we wouldn't bitch about the imprecision. It did mean that the second fire team made it to the rendezvous point fifteen seconds faster than my batch. Fifteen extra seconds to get their breath back.

Nuyi was the last man to reach the rendezvous and throw himself on the ground. He was not audibly gasping, but he had extended himself as much as he could on the sprint. More than any of the rest of us, he needed a few seconds to let his lungs catch up.

A few seconds was all we could afford. We had to move farther from the LZ. The trails our sleds had carved out coming to a halt were bright arrows in infrared, and it might not take long for the IF to put troops on us, or artillery, if they had any in range.

Ten seconds. Twelve. Fifteen. It wasn't long enough to let all of us recover completely, but it would have to do. I sucked in as deep a breath as I could manage. "Let's get moving. Iyi and Oyo, on point. Get up in the trees as soon as you can. You know the heading to take?"

"We know," Iyi said. He and his twin started moving, more rapidly than I expected. Each carried little more than thirty pounds, half of that weapons and ammo, but it was as much a load for the biraunta as what I carried was for me. I put Nuyi next in line, then followed, with Wilkins behind me. Souvana followed Wilkins, then Fang and Claw, Jaibie, and Kiervauna on rear guard. We did not walk in a straight line, one behind the other, but were spread out, alternating left and right, keeping three to five yards between men. This time Souvana did not question my arrangements.

The temperature would have been comfortable, had I taken time to notice. It was night, late spring, and we were far enough north that the low might reach the upper forties, with a gentle breeze. We weren't going to have our strength sapped by heat and humidity, not at night. I wanted to get the biraunta up in the trees, where they would be more comfortable, while I could. It wouldn't be as much help as it had been back on Dancer. This area was not so completely forested. There were plenty of clearings, tracts of virgin prairie—long grass, bushes, and so forth. Each time we reached one of those areas, the biraunta would have to come down and move with the rest of us.

We were not moving directly toward any of the towns or concentrations of enemy troops. A direct line would be too obvious, too easy for the IFers—Ilion Federation soldiers—to meet. We were on a heading to nowhere, in the middle of empty forest. From there we would swing around to start hitting the enemy from an angle we hoped they wouldn't anticipate, to pin those troops down so they couldn't be moved to oppose the line battalions when they hit the dirt just before dawn.

Time does strange things in your head when you're

in a position like that. It seems to go both slow and incredibly fast at the same time. The mind speeds up, which can give you the impression that everything outside your head is crawling in slow motion. At least it gets that way for me. I have to keep looking at the timeline on my helmet display to keep track and avoid getting disoriented.

Six minutes after we came out of the sleds, we were half a mile from them, at a thirty-degree angle from the trail they had left coming in. We reached a clearing, and I had Oyo and Iyi take us around the one side of it that offered *some* cover—tall underbrush, a few scrub trees, and high grass that had a few animal paths through it.

When we get to the far side, I promised myself, *we'll take a five-minute break.* We all needed it.

THERE WERE ALMOST CONSTANT REPORTS ON the command channel, but not from on the ground. We received updates from one of the ships, keeping us apprised of enemy movements and so forth. Our orders were not to respond, or to use the command frequency for anything unless we were directly engaged with the enemy. And we were to use our lower-powered squad frequency as little as possible. Those can be detected if an enemy is close enough and listening. Radio silence was not an obstacle for us. It's standard for spec ops. We're the ghosts goosing the enemy from behind, working in areas he thinks are secure, providing security nightmares for the enemy brass. Most of us like that sort of image.

In our first fifteen minutes on the ground, the enemy troops scarcely had time to begin reacting. Apparently they had all been caught in their camps. They had been alerted when the fight started in space, but had not moved far from those camps when we came in. Most were under attack—or the threat of attack—from the aerospace fighters that were covering our deployment.

We had spread our landings over a wide enough area that the enemy also had to feel some uncertainty over where to head first. Which landings were feints? Which were real? They might not even be certain in those first minutes if there had actually been troops in the dozens of airsleds the shuttles had dropped. The longer the enemy took to buck those questions up and down the chain of command, the better our odds were.

A FIVE-MINUTE REST WAS ENOUGH TO GET US all back to normal breathing, ready to go on for however long we needed to before the next break. We don't spend all that time in garrison working on physical conditioning just so we'll look pretty showing our muscles. Strength and endurance are more important weapons than the rifles and grenades we carry.

Stealth is important as well. I won't say that an expert tracker could *never* follow us, but it would be slow work. Rangers learn how to minimize evidence of their passage, to avoid breaking twigs or leaving obvious footprints. We don't make smoky campfires or leave identifiable litter.

The beginning of a mission calls for caution, a chance to get the mind-set right, and make sure that you're not making casual mistakes. Sometimes that's not possible, but when it is, a leader has to take advantage of it, especially with a new team. Our schedule wasn't all that tight just yet. We could take those few minutes here and there.

We moved east-southeast for three miles in thirty minutes—extremely good time cross-country over rough terrain with full loads of gear. Then we took another five minutes—time to get off our feet, take a little water, and snack on energy bars—before we changed direction and started toward our first target.

Our target was two miles away when I stopped the squad and brought everyone together to lay out our plan of action. We turned off our transmitters, lifted face-plates, and whispered. There was no enemy close enough to eavesdrop on that. I couldn't be certain there were no electronic eavesdroppers who might hear any radio transmissions. It wasn't that they might *understand* what we said—the encryption scheme we use to scramble transmissions makes that virtually impossible—but if they could detect our signals, they could locate us, to within inches if their gear was as sophisticated as ours.

I opened my map and centered the view on the target, then increased the magnification so that only an area about two hundred yards across was visible on the screen.

"Intelligence thinks that the IF is using this building as an armory," I said, tapping the image of the building on my map. "We don't have any information on the construction other than what we can see—a brick exterior two stories high. I do know that the bricks the divotect generally used here are about ten inches by twenty, and five inches thick. Sometimes there's a metal frame under the skin, sometimes wood, sometimes neither—just beams set right into the wall.

"If it is an armory, any ammunition will likely be stored on the ground floor. We'll plant explosive and incendiary charges here and here." I pointed at two spots near one corner of the building, on the east and north sides. "That gives us our best chance of setting off secondary explosions inside and toppling the structure, or at least burying any munitions under enough rubble to make it difficult for them to get at them anytime soon."

"Floor level is likely to be at least this far below the outside grade," Nuyi said, holding a hand about eighteen inches from the ground. "My people like to feel that they are at least partly below ground level when they can, and that building was constructed by divotect."

I nodded. "Good point. We keep our charges low on the outside, and angle them down, inward, and toward each other. Souvana, you'll take your fire team in to plant the charges. The rest of us will cover you from along this line." I indicated an area 120 yards away. The trees had been cleared around the village out to nearly that distance. Some of that work had been done within the past few days. Where the trees and underbrush had been bulldozed, the ground was still loose and damp. There was still earthmoving equipment on the scene, so the defenders probably planned on widening the open area around the buildings to give them better lines of fire.

Souvana nodded, but his eyes were fixed on the map. "If you will be here, then I think my team should come in from over here." He indicated a point along the edge of the tree line about eighty yards from where my fire team would be. "In here, out this way. This will give us our best route and leave you with a clear field of fire should that be needed." He traced a line with his finger.

"Okay, that looks good," I said, nodding. "That keeps our fields of fire away from the buildings where we think the divotect laborers are quartered. We do hope to get in and out without being seen, but in case we are spotted, that gives us a good shot at getting your people out safely." Despite their bulk, the porracci were good at moving stealthily—obviously better in the forest than out in the open, but it would still be dark when we made our move.

"If we get separated, we'll rendezvous at this point." I scrolled the map slowly, then indicated a location half a mile from the target, east-southeast, in a somewhat wilder stretch of terrain—heavily forested hills cut by a number of narrow but deep gullies. We could lose ourselves in that kind of country, and a regiment of hostiles would have a hard time finding us.

"Let's get moving." I waited to make certain no one had any questions, then pulled my faceplate down and gestured for Iyi and Oyo to head out on point. We would have forest until we reached our position for our attack on the suspected armory.

Two of the groups in the battalion had already struck. One of them, a two-squad team from C Company, was in a firefight, having difficulty breaking contact. The fleet had dropped several missiles on concentrations of the enemy. The more confusion going on, the easier it would be for us to strike and get lost in the forest before the small garrison we expected to be guarding the munitions dump could react.

It took us only twenty minutes to get into position, including a crawl over the last twenty yards of forest to the final line of trees and undergrowth. The IF attempt to shove the forest farther away from the village left piles of debris in front of us, providing extra cover. I could see two sentry posts near the collection of small buildings that had been a divotect mining village, and noted our target. There was one sentry walking a post across the front of that—on the far side of the building from us, guarding the front entrance.

My fire team was just far enough back from the edge of the wooded area to keep from showing a glint of starlight off rifle barrels. Nuyi had his grenade launcher out and ready, with his rifle lying on the ground next to it. The rest of us had our rifles pointed into the village. We hoped to avoid a firefight, but we had to be ready for one.

Souvana had taken his fire team off to the side, moving in toward the departure point he had indicated. The timing of the actual assault would be up to him. His men would move in as quickly as they could while attempting to remain hidden from enemy view.

The rest of us waited. I divided my attention between scanning the village for threats and looking for Souvana's team to start working their way from the woods to the target. I assumed that they would try to take out the one sentry who might be in position to spot them. My guess was that either Fang or Claw would be given that assignment. They were hunters, through and through.

Seven minutes. Even though I was anticipating the move and knew where to look, I almost missed the emergence of the second fire team from the woods— low, fast-moving shadows. Souvana was the first to emerge from cover. I could tell that from his size and the way he moved. Kiervauna was next. My guess was that the porracci were carrying the explosive charges and would take care of affixing them to the target while Jaibie and the two ghuroh covered them.

A blur of movement drew my attention off to the side, and I saw one of the ghuroh hauling that sentry to the ground. No sound carried from that encounter. As long as that sentry wasn't due to be relieved or make a report

within the next few minutes, we would be okay on that
count.

I moved my attention back to the target building and
lined my rifle up with the far corner, where the other
sentry came into view briefly at the end of his post. He
appeared, did an about-face, and disappeared. The sentry
was tonatin, as were the other two we had spotted. That
fit with the intelligence we had, that the IFers left on
Dintsen were likely all tonatin.

Souvana and Kiervauna separated, going to their re-
spective sides of the building, twelve feet apart. Souvana
was the one more likely to be spotted by the sentry at
the front of the building. All the guard would have to
do is glance to his right at the corner. He hadn't done
that in the three circuits I had watched, but it hardly
seemed credible that he would be so careless. Had it
been me walking that guard post, I would have scanned
as far around as I could every time.

One of the ghuroh slid along the side of the building
past Souvana to get into position to take out that sentry
should he give any indication of seeing what was going
on. I couldn't tell if it was Fang or Claw.

The porracci needed less than thirty seconds to place
and arm their explosives. As they moved away from the
building, the ghuroh along the side moved as well, staying behind them, keeping his attention on the corner
where the tonatin guard stopped and turned after each
pass. I kept scanning the village. We were a long way
from being clear.

It wasn't until the last of Souvana's men reached the
trees that I signaled for my fire team to start pulling
back. I wasn't tempted to stick around to watch the
fireworks. When the explosives went off, we would hear
them. By that time I hoped we would be far enough

away that the enemy wouldn't have any idea where we might be.

Moving away from the village, I dropped back to the rearguard position. That wasn't according to doctrine, but you have to be pragmatic. I wanted the biraunta out in front, and I trusted myself more than I trusted Wilkins to watch to make certain we weren't leaving a plain trail.

We were within a few dozen yards of the rendezvous when we heard the explosions—two major blasts a second or so apart. Ten seconds later there was a series of smaller blasts, stored grenades or rockets going off. When I glanced back toward the village, I could see a dirty orange glow behind the trees, spreading and climbing.

"Good job," I told Souvana and his men when we met. "In and out without a problem. Looks like the intel was right on the money. They sure had something explosive in that building. Now let's get moving. We've got more work to do."

WE HIKED FIVE MILES IN AN HOUR, GOING through the roughest terrain we had encountered since hitting the ground, pushing hard. Before we hit the enemy a second time, we wanted to get farther than they might expect possible. If we could do that, they might overestimate our numbers and spread themselves too thin to try to counter more teams than they had to. By that point most of the spec ops squads had hit the enemy at least once, and a couple of the teams had made their second strike. We were circling our area of operations clockwise, this time heading toward where a company of IF troops had moved during the landing operation. According to the latest update, those troops were still in their assembly area, half a mile from their barracks.

I had a short call from Tonio. The platoon's second squad was in a firefight of its own.

"Don't break radio silence," Tonio started. "I know about your first hit. Good work. We'll be moving toward a rendezvous with you after the main landings if we can get away from this little fracas. I've got one man down. I think we've come across tonatin who are more than just rear-echelon prison guards."

Tonio's voice showed no emotion. Even over the radio, he was whispering, controlled. I waited a few seconds to see if he had more to say. I could hear gunfire over the link, but not too close. Okay, we had some tough hostiles. It was too much to hope for that they'd all be second-line troops.

"THIS ONE WON'T BE SO SIMPLE," I TOLD MY people when we stopped for a break. "They're in a defensive perimeter and looking for trouble, unless their brass has decided to move them." It would be easier to hit the enemy while they were moving; we could set an ambush to strike, then move to repeat the process as often as possible, but our goal was to pin them down.

"They're in a prepared location. We have to expect sentries, or electronic snoops planted well out from their perimeter, and there's a good chance they'll have land mines planted, so we need to be extra careful." I wanted to make sure I gave them all the cautions, even though most of it shouldn't have been necessary.

THE TWO-SQUAD TEAM FROM C COMPANY MAN-aged to break contact, but four of their men were killed.

The platoon sergeant who had been running the operation broke radio silence before they disengaged from the IF force they had been exchanging fire with. The survivors, including several wounded, were moving as quickly as they could, with the enemy in hot pursuit. That wasn't what the plan had been for that team, but it did tie part of the enemy force down. It looked as if that team had run into front-line troops, too, just as Tonio had.

Our main landing was imminent. The assault shuttles for the line regiments were beginning to separate from their ships, gathering for the dash to shore. Line soldiers ride their shuttles all the way to the ground instead of getting dropped in airsleds. They would have all the air cover the fleet could provide, which meant that those of us already on the ground couldn't count on any help if we got in over our heads.

My squad's job was to hit our next target before those IF soldiers could move to intercept the main landing force. I gave my squad a short rest; then we started moving again. I was beginning to feel that time was running short.

TEN MEN AGAINST TWO HUNDRED—MORE OR less. We weren't expected to wipe out an entire company of enemy troops with mad heroics, just to keep them busy while minimizing our own risk. I brought Oyo and Iyi down out of the trees before we got close to our target. Though they might be able to score a few hits quickly, they would be too vulnerable to return fire, as they had been during that training exercise on Dancer. I wasn't going to sacrifice them to no good purpose.

We split into fire teams and moved toward different

points on the enemy perimeter, and the men in each team spread out into skirmish lines. You don't want your people clustered so tightly that a single grenade or land mine can take out more than one man. In this case we also wanted to give the impression that there were more of us than really existed, attacking along a broad front, or that we were a feint intending to draw the enemy out of its defensive perimeter so a larger force could close in and finish them off.

The final two hundred yards went extremely slowly. We were crawling, taking a lot of time looking for electronic snoops or booby traps. A snoop might show only a small knob above ground or be concealed in the joint between a tree branch and its trunk, but it can have a microphone, a camera, or both, and by the time you spot it, either visually or through its electronic signature, it has almost certainly spotted you. Mines or other booby traps can be even harder to locate without setting them off, but our helmets do have detectors built in. Their range is limited, and it can take a couple of seconds for explosives to register.

We were planting snoops and booby traps of our own, something to catch anyone who came after us . . . with a little luck.

I had to detour around one mine—carefully, since I couldn't be sure what might trigger it. I couldn't count on the probability that it would be command-detonated— that is, that it wouldn't go off until someone in the enemy perimeter triggered it. The thing might have a trip-wire too thin for me to spot, or a pressure pad buried near it.

I got to within 120 yards of the enemy perimeter before I decided that I was as close as I was likely to get without triggering an alarm. Then I waited, giving the rest of my people time to get as close as they could. The signal to start the attack would be mine. I was to fire the first shot. Or, if the enemy fired, we would all start up together.

A report on the command channel informed me that the rest of the regiment had started in toward their landings. I scooted forward another few inches until I had a clear line of fire. I increased the magnification of my faceplate and scanned across the few degrees of arc my rifle could move without losing sight of the enemy line, then took in a breath and held it while I squeezed off a short burst of rifle fire.

BEFORE MY FIRST BURST ENDED, THE REST OF my team had started firing—rifles and grenade launchers. One man in each fire team had a grenade launcher; two others carried several spare four-grenade clips to keep him supplied. I slid a little to my right until I had another decent position, then fired again, spreading several short bursts across as much of the enemy line as I could see, rolling more to my right after each burst.

The IF company had started to return fire, but wildly, so I had muzzle flashes and the outlines of enemy helmets to target. For the most part, I concentrated on shooting and moving, staying flat so I wouldn't give enemy riflemen much of a target. But I also kept an eye on the timeline of my helmet's head-up display. We didn't dare stay close very long or the enemy commander would have soldiers out to try to flank us, or they would start dropping barrages of grenades around our positions.

Less than two minutes after I fired the first shots, I started angling away from the enemy. If they remembered their instructions, the rest of my men would be doing the same. Just in case they didn't, I said "Start disengaging" over the squad frequency. At the moment, radio silence was unnecessary. The enemy knew we were close, and no matter how good their direction finders might be, they couldn't get as much from them as they could by spotting our muzzle flashes.

Each fire team would attempt to regroup 250 yards farther out—beyond the range of rocket-propelled grenades, RPGs—and too far out to have to worry too much about enemy rifle fire, as long as we stayed low. There were too many trees between us and them. Then the two fire teams would move toward rendezvous.

The enemy gunfire was heavy but still not well directed. Most of the rounds passed well overhead. Once, after I had started crawling backward, a small limb fell on me after it had been cut by rifle fire. For maybe two seconds I froze where I was, startled, needing that time to realize what had hit me, and to reassure myself that I had not been injured. Then I moved, faster, anxious to put more distance between me and the enemy.

I spotted Nuyi on my right as my fire team started to come together. The IF rifle fire had started to slacken, coming in batches, often separated by five to ten seconds of near silence. An occasional enemy grenade was also going off—most at least sixty or seventy yards away. The tonatin soldiers evidently thought we were closer than we were.

Oyo and Iyi came into view on my left, too close together, but both uninjured. Fred Wilkins was the last to reach the rendezvous. He was also unhurt. I wasn't going to get on the radio to ask Souvana about his team. Since we were trying to break contact with the enemy, I didn't want to use the radio.

I used hand signals to communicate with the others in my team. We would move back another hundred yards. Souvana's fire team was to meet us there. Then we would slide around the enemy perimeter and take another stab at them.

Our line battalions were beginning to land on Dancer.

I had just spotted Souvana, right where he was supposed to be, when I had a call from Tonio. This time he didn't sound quite so calm and collected.

"Dragon, we're in a bit of a fix here. Break off what you're doing and head toward my coordinates. We'll try to hold out until you get here, but don't waste time. Just click your transmitter to acknowledge."

CHAPTER 10

I READ **TONIO'S** POSITION THROUGH OUR LINK
to the regimental command center, transferred to my
map. I took a quick look at that, then went to Souvana
to tell him there was a change in plans. He listened, then
nodded abruptly. I went to fill in the members of my
fire team, and he turned to explain the situation to his
people. We conducted our briefings face to face, not
over the radio. We were ready to move thirty seconds
after I had clicked my transmitter to let Tonio know that
I had heard him.

Again, I put the biraunta out as our scouts, up in the
trees where they had swinging room. I had Souvana cut
Fang and Claw out to bring up the rear. They were to
stay fifty yards behind us to stop any IF pursuit long
enough to let us get clear. With the biraunta and the
ghuroh separated from the rest of the squad, I hoped I
had minimized the chances for any friction that might
sap our . . . efficiency, but the disposition was right even
without that. The biraunta were best deployed as scouts
in the forest, and it had to be either the porracci or the
ghuroh in back.

I hoped that the company we had struck had orders to stay put, but I couldn't take a chance. We wouldn't do Tonio and second squad any good if we brought a couple hundred more enemy soldiers into the fight. If the tonatin company we had attacked came after us, we had to slow them down, and my estimate was that the ghuroh would be the best for that job. They were less likely to get too hooked on a fight to withdraw when the time was right. I had Souvana tell Fang and Claw to hang back until they were certain we weren't being followed, then close the gap by half.

We moved quickly. For part of the distance, we were retracing our earlier course—we knew there had been no enemy force along that. Even if nothing slowed us, we would need at least forty minutes to reach Tonio. If second squad was in as hot a spot as I feared—and Tonio would hardly have yelled for help if they weren't—forty minutes might not be soon enough.

I pushed my people harder, and I switched one of my radio channels to monitor second squad's frequency. There was very little talk, but I could hear the fighting—gunfire, grenade explosions, and an occasional cry of pain. It was all I could do to hold myself in. We couldn't run the whole distance, not and be in any condition to fight when we got there. If Tonio and his people couldn't hold on for those forty minutes, there was nothing we could do.

Except try to even the score once we got the chance.

TONIO'S BLIP WAS MOVING ON MY MAP, slowly, toward us. My head-up display tracked that motion. I didn't know how many effectives he had left or how many wounded they might be carrying. *Keep mov-*

ing, Tonio, I urged silently. Every yard they moved in our direction was a yard less we had to cover, a fraction of a second less until we could help.

I dropped out of the line of march until Souvana reached me. He stopped just long enough to whisper that Fang and Claw had rejoined the squad and were in their proper positions. Fang had reported that the enemy had not come out of its perimeter or put out patrols to look for us in the time they had watched.

"That's one break," I whispered, then hurried back toward my position near the front of the squad. Being able to move a little faster for a few seconds felt good. It let me work off some of the tension I felt.

THERE WAS ONE MORE CALL FROM TONIO, twenty-five minutes after we had started moving toward him. "Hurry, Dragon. We can't hold on much longer. We're up against two companies."

We were still five minutes away, maybe half a mile. Tonio and his people had moved farther than I had hoped possible. We had been able to hear the firefight for several minutes—gunfire and grenade explosions, getting louder as we got closer. I saw a brief glare in the distance, almost hidden by trees. The orange glow of an explosion was quickly lost to the night. The noise was damped even faster, and we were still far enough off that it sounded like the pops of small firecrackers.

Plans? There wasn't time for anything fancy. All I could do was spread my squad along a skirmish line and get into the fight, as hot and furious as we could, and hope it would convince the enemy that we were numerous enough to give them more trouble than they wanted.

I used hand signals to disperse my people. Everyone

realized that there would be nothing elegant about this. We were just trying to save our comrades, buy enough time to let the operational commanders free up a fighter or two for close air support, or for more of our spec ops team to reach the fight. The operations team running the show from the ships knew about Tonio's situation, and that we were heading toward them. So far I hadn't heard of any other teams moving to help us. We had been closest.

I had to stop for ten seconds, to catch my breath. Everyone stopped when I did. We were close to the fight, very close. Spent rounds were hitting trees near us, or cutting through leaves and branches—all well above our heads.

Two quick, deep breaths, and a reminder to breathe normally, not hold it. I glanced to either side, then signaled for the squad to disperse more than it was, and to advance again. Thirty seconds later I could see hostile muzzle flashes. I waited another ten seconds, then gave the command to open fire.

EIGHT RIFLES AND TWO GRENADE LAUNCHERS. Those of us firing rifles were profligate with ammunition, using long bursts instead of short, spraying enemy positions. The grenadiers spit out their clips of grenades as quickly as they could. When they ran out of ready ammunition, they switched to their rifles as well. The impression we wanted to create in the enemies' minds was that we were a lot more soldiers than we actually were.

Ten soldiers with fully automatic weapons can put down one hell of a lot of fire. We moved while we fired, especially between bursts. Up, down, move to one side or the other. We did what we could to keep *some* cover in front of us, but movement was more important—not just to give the impression of numbers but also to make it harder for the enemy to target us.

The IFers switched their fire toward us, which gave us a chance to spot the extent of their line, an arc of 150 degrees that had been focused on Tonio's position. Although I followed a wildly staggered course, that was where I headed as well. I wanted to get in and see just what he had left. It was even worse than I had expected. Of the eleven soldiers the team had started with, only three were still alive and able to fight—Tonio, Sergeant Chouvana, and one biraunta.

"I've got four others wounded too badly to fight—if they're still alive," Tonio told me when I dropped to the ground at his side. "Up ahead, between ten and thirty yards out. We had to leave them. I know the other four are dead." The three effectives were short on ammunition. Tonio was using a porracci rifle, and he was down to the last magazine for it.

"Do we stick it out here or try to recover your wounded and then pull back?" I asked.

Tonio shook his head, almost violently. "I don't think we can get to the wounded without losing more men, but as long as we're here the enemy can't get to them either."

"You're probably right," I said. "But we don't have endless ammunition. The way we're going, it'll be a miracle if we can keep this up for another ten minutes."

"It'll be twice that before we can get any air support in, even longer before anyone can get to us on the ground."

"I know you're not going to like this, but we may have to leave the wounded—for now. Try to draw the enemy away from them with a fighting withdrawal."

He hesitated before he replied. "You're right, I don't like it, but there's really nothing else we can do." His voice was tight, each word clipped short. "But we need to stay engaged with the enemy as long as possible, force them to move with us."

No, it wasn't a heroic decision. It also wasn't an easy decision. But it was the *proper* decision. We were going to leave four men who might or might not be alive rather than attempt to rescue them and get them to medical treatment, but that gave the rest of us a better chance to survive and continue the fight. Last stands are seldom the right choice.

It wasn't until Tonio started to get up that I noticed that he had been wounded. There was a nasty burn and gash across his left biceps where a bullet had scored the flesh but had not penetrated. Apparently he had done considerable bleeding and had not managed to bandage the wound. Second squad's sergeant, the porracci Chouvana, was also wounded, but I didn't notice that then. It didn't slow him down.

I passed the word to my men to start withdrawing toward the southwest, away from the people we were going to leave behind. "Start taking it easy on ammo," I said. "Hard telling when we'll be able to get more."

The biraunta from second squad started backing away from the IF force. He was three feet from me when he was hit by three heavy-caliber bullets. They stitched across his neck, just below the lip of his helmet faceplate, and damn near severed his head. The impact blew the biraunta back into me, nearly knocking me to the ground. I felt hot, sticky blood splatter me as I steadied myself and let the biraunta finish his fall. I had to wipe blood from my faceplate so I could see.

There was no point in taking the few seconds I would have needed to feel for a pulse. The biraunta was dead, or so close to it that nothing anyone could do would save him. I used those seconds to take his rifle and strip his web belt with its ammo pouch from his waist. Besides the magazine in the rifle, he had only two more loaded magazines in the pouch.

"Rest in peace," I whispered. That was all the time I could give to the dead.

WE DID NOT RUN STRAIGHT AWAY FROM THE enemy. We moved at an angle across the front, slowly drawing farther from them. The sound level of the fight had already declined once I told my men to conserve ammunition. They went back to firing single shots or short bursts instead of holding triggers down and spraying. An orderly withdrawal from a firefight is one of the more difficult maneuvers, especially when you're facing significantly superior numbers. It's too easy for something like that to turn into a rout, and that was the last thing we wanted.

We worked our way gradually farther from the IFers, hoping to draw them away from the wounded we had left behind. My estimate was that the enemy force was closer to one company than two, but I couldn't be certain. For a few minutes it looked as if the enemy would come after us. They were moving, and attempting to keep us under fire. Then I noticed that they weren't getting closer. They were moving away from where they had been, but at a diverging angle.

"They're withdrawing, too," I told Tonio. I had stayed

close to him after seeing that he was wounded and show-ing the effects of blood loss.

He stopped moving and sank to one knee before look-ing off toward the enemy. At first I wasn't sure why he had knelt. I suspected that he was just getting too weak to stand. He shook me off when I offered him a hand up. "I'm okay. Just trying to get steady. Hold your men up for a minute."

I passed the order on my squad channel.

"They *are* pulling away," Tonio said after watching for most of that minute. "They're angling away faster than we are. They must want to break contact."

"Maybe just part of them," I suggested. "The rest could be waiting to see what we do."

"You mean sucker us into going back for our wounded." There was no question in Tonio's voice. "It's possible."

There was no need for me to say anything, so I didn't. I just waited for Tonio to decide what we would do next.

"We'll go back partway, stick farther away than Chouvana and I were before. When we get into position, send two of your men to check on our wounded. If any of them are still alive, we'll move in to get them."

"Oyo and Iyi," I said. "They'll get in without diffi-culty, and they're smaller targets. How about I send two others off to make sure that all the IFers have actually left?"

Tonio hesitated, then nodded.

I GAVE THE ORDERS TO CEASE FIRING AND move. This was an opportunity to disengage . . . if the tonatin IF force wasn't just suckering us in. I gave Iyi and Oyo their orders, then told Fang and Claw to go in on the south side to see what they could find about the IF force's movement.

"Be ready to give Oyo and Iyi support if they run into trouble," I told the two ghuroh, "but don't initiate a new firefight. That's the last thing we want."

Once the four men started off on their missions, the rest of us moved as well, and we went back to radio silence.

We moved slowly and silently, more concerned with stealth than speed. The wounded would have to hold on that much longer . . . but that was the way it had to be. Maybe the enemy wouldn't forget about us, but we did want them to lose track of exactly where we were. Iyi and Oyo climbed into the trees and moved more rapidly than those of us on the ground. Once they reached the casualties from second squad and were able to determine if any of them were still alive, then there might be some call for speed from the rest of us.

Twice during the seven or eight minutes we took to get into position I saw Tonio lean against a tree for an instant, rest his head against the trunk, and take in an exaggerated breath. It was clear that his wound was affecting him, but as long as he didn't collapse or ask for help, I would keep quiet—at least until we had those wounded men accounted for.

Dead silence. The local birds and animals hadn't started making noise after the bedlam of the fight—if there were any birds or animals left in the area. The gunfire and grenades had done considerable damage to their habitat. The acrid smells of explosives and the liquid propellants most of our rifles used were heavy. I saw a couple of animal carcasses on the ground, innocent bystanders who hadn't managed to escape.

We reached the spot Tonio had chosen and went into

a tight defensive perimeter, each man taking the best cover he could. Once everyone had checked to see how much ammunition he had left, we waited almost without movement. *The biraunta should have reached the wounded by now,* I thought. *They won't break radio silence,* I reminded myself. *They'll come here to tell us what they've found. One of them, at least, if any of the wounded are still alive.*

I kept my eyes on the branches above and to the east, toward where second squad had been chopped to pieces, looking for movement or a familiar infrared signature. It was nearly ten minutes before Oyo dropped out of the tree over my head.

"There are two still alive," Oyo whispered to me. "One porracci, one ghuroh. I don't know if either can survive until we get them to help. Iyi remains with them."

I glanced toward Tonio to see if he had heard. But Tonio was on his knees, slouched against the next tree trunk, sliding toward the ground. I crawled over to him as he fell sideways. There was still a pulse in his neck, but he was unconscious.

I CURSED SILENTLY WHILE I PULLED THE FIRST-aid pouch from my belt. It didn't take long to get a bandage over the wound on Tonio's arm once I got him laid out on his back. The bandage was impregnated with medical nanoagents that would get inside the wound and into Tonio's system, helping the body create new blood while they cleaned and started to heal the wound. They also provided painkillers.

"Souvana, I'll keep Chouvana and Nuyi here with me. You take the rest of the squad and bring the wounded back—give them what help they need there to give them a chance."

"I'll go with them," Chouvana said. "They're my men."

"I can't order you not to," I told him, "but I think you'll do your men more good by taking care of that wound of yours first. Besides, if we have to move Tonio before the others get back, I'll feel a lot better if I know you're here to help keep off the enemy." No, it wasn't empty flattery. If the situation came up, I *would* feel better with a porracci sergeant to cover my back.

He hesitated, then said, "Very well," and took off his first-aid pouch. One of the items that hadn't caught up with the reality of the 1st Combined Regiment yet was medical gear. Each species had its own medical patches and injectors, with the nanoagents tailored for their own kind. Sure, there're not a hell of a lot of differences among us, but those slight differences can mean that a patch that will heal a human in thirty minutes (or thirty hours, depending) might take ten times as long to heal a porracci or a biraunta . . . or do no good at all. We had been assured that they could do no harm, though I remained skeptical of that.

I checked Tonio's pulse and breathing. His breathing was slow and shallow, the pulse under sixty beats per minute; his face was pale and clammy. *You should have put a patch on that a lot sooner, Tonio,* I thought. *Saved us both a lot of problems.*

There was nothing more I could do for him then. I had to give the medical patch time to work. Fang and Claw returned ten minutes after I had sent Souvana to get the other wounded men.

"The enemy continues to withdraw," Fang said, whispering next to my ear. "They have left no one behind."

"At least we caught a break there." I didn't question his statement. He wouldn't have said it quite that way if he hadn't been certain. Ghuroh males are primarily hunters by instinct and training, as opposed to being instinctive warriors, the way porracci are. "Sergeant Xeres is unconscious. Sergeant Chouvana is hurt." I gestured in the direction the squad had taken. "I want you and Claw to go out to meet them. They might need help."

Fang and Claw started moving away. There was one other reason I sent them. The more nonporracci who were around, the less nervous Oyo and Iyi were going to be.

IT WAS ANOTHER FIFTEEN MINUTES BEFORE THE squad returned with the wounded. The porracci, Private Tiavauna, was in desperate shape. His left arm had been blown off below the shoulder. There had scarcely been enough arm left to get a tourniquet secured above the wound. Tiavauna also had several shrapnel wounds and had lost considerable blood. His fur and uniform were soaked with it. He was unconscious, but his remaining limbs were twitching spasmodically. After taking a quick check of his condition, I didn't think he had any chance of surviving long enough to get a shuttle in to evacuate him, but we couldn't give up on him as long as he was still breathing.

The ghuroh, called Slash by his comrades, wasn't hurt as badly, but he wasn't going to be able to do much for some time—*if* he survived until we could get him to qualified medical help. Among other wounds, he appeared to have a serious spinal injury. Before carrying him away from where he had been hurt, my people had fashioned a stretcher from tree limbs and had bound

Slash to it in order to avoid further complicating the spinal injury.

Tonio was still unconscious. I squatted next to Chouvana for a conference. We were both buck sergeants, and I wasn't certain who had seniority. For the moment, leadership had to be by committee of two.

"We've got to get them to the doctors," I said. "It's the only chance either one has."

Chouvana made a complicated growling noise that my translator button didn't attempt to interpret. Then: "Tiavauna will not survive, no matter what we do, but the ghuroh has a chance. And Sergeant Xeres will live. He should recover even without evacuation."

"The way I see it, we've got two problems," I said. "First, we're not far enough from that IF force to call for help, or to secure an LZ for a shuttle. Second, I don't know if there are any shuttles available."

"We can do nothing about the second problem. If we do not call for help though, neither Tiavauna nor Slash will live."

"Make the call, then move northwest, away from the enemy force we know about?" I suggested.

"That is all we can do," Chouvana said, "pass the decision to our superiors."

I WAS HESITANT ABOUT BREAKING RADIO SI-
lence, but while Tonio remained unconscious, Chouvana and I were the ranking men. We might pass some of the buck up the chain of command, but we had to make the first decision. I had the others get the three unconscious men ready to move, and put my biraunta out as sentries. I switched channels and made the call. I gave headquarters the situation in as few words as I could manage,

keeping my transmission time to a minimum.

"Mark an LZ and set up a perimeter. We'll get a boat in as quickly as we can," the duty officer said. "It might be a while."

"We need ammo resupply as well, for all our people," I said. "We're all just about out."

There was a brief hesitation before the officer said, "We'll have to bring you all out. We're not set up for resupply yet."

WE MOVED NORTHWEST FOR THREE HUNDRED yards before we found a clearing large enough for a shuttle. There was no way eleven of us could set up a secure defensive perimeter. We could scarcely scan the area to make sure that no enemy force could penetrate without being spotted. I put my men in an arc covering the section of the perimeter closest to the enemy force we knew about. Then I had Iyi and Oyo plant snoops near the far side of the clearing.

There was no need to transmit the LZ's coordinates to headquarters. They would have a fix on my helmet electronics—on all of our electronics, if everything was working. That would tell them where to send the shuttle.

It was close to dawn. There was already a clear line marking the eastern horizon, a lighter gray to the night sky. I was uncomfortably certain that the shuttle would not make it under cover of what was left of the night. We would be burning away from the surface in daylight, visible to any enemy soldier with a shoulder-fired rocket launcher. The lighter that area on the horizon got, the more my stomach churned.

To keep busy, I checked our wounded. To my amazement, Tiavauna was still alive, though his pulse and respiration were so depressed I almost thought I was imagining them. *Porracci are tough,* I told myself. *Maybe he can make it, despite how badly off he is.* I wasn't fooling myself. I knew it would take a miracle for him to survive until a shuttle came and got him to the infirmary on one of the ships. Tiavauna might die at any second, even though the twitching had stopped.

Slash was breathing more regularly than he had been, and his heart rate had increased to eighty—not too low for a ghuroh, Claw informed me; one hundred would be "normal." Fang and Claw had carried his stretcher.

Tonio seemed to be getting close to waking up. I heard a few soft groans from him, and his head moved from side to side a couple of times after we reached the LZ. The way he was acting, he might almost have been having a bad dream.

I felt as if *I* were having a bad dream. There had been more work scheduled for us—two additional strikes before daybreak. Running out of ammunition early and having to be evacuated with the remnants of second squad had not been in the plan.

Now that we were lying around waiting, I had time to catch up on the reports on the battle as a whole, There were other units in trouble. We weren't exactly getting our butts kicked, but the invasion was not on schedule, and we were taking heavy losses. Several other spec ops teams had run into trouble. Some of the line companies had been pinned down where they came out of their shuttles, and none of them had achieved their initial objectives on time.

A few shuttles hadn't made it to the ground safely, but the reports I heard did not mention specific numbers.

We had been at the LZ for twenty minutes when I had a call from operations to tell me that a squad from our company's fourth platoon was going to rendezvous with us in fifteen minutes to evacuate on the same shuttle. They also had seriously wounded men to get out.

There was no ETA for the shuttle.

TONIO **REGAINED CONSCIOUSNESS JUST BE-**fore the squad from fourth platoon reached us. He was never really alert, but he opened his eyes and mumbled a few indistinct words. I gave him a sip of water and a summary of what was going on, not certain that he could hear or remember. He mumbled something else I couldn't understand, then closed his eyes again.

The squad from fourth platoon was coming in when Tiavauna went into convulsions—violent and noisy; audible for a hundred yards. The convulsions lasted twenty seconds before he settled into silence. And death.

THERE **WERE ONLY SIX MEN LEFT OF THE NEW** squad, four of them wounded. Three of the wounded were able to walk, or hobble along on their own. Their wounds had been patched. The platoon sergeant and the corporal were both among the dead they had been forced to leave behind. The two lance corporals, a divotect and a ghuroh, were happy to have someone higher ranking make decisions.

"We take care of our wounded and wait for pickup," I told them.

"Do you know yet how long we must wait?" the divotect asked.

I shook my head. "No idea. We just have to settle in. Get your people into the perimeter. How are you for ammunition?"

"Short," the ghuroh said. "Very short."

"Join the club."

THE SUN STARTED TO LIFT ABOVE THE HORIZON.
I continued to monitor the command channel, listening
to reports in both directions. Units actively engaged with
the enemy were not subject to radio silence—there was
little point when the enemy knew where they were—and
the line companies weren't as restricted as spec ops in
any case.

In the thirty minutes after the squad from fourth platoon reached us, there was no radio traffic directed to
us, no hint of when the shuttle might come in. I had the
men from fourth platoon give up their snoops and had
my people plant them, extending our coverage of the
area around us. I was nervous. There were too many
enemy around, and I wasn't certain that our people
would spot any enemy units moving toward us fast
enough to let us get away.

The way I saw it, we had no chance in a firefight, not
against any force larger than a platoon. If the enemy
found us, we would have to run and try to establish a
new LZ somewhere else.

I did hear about other medical evacuation flights while
I listened to the radio. I don't know how operations decided who got pick-up first; they could hardly triage casualties by remote control. I *wanted* to call to remind
operations that we needed help, but I didn't. Breaking
radio silence again would do no good . . . and might do
a world of harm.

Wait. It wasn't easy. I forced myself to eat a field
ration pack—more tasteless than ever—and washed it
down with water. The sun kept inching higher. It was

completely above the horizon. Tonio continued to hover at the edge of consciousness, moaning occasionally, moving a little. I tried talking to him several times, but he didn't respond.

Slash didn't seem to be improving either. He may even have lost ground. His pulse was slower, weaker. Either Fang or Claw was with him almost all the time. Sergeant Chouvana was sitting with his back against a tree trunk, slouched low, trying not to show any weakness from his wound. I *thought* he was hurting worse than he let on, but he shrugged off my questions. Humans are amateurs at the macho game compared to porracci.

It had been more than two hours since my call for a medevac shuttle before I heard from operations again.

"Your pickup is on the way in, ETA twelve minutes. The shuttle will be landing from west to east. Have your people ready to go when it touches down. There is an enemy force estimated at two companies moving toward you. They could reach you in fifteen minutes."

That's cutting it too damned close, I thought, but I simply clicked my transmitter to acknowledge the message.

"We can't cut loose a fighter for close support," the officer in operations continued.

I pulled everyone in close and passed along the news—both the good and the bad. "As soon as that shuttle comes in, we need to start moving the wounded. We can't afford to waste even seconds or the enemy will be close enough to pop us out of the sky before we get out of range. Let's move around the side of the clearing—will be that much closer to where the shuttle will stop."

Proper procedure would call for us to stay under cover of the trees while we worked our way *cautiously* around the clearing. But we might not be able to do that in time, so we cut across the open space. The men carrying the stretchers went first, then the walking wounded, while the rest of us brought up the rear—and spent most of the time looking over our shoulders.

We did get down in the long grass once we were as close as we could get to where I *thought* the shuttle might end up. If the enemy was moving faster than the estimate, we would be out in the open without effective cover. I put everyone in a perimeter of sorts, around the wounded, but grass won't stop bullets.

Two minutes remained until the shuttle's ETA. Operations didn't call back with any revision of that, or the ETA for the enemy force. I don't think I've ever sweated so much in my life, or been so frightened. Even after I spotted the shuttle on its approach, I feared that the enemy would arrive in time to bag us and the bird. Lying still and waiting was torture even though I knew we could do nothing else.

"Once that shuttle gets down, we pick up our wounded and run like someone was sticking bayonets up our asses," I told my men.

The shuttle pilot showed guts. His wheels didn't clear the trees at the far side of the clearing by twenty feet. He switched the jets to full thrust in reverse before the shuttle touched down. The noise was *loud*. Even if the enemy hadn't seen the shuttle, they had to be close enough to hear it. And they might be closer than we thought. Operations had only given an *estimate* of how long it would take them to reach us.

I didn't wait for the shuttle to brake to a full stop. I was on my feet and moving before it was halfway across the clearing. So were the rest of the men with me. The pilot turned the shuttle around, skidding through 180 degrees with the last momentum of his craft, and two passenger hatches popped open.

I think we set a record for boarding. The shuttle's crew chief shut the hatches and yelled, "Strap in fast."

By that time the pilot was already pushing the throttles forward again and we were rolling across the clearing.

I didn't *start* to relax until we were five miles high, beyond the reach of shoulder-fired missiles, burning for orbit.

CHAPTER 11

THE FLEET'S COMBAT FIGHTER SCREEN TOOK us under their wings once we were halfway to *Tarsus*, the transport that held the regiment's main infirmary. There were two medtechs waiting for the wounded just past the airlock between the hangar bay and the rest of the ship. Just about everything they might need to keep a serious casualty alive until the doctors could get to them was right at hand.

An abarand staff sergeant was there to direct those of us who weren't wounded off in the other direction. "The galley has hot food waiting. We've got a room for you to take off your gear and leave it. The heads are close by. Do what you need to and get cleaned up. I'm afraid we can't supply you with new uniforms, but we can handle ammunition—for everyone."

That was more than I really expected, but then, my expectations could hardly have been lower than they were. "How long before we go back in?" I asked. "My squad is intact."

The abarand sergeant smiled. "I have no idea. Things are rather . . . fluid just now. Get cleaned up, eat, and relax. We've got beds available. After you eat, catch some sleep if you can. That's always a wise option."

TARSUS WAS A HUMAN SHIP, DESIGNED FOR HU-
mans. The other species made do with the arrangements in the head—latrine. There were no insurmountable obstacles. It was while I was taking a hot shower that exhaustion caught up with me. It had been more than thirty hours—and several dozen light-years—since I had slept, and enough of those hours had been active that my body wanted sleep even more than food. But we all trooped along to the galley, mess hall, and stood in line for hot food. *Get it while you can.*

The galley was equipped for all the species, with "native" food for each of us. There also was plenty of hot coffee. I lost count of how many cups I drank. I wasn't concerned that it might keep me awake if we actually got a chance for sleep. There was a nagging pessimist dancing around in the back of my brain that kept telling me that we'd no more than stretch out before someone would tell us to get ready to head back down to the surface of Dintsen.

I figured any sleep I *did* get would be gravy, even if it was only five minutes. We sat in the galley until everyone had finished eating, then trooped along the passageways until we reached the compartment with beds. No one had said much. We were all beat. Even Souvana was looking as if he were about ready to drop—something none of our training had managed.

Since I was in front of the group, I flopped on the first empty bunk. There were already about twenty others in the room, sleeping. I don't know if my bunk's springs had stopped vibrating before I was asleep. I might have been out before my head touched the pillow.

It was more than five hours later before someone came in and woke me. With difficulty.

I was so deep in sleep and groggy that at first I didn't recognize the voice that kept saying my name. I was slow to feel that my shoulder was being shaken as well. My brain tried to construct a dream to contain the sensations and let me continue sleeping, but to no avail. Somehow I managed to sit up, with my feet on the floor, before I was all the way awake, before I realized that it was Tonio trying to rouse me.

"What time is it?" My mouth was dry. The words came out thick, and got lost in a gaping yawn while the last fragments of dream got lost in consciousness.

"About sixteen hundred," Tonio said. "Four in the afternoon." Dintsen's day was about twenty minutes longer than Earth's, a small enough difference to ignore over a short haul.

"What are you doing back so soon?" I asked after another yawn. My eyes were tearing, so I wiped at them with my forearms.

"They filled my tank and patched my arm. 'Returned to duty.' "

I rubbed at my eyes some more, then ran my hands over the stubble of beard on my cheeks. "How's it going down below?" I wasn't sure that I wanted to ask that question, or have it answered, but I couldn't hold it back.

Tonio shook his head. "They haven't told me much, but I've seen enough long faces to know it isn't good. We've got a briefing in"—he looked at his watch—"forty-two minutes. That gives you time for a trip to the latrine and a shave, maybe even for a bite of food if you hurry."

"We're going back in?"

"That's my guess." Tonio shrugged. "They didn't bring us all this distance for a furlough. Get cracking. You're using up your time."

"What about the others?" I gestured around, looking around at the men from my squad. I stood and started stretching.

"Let them sleep while they can. The briefing is for sergeants and up, everyone fit for duty, I guess."

THE ROOM WE WERE LED TO WAS SET UP WITH several rows of chairs facing a table with a lectern on it, and chairs flanking that, facing out.

Sergeants and up. There were two junior lieutenants—one a ghuroh from A Company's third platoon, the other a human from one of the line battalions—at the briefing. The rest of us were sergeants of one stripe or another. Of the noncoms, the highest ranking was First Sergeant Halsey of Ranger Battalion's B Company. There were two platoon sergeants, one staff sergeant, and seven buck sergeants besides me. Most of us were from Ranger Battalion. There were only three soldiers I didn't at least know by sight. About half the noncoms had blood on their uniforms, and rips. Short of missing limbs, serious spinal injuries, or badly chewed-up major organs, four hours in a medtank—medical repair tank—will take care of most injuries.

We waited for the briefing to start. There was a coffee pot in the room, and we all drank coffee. That's one human vice most of the other species had adopted—at least in the 1st Combined Regiment. A petty officer from *Tarsus*'s crew came in to tell us it would be a few more minutes. We had been waiting fifteen minutes by then.

The few conversations had been almost whispered, and short.

Mostly we asked each other if anyone knew what was up or what was going on. No one seemed to know what the briefing would be about, and no one had any encouraging news about what they had seen on Dintsen. No one really *knew* anything but what they had experienced personally, and everyone who had been brought up to *Tarsus* had either been wounded or had been in a unit that was hit badly, so the stories tended to be rather one-sided.

The wait had gone on nearly half an hour before the door opened again and Lieutenant Colonel Hansen walked in. He was a surprise. The sour look on his face wasn't. We all stood at attention and held it until the colonel told us to be seated.

"Sorry you had to wait so long," Hansen said. "My shuttle ride over from *Alexandria* had to be delayed while we cleared the space between ships." He tilted his head forward for an instant and sucked in a breath. What he hadn't said came through loud and clear. The enemy still had fighter assets that could threaten the fleet.

"We knew this would not be an easy mission," he said when he looked at us again, "and—so far—it hasn't been, as most of you are already aware. Enemy resistance has been fierce, and our estimate that most of the IF troops on Dintsen would be other than first-string assault forces appears to have been, ah, overly optimistic. We are behind schedule." He shrugged. "I expected that. Most operational schedules are overly optimistic."

I caught myself wondering how often he would use the term "overly optimistic." *We screwed up,* I thought, *but we knew this whole operation was screwed from the start.*

"The good news is that the fleet is mostly intact and that we have parity with the IF space forces here, and a slight margin over them in aerospace fighters—and the advantage of having abarand flyers and fighters for half of our complement." *Parity* with the space forces, not the superiority we had been told before the dance started. I didn't miss that in what he said. "The bad news is that the Ilion Federation outnumbers us by more than two to one on the ground, and they're . . . not making many mistakes. We have taken more casualties than we allowed for." He hesitated, then shook his head—minimally.

"We still have freedom of movement on the ground, and we are still—mostly—on the offensive, and that gives us some advantage. As long as we can keep that momentum, we have a good chance of meeting our objectives. But we can't slack off, can't give the IF the opportunity to blunt our attacks and go over onto the offensive against us."

Come on, get on with it, I thought. *Drop the other shoe. What are you going to drop us in this time?*

"Those of you from the line battalions will be put back on the ground, returned to your own units, or used as replacements in other units that have holes to be filled. You will be contacted individually about your assignments.

"We can't return those of you from Ranger Battalion to your units immediately. The spec ops squads are too separated and fragmented to make that practical." And some of those units had been chopped up so badly that there was no one for them to go back to; the colonel didn't bother to say that, though. There was no point in parading the painfully obvious through our ears.

"Lieutenant Deliatwelayen will lead a team made up

from the spec ops people here, built around Platoon Sergeant Xeres and Sergeant Drak's squad from B Company. Not all of the spec ops men will be part of this team. Those who are not will be held on *Tarsus* for the time being, until we can deploy you effectively."

Sergeant Chouvana and the men remaining from his squad would be part of the pick-up team, along with half a dozen other men who had been brought up to *Tarsus*. Colonel Hansen dismissed everyone but those of us who were being sent back in with the ghuroh lieutenant.

"Move in closer," Hansen said when the rest were gone. He came around from in back of the lectern and turned a chair to sit facing us—Lieutenant Deliatwelayen, Tonio, Chouvana, and me.

"Some coffee, Colonel?" Tonio asked, and when Hansen nodded, Tonio got up and filled a cup for him. The colonel took several spaced sips before he started talking again.

"My operations staff is putting together the details of this mission now. There will be someone to give you a detailed briefing on it shortly. You won't be going in for several hours yet. After dark.

"The situation is this: The line battalions are moving on the Dintsen capital, which is also the headquarters and central strong point of the IF occupation. Our people are not moving as rapidly as we hoped. They've got four battalions of IF soldiers in front of them, and harassing their flanks, and there is another short regiment moving to reinforce those troops. Your job is to prevent them from doing so, for as long as you can, hopefully until we degrade the IF units we're pushing against now enough to let us break through into the capital. We have several spec ops teams operating against them already, and we're getting fighters in to hit them from the air when we can, but it hasn't been enough, and we've taken heavy casualties."

"Colonel?" Tonio said, raising his hand about halfway. Hansen nodded. "Have we managed to determine yet if there are any surviving divotect military units on the planet?"

"There don't seem to be," Hansen said. "If there are small units, or individuals, still free, we haven't spotted them and they haven't contacted us. We have to assume that we're not going to get any help from that quarter. And there is no sign of divotect civilians trying to rise against the IF occupation, or any resistance movement. We don't know how many divotect civilians remain. The tonatin forces have not exterminated all of them. We know they've kept many thousands of workers alive and under guard. Beyond that. . . ." Hansen shrugged. "We just don't know."

"Do we really have a chance here, or are we just buying time for the Alliance with our lives?" That was Chouvana.

"Buying time is important," Hansen said. "It gives the Alliance time to get more units trained, more weapons and ships built. If we can keep the Ilion Federation from attacking the core divotect worlds, we might save millions of lives, maybe hundreds of millions. But, with all that said, yes, I do think we have a chance to win on Dintsen, providing the Ilion Federation isn't able to bring in reinforcements before the issue is settled. We've taken it on the chin so far, but . . . we're performing well despite that. I think we've proved the validity of the combined unit concept." His smile was weak.

"If anyone ever learns that," I said, under my breath. I was surprised that Hansen heard.

"They'll learn about it," he said. "We've been sending

message rockets out every three or four hours with detailed reports. We're a bastard unit with unprecedented problems, too many different weapons and types of ammunition. Our communications aren't as good as they should be. We're not working together as well as we could be. But we're fighting bastards for all that, and we're learning fast."

THE OPERATIONAL BRIEFING TWENTY MINUTES later was mostly an exercise in studying maps, with the enemy's route of march marked, along with possible avenues of attack. Since we wouldn't be heading in for three hours, everything remained tentative. The only solid information was that we would be going in all the way aboard shuttles. With the situation on the ground what it was, it hadn't been possible to retrieve many airsleds. That was what the captain who briefed us said. Mentally, I translated that as we hadn't retrieved *any* sleds. The idea is, you do that when you've got the engagement won—or have local air and ground security so you don't lose shuttles during the operation. Airsleds are expendable; you don't risk more important assets recovering them. Not that I would miss having another sled ride.

By the time we got back to the barracks compartment, some of the others had started waking up. Chouvana and I woke the rest of the people in our squads, and the few others who would be going in with us. We gathered off to the side, away from the rest of the men in the compartment—some of whom were still sleeping—and Tonio laid out the bones of the mission and the lines of command and communication within the team. Lieutenant Deliatwelayen would lead the mission, with Tonio as his second. Then Chouvana and me. I would have my squad. Chouvana would have the remnants of his and the added replacements. Chouvana took his pick-up squad out in the passageway to get everyone acquainted—and to tell them what he expected from them.

We all went back to the galley then. Everyone ate, knowing it might be some time before we had hot food again . . . if this didn't turn out to be the condemned men's last meal. I wasn't particularly hungry, but I forced myself to eat.

Afterward, we gathered our gear, drew ammunition and grenades, and ran performance checks on our electronics. That was better than twiddling our thumbs until it was time to head to the hangar and our ride back to the surface of Dintsen.

IT **WAS PAST 1900 HOURS WHEN THE CAPTAIN** from Colonel Hansen's staff gave us an update on the situation—how far the regiment we were supposed to slow down had traveled, the latest estimate on numbers, where the other spec ops teams were, and so forth. The captain laid it all out for us on the maps.

"There remain almost eight miles between the two Ilion Federation units," Lieutenant Deliatwelayen noted, moving his finger between the two on his map. "Captain, have these troops been moving all day?" He indicated the reinforcing regiment, the unit we were being thrown against.

"Since just after dawn," the captain said, nodding. "Moving, or defending themselves against our attacks. We've kept them as occupied as we could."

"That must decrease their efficiency," Deliatwelayen

said. "They will be looking for an opportunity to rest, to allow their men time to sleep."

"It's not enough yet for it to degrade tonatin performance significantly," Tonio said. "I would suspect that they could go without sleep for another sixteen to twenty hours, at a minimum, before they get too groggy to be extremely deadly. I've faced them before, Lieutenant—before this campaign."

"So have I, Sergeant," the lieutenant replied.

"Sorry, sir, I was forgetting," Tonio said.

Deliatwelayen brushed aside the apology. "I believe it is time for us to move to the shuttle."

The captain from operations nodded and we all got to our feet. That walk felt a lot longer than it was.

CHAPTER 12

THERE WAS ONE THING I HAD ESPECIALLY NO-
ticed while we were drawing weapons and ammunition.
Without exception, every soldier in the team had taken
more than a "standard" load of ammo, cramming extra
rifle magazines anywhere they could be stashed, hooking
a couple of additional hand grenades on their harness,
an extra pouch of RPGs for each fire team's grenadier.
No one told them to do it, and the privates and lance
corporals were the first to draw ammo. They didn't even
have the example of the lieutenant and sergeants to suggest it.

I carried four more magazines for my rifle than I had
when we went in the first time . . . and I had carried two
more than the "standard" load that time. I figured that I
wouldn't have to tote that extra weight for long, and it
could do a lot more good if I had it on me than if it sat
in the armory aboard ship.

When we got into place in the shuttle—in web seats
that were uncomfortable, but infinitely less so than the
sleds—we had more waiting, with no explanation of
why or how long it would be. Maybe we were waiting

for fighters to clear space for us. Maybe . . . well, the list of possibilities was long.

I looked along the row of my people—soldiers in camouflage fatigues, web belts and pack harness, battle helmets and boots. Each man had the faceplate of his helmet down, and the tinted plastic effectively hid facial expressions. Most had their heads down, at least a little.

Souvana was an exception. I couldn't see his face any better than I could the others, but I was certain he was staring at me while I looked at him; the fingers of his left hand worked, clenching and unclenching the forestock of his rifle.

Iyi and Oyo sat motionless; not even their tails were moving. That said a lot, and not good.

Nuyi sat like a lump, with his chin almost touching his chest. With my divotect, though, that wasn't extraordinary. At his cheeriest, Nuyi was melancholy. If he had been human, I would have considered Nuyi clinically depressed. For a divotect, he was almost normal.

Tonio sat with his map open on his lap, staring at that, one hand occasionally adjusting the screen. The other hand held his rifle against his leg. Before long he would probably have the topography of our new area of operations committed to memory.

Fred Wilkins had both hands on his rifle's forestock; the impression I had was that he was nearly using it to hold himself erect. His knuckles were white from the pressure he was exerting. Wilkins had been even quieter than usual since we were told we were leaving Dancer, and since I had dressed him down early in training there he had been the least talkative of anyone in the squad but Kiervauna and Nuyi.

Kiervauna sat tensely, leaning into his safety harness, as if challenging it to hold him. Occasionally he glanced at Souvana or Chouvana, the two other porracci. At other times he looked my way, but never for long.

Our lieutenant seemed busy. He had a map open, but he was not staring at it as fixedly as Tonio. The lieutenant was looking around at the men he would command. Maybe he also had a conversation or two going on the radio; I assumed he did. At a minimum, he would be monitoring the command channel to try to keep informed about what was going on below.

Jaibie alternated between sitting motionless and fluttering his arms, wings, at his side. That was fairly standard for him, especially when he was nervous. Those wings might not let him truly fly, but they could help him stay cool.

During most of the time we waited in the shuttle aboard *Tarsus,* Fang and Claw had their heads together, conversing too softly for me to hear what they were saying. I didn't know the ghuroh as well as I knew the other members of my squad, but what I had seen of them in action was encouraging.

Me? Hell, I was at least as nervous as any of my men, fighting the intrusion of fear by studying everyone else. That let me keep my mind off me. I *tried* studying my map, but I had difficulty focusing on that for long. Any distraction was welcome, anything to keep from thinking about what might lay ahead, anything to keep my mind from dipping far into the past as well. Memories would lead to places I didn't want to visit—like the fact that if I died, there would be no one on Earth to mourn me. I hadn't had any contact with my parents—the only family I had—since I enlisted in the army. They had been against that . . . but their opposition had not stopped them from using the exemption granted by my service to get on an emigration list and moving out to one of the colony worlds. I had written them a couple of times early on, but they had never answered.

WE HAD BEEN IN THE SHUTTLE FORTY-FIVE minutes before we heard anything but our stomachs growling. Our lieutenant told us it would be another ten minutes before we were launched, but he had no explanation why. Maybe he had been given none. Maybe he didn't feel that we needed to know. I wasn't that good second-guessing human officers, let alone ghuroh.

I watched the timeline on my head-up display after the lieutenant said we had another ten minutes. That held much of my attention for the next several minutes. That and continuing to watch the others. I knew less about the people in the squad thrown together under Sergeant Chouvana. Whatever the individual capabilities of those men, they hadn't trained together, they didn't know each other, how they would react to . . . whatever. That was a weakness.

Ten minutes. Eleven. Eleven and a half. *Don't get your bowels in an uproar,* I told myself as the seconds started to drag into ages. *Nothing in the army ever goes exactly on schedule.*

I sucked in a long, deep breath and held it for nearly a minute before I started to let it out, trying to do that slowly and smoothly. I would have made it, too, except that about halfway through the process, the shuttle's pilot gave us the warning that we would be launched in thirty seconds.

I'VE GOT A PRETTY GOOD HUNCH WHERE THE cliché "Ignorance is bliss" came from. My bet is that it started with some soldier who was on his way into combat not knowing what the hell lay ahead but fearing that the reality would be more terrible than his worst nightmare. Your mind tortures you with what *might* be waiting, and that brings knots to the stomach and rivers of sweat to the rest of the body. But I've seen times when ignorance *was* better than knowledge. The situation Tonio and I—and the rest of our battalion—had faced when the tonatin started this war by attacking Dintsen was one of them. I just hoped I would be around to have nightmares about this campaign the way I still did about the other.

We counted down the final seconds until our shuttle was blown out of the hangar by compressed air jets; then we counted the seconds until the shuttle's rockets lit and we started accelerating away from *Tarsus* and toward Dintsen.

We got off lucky last night, I told myself, looking around at my squad as acceleration brought back a sensation of weight after the seconds of weightlessness, *luckier than a lot of other squads. How far can that luck run? Is this* our *turn to get chopped up? My turn?* I'd been in the army a long time before I realized that I wasn't immortal. The Bunyan Rebellion didn't do it. I saw a little combat there, but nothing really . . . desperate. When we got chewed up and spit out on Dintsen at the start of this war, I saw a lot of men die. For a time I waited to join them, resigned to death. I didn't see any chance of surviving that battle. But I did. Somehow.

You've had almost a year of gravy. Just do what you can to make sure you get back this time, with your men. I closed my eyes and said a silent prayer. That couldn't erase my fears, but it did make them a little easier to live with.

I opened my eyes and looked at Tonio. He had put his map away and was looking around like I was. Tonio would know how I felt. I was sure he must feel something similar. We had been through that time in hell together. And, like me, the army was the only family Tonio had.

The shuttle started to tremble in a new fashion as we entered Dintsen's atmosphere, still accelerating, though the pilot had started to ease off on our angle of approach. The knot in my stomach moved and seemed to press in another direction.

"Lock and load," our lieutenant ordered on his all-hands channel. Everyone had loaded magazines in their weapons. We automatically ran the bolts to put a round in the firing chamber after putting the safeties in the "on" position. We would take the safeties off once the shuttle was on the ground.

I wiped my hands on my trouser legs, one at a time, getting rid of the sweat that had accumulated on my palms. I swallowed hard. *Not much longer,* I told myself, and within seconds the pilot had come on the intercom to tell us that we were within three minutes of our LZ.

"Remember your assignments," the lieutenant said. "When we hit the ground, everyone out and away from the shuttle quickly. Initial perimeter until the shuttle takes off. Then we move." He switched to the noncoms' channel then.

"We should be two miles from any hostile forces when we land, if the intelligence we were given remains correct. But we cannot afford to assume that until we can see for ourselves. Keep your men alert, and make certain you stay alert yourselves. We have no room for error."

Ain't it the truth, I thought, swallowing again. *That's what this crap is always about.*

"We'll hold our own, Lieutenant," Tonio said. "We'll do everything possible."

"We continue to fight as long as there is one man left with one bullet," the lieutenant said, and I groaned silently. Maybe I should have expected that sort of gung-ho attitude from a ghuroh lieutenant, but it still hurt to listen to that manure.

"We'll do what we can, Lieutenant," Tonio said. "Suicide rarely helps."

Good for you! I thought. I wanted to cheer. But then the pilot gave us the one-minute warning.

THEY MAKE THE BOWS AND BOTTOMS OF THOSE shuttles tough. Since most assault landings aren't going to be on prepared landing strips, shuttles have to be able to take whatever the ground offers—stumps, rocks, metal hazards planted by an enemy. Whatever.

Our pilot seemed determined to put his boat to the test. We came in hot, with the pilot waiting to throw the engines into full reverse until the last possible second. We didn't so much touch down as bounce in, and the shuttle hit something solid after the second bounce. We lurched forty degrees to the right before the boat came back down on its wheels and skids and stayed on the ground. I sat with my feet braced in front of me and held my rifle with all my strength as we got bounced around, thrown against our safety harnesses, then against the back of the seats, then forward and sideways. It was as bad as the worst airsled landing, and in a sled, at least you don't have that far to bounce. There isn't room to be a tennis ball.

I heard someone throw up, maybe two people, but I didn't look to see who. I was satisfied when none of the stuff hit me.

The bucking bronco ride seemed to last forever, and at the very end our pilot skidded the shuttle around 180 degrees and went to forward thrust to bring us to a halt. We tilted 40 degrees to starboard for a second or two during the turn. Then we stopped and the hatches sprang open. The pilot and our lieutenant both screamed, "Up and out!" almost in unison.

I slapped the quick release on my safety harness, lurched to my feet . . . and almost fell. The shuttle hadn't *quite* come to a complete halt. I had to catch myself on a stanchion and hold on for about three seconds before things stopped moving around me.

Tonio was also yelling for everyone to move, and Chouvana and I added our voices. I shoved two men past me toward the nearest hatch, then fell in behind them, pushing them forward.

We scrambled out of the shuttle running, then fanned out to set up an initial perimeter fifty yards away to cover the takeoff of the shuttle. I had scarcely dropped to the ground before I heard the pilot run his throttles up to maximum and start his takeoff run. My face was already as close to the dirt as it could get, but I still tried to duck. Some instinct, I guess, some fear that the shuttle might run me over.

No one got run over. The shuttle was off the ground and tilted back to burn for orbit as our lieutenant got to his feet and shouted—over the radio—for us to get moving. No one needed much urging. The standard procedure is clear: *Get away from the LZ as fast as your feet will carry you, before the enemy can drop any nasty surprises on your head.*

*　　*　　*

IT WAS RAINING, A LIGHT MIST, JUST ENOUGH
to clean the air. It wasn't heavy enough to pose any sort
of obstacle, and there wasn't enough mud to bitch about.
The clouds were thick enough that we couldn't see the
stars, but as long as we had working helmets and ships
overhead, we had no need to navigate by them.

The lieutenant set the direction of march, but I
checked my own compass anyway. I would have done
that no matter who was leading the mission. Some things
you never take on trust if you have any alternative.

We jogged until we were under cover of trees and
away from the clearing. Then we slowed down while
the lieutenant adjusted our order of march, and changed
our heading thirty degrees to the left—in case the enemy
had managed to get a fix on us while we were out in
the open. My squad got the point. That made sense. We
were the squad that had trained together.

I put Oyo and Iyi up in the trees and set Wilkins on
point on the ground. I was behind him, with Nuyi following me. Tonio moved into position after Nuyi. Souvana was in the middle of his fire team, with Fang and
Claw in front of him, and Kiervauna and Jaibie behind.
The lieutenant got in the middle, between the two
squads, and Sergeant Chouvana was near the rear. We
kept our spacing fairly loose, holding five to ten yards
between men.

WE DID NOT ATTEMPT TO RACE THROUGH THE
forest, despite the urgency of closing with the enemy
quickly. We picked our way with due caution, alert to
the possibility of running into an ambush or stumbling

across an enemy patrol. If the enemy had an entire regiment moving, they would certainly have patrols out on every side, perhaps in as much as company strength. We didn't want to get bogged down fighting a patrol. That might not slow the enemy's main force at all. And *that* was our objective.

This section of Dintsen had not been settled by the divotect. It was tropical, not temperate, and even late at night the temperature was eighty degrees. The light rain did not provide significant cooling, and there was no breeze worth mentioning. Once we were under the trees, we got even less water and less breeze. The air was stagnant; it felt heavy.

I had no problems with concentration after we arrived on the ground. If you let your mind wander, you can get in deep trouble fast. Every man was watching, eyes moving, heads swiveling, weapons tracking from side to side, looking for any hint of a threat. Our night-vision systems give us about 80 percent of what we could see in broad daylight. All of the systems are similar, different in detail but about equal. You just can't see quite as far or with quite as good resolution as in daylight. Most times, though, it's good enough.

We were maintaining strict radio silence, not even using the low-powered squad channels. We used hand signals to pass orders, and when anyone needed to get a message to us, they either used hand signals or came over to whisper the message. That was second nature.

The lieutenant had told us that the LZ was two miles from the nearest known enemy positions. Those would be outlying patrols, I thought. The enemy main force would be perhaps half a mile farther. We would try to avoid the patrols by getting between them and the main force they were supposed to be screening.

If we succeeded, we would have one "free" shot at the enemy regiment before we had to start worrying about defense—getting our butts away before they got sawn off—as well as offense. We would try to pick the location of our first encounter to give us as much maneuvering room as possible: good lines of fire for the attack, and a better avenue for our escape. *Escape*—that's really not the right word, since we would be coming back to hit the enemy again and again as long as our luck held (or until our line battalions got into Miorawinn, the capital of Dintsen), but it's as close as I can come.

I didn't waste time thinking about that just then. I might not be the brightest man in the army, but I'm not stupid. You have to concentrate, pay attention to what's right around you and to where you're going to take your next step. You can't just look off into the distance. You have to give some thought to the next couple of feet and to what's right at either side. It wasn't inconceivable that there could be mines or booby traps planted.

We took thirty minutes to cover the first mile of forest. Our maps gave us a moving fix on the various segments of the enemy regiment. They were not maintaining electronic silence, so our ships had them pinpointed and fed the information to our maps—only a minute or two slower than "real" time—whenever one of the enemy used his radio to transmit. When we stopped for a few seconds, I took my map out and estimated that we were perhaps three-quarters of a mile from the flanking unit that was between us and our target. The lieutenant changed our course by a few degrees, aiming to pass behind the flanking patrol.

The danger was that even if we picked our route properly, the enemy patrol might have a fire team or a squad hanging back, maintaining electronic silence to spot any-one like us. We were *supposed* to be good enough not to get caught like that. That's why we spend so much time training to move with all possible stealth. We were the mouse out to bite a lion on the ass.

TEN MINUTES LATER, IYI CAME BACK AND dropped to the ground near my position. "We spotted the enemy flanking patrol," he whispered. "Platoon strength or a little more, about three hundred yards." He pointed, a little right of our line of march.

"You're sure it's only a platoon?" I asked after sig-naling for Wilkins to hold up. We all went to the ground, watching in every direction. "I'd expect closer to a full company. Could it be split, with the rest farther back?"

Iyi shook his head. "We were careful to look for that. If there are more, they must be considerably farther in front."

"Any trailers hanging back from the main patrol?" I asked.

"Four tonatin, a hundred yards behind the rest."

"Okay, come with me while I tell the lieutenant."

I dropped out of the line of march and moved back to where our team leader was. Tonio hurried to join us, and Chouvana was only a couple of seconds behind him. The lieutenant stepped out of the line to hear my report; then he gave Iyi orders directly.

"Get back out there and move past the flankers, but keep those trailers in sight. We'll come around behind them. Make sure the two of you get down on the ground and out of our line of fire before the shooting starts."

"We will," Iyi said. "Is there anything else?"

When the lieutenant said no, Iyi climbed the nearest

tree and started moving quickly back toward his brother.

"They're good, Lieutenant," I whispered, and Tonio nodded his agreement.

"I have no doubt of that," the lieutenant said. "All of the biraunta I have seen have been good at scouting. Here is what we'll do." He needed little more than a minute to lay out his plan of attack for the three of us, then sent us back to our positions and gave the signal for the team to start moving again.

OUR PROGRESS SLOWED BY HALF, AND IT HAD not been all that fast before. I was keyed up. That was good, proper, as long as it didn't get extreme. You need the edge, the adrenaline. It helps you to focus. It gives your reactions a little extra speed when the crunch comes. It can help you stay alive.

We heard shooting when we were four hundred yards from the nearest IFers. For an instant the gunfire startled me because it was coming from too far away, and not quite from the expected direction. I needed a second to realize that one of the other spec ops squads must be hitting the enemy from the other side.

I glanced back toward the lieutenant. He made a short pumping gesture with his right arm—just once. That meant that we should speed our pace, but just a little. I nodded—an exaggerated gesture to make sure the lieutenant saw it—then repeated the arm pump for Wilkins on point.

Might have been better if they had waited another five minutes to hit, I thought, *but this should distract the IFers for a moment.* The diversion was nice. Theoretically, well-trained soldiers not directly involved in the firefight would ignore it and continue to watch their own sectors even more carefully than before, in case the first attack *was* a diversion—but that's easier said than done for all but the very best.

I would accept any advantage I could get.

THERE WASN'T A WHOLE LOT OF UNDERBRUSH. Ground level was fairly clear between tree trunks. We were going faster than before, angling around to make certain we didn't stumble over the fire team that was trailing the flanking patrol, but we still moved with caution. The trailing enemy fire team couldn't be far off, maybe eighty yards to the right and forty yards ahead of the point, if they hadn't simply gone to cover when the shooting started. I hoped that either Iyi or Oyo would come back to warn us if that had happened.

Time didn't seem to be working right, but that was familiar. When the brain speeds up, everything else appears to slow down.

I adjusted my grip on my rifle, bringing it closer to firing position, shaving a small fraction of a second from the time I would need to react if we came under fire. I could see the men in front of me doing the same thing. Wilkins already had his rifle to his shoulder.

Five minutes. The level of gunfire in the distance decreased suddenly. My guess was that our spec ops people on the far side were attempting to disengage before they could be surrounded . . . or obliterated.

I looked to my right and did a more careful-than-usual scan, trying to pick out where the flankers' trailing fire team might be. If I had judged our advance correctly, those four tonatin should be directly to my right and eighty yards away. I looked for movement but didn't spot any. That didn't prove anything one way or the other, but I gave that side more of my attention through the next couple of minutes. Just in case. It was a nervous itch that I couldn't quite scratch.

Two minutes later, the lieutenant signaled for us to move from line of march to a skirmish line. Sergeant Chouvana and I moved our teams, putting each man three to five yards from his neighbors on either side. The enemy regiment's main force couldn't be too far away. It was time to get ready.

We slowed down again, just as Iyi and Oyo rejoined us.

"The enemy main force stopped in place when that shooting started," Oyo reported. "After a minute or so, they detached one company to attend to the threat. Then the rest started moving again, but more slowly."

I ran along the rear of our skirmish line, bent low for caution, to tell Tonio and the lieutenant. They weren't too far apart now, just a few steps behind the line.

"We move to within RPG range and hit them with grenades first," the lieutenant said. "Then we open up with everything we've got until they start to come after us. Then we head due south." That was to our left. "Make sure your grenadiers have real targets in sight before they open up," he added.

It was less than three minutes later when I spotted movement in the enemy column. It was time to throw the dice, even knowing that they were loaded against us.

CHAPTER 13

ACCORDING TO THE BEST INFORMATION WE had, the average IF regiment numbered about four thousand men—but could run as high as five thousand. The regiment we were about to attack was estimated at forty-two hundred men, probably 90 percent tonatin.

Twenty-two men against more than four thousand? That doesn't *have* to be suicidal. As long as we hit smart and moved fast, there was no way the enemy could bring more than a small fraction of that number against us. You don't stop what you're doing and throw everyone against a small threat. If you do, you never get anything accomplished. Besides that, a large military formation has a certain inertia, and physical limitations. On the march, a regiment spreads out over several miles. When we got within striking range of the regiment's right flank, probably three-quarters of the enemy were more than half a mile away, with some of them well over two miles off. It takes time to move men, time to decide where to move them, and so forth.

Our major concern was to remain mobile. If we didn't let the enemy pin us down until they could bring more

people to bear, we had a good chance of confusing the
enemy, slowing them down, and causing a fair share of
casualties without suffering too many ourselves. And
those were the tactics that were supposed to be our bread
and butter.

We reached our position. Each man took what cover
he could find. At the lieutenant's command, the grenadiers started popping RPGs toward the IF force, moving
their point of aim with each shot, looking to spread the
destruction as much as possible. Before the first grenade
exploded, the grenadiers had all shifted position. Then
the rest of the team opened up with rifles.

I counted seconds mentally while I lined up targets
and fired. When the targets started dropping to the
ground for cover, I lowered my aim and continued to
spray short bursts into the area. My count had only
reached fifty seconds when the lieutenant came on the
radio.

"First squad, shift left behind second squad. Second
squad, follow first squad then. Compass heading one-
six-five." That would take us slightly farther from the
enemy and toward the rear of the regiment. I switched
to my squad channel and ordered my men back, and took
the rear position while we edged farther from the enemy
and ran behind the positions Chouvana's squad held.

It was only then that we started taking return fire, and
most of that was well over our heads. Most, not all. A
large-caliber bullet hit a tree trunk at about eye level,
just in front of me and a little to my right. Splinters
struck my helmet and made me drop to the ground. Then
I saw dirt and leaves pop up from where another slug
had plowed into the dirt.

As I got back to my feet and started moving again, I
saw that Jonnie Tenzik, one of the humans added to

Chouvana's squad, had been hit. I changed course to go to his aid. He had taken a bullet through the left shoulder—in and out. The bullet had to have come from a tonatin weapon. Their standard infantry rifle fires roughly .40-caliber ammunition.

I got a medicated bandage wrapped around Tenzik's shoulder, covering both the entrance and exit wounds, and took one of the straps used to hang gear from the side of his pack harness to fashion a sling for the arm. Tenzik was stunned, not yet feeling the full pain of his wound. If he was lucky, the painkillers in the bandage would take effect before the pain took hold.

I helped Jonnie to his feet, pulled his right arm over my shoulder, and got him moving, slowly. He stumbled with almost every step, and his level of consciousness was slipping quickly. A ghuroh from Chouvana's squad came to my aid and took over the work of toting Tenzik. Ghuroh are stronger than humans, pound for pound. Except for the abarand, maybe, I guess that's true of all the other sentient species in the Alliance.

A wounded man was going to slow us down. But we wouldn't leave him for the enemy, and there was no way we could get a shuttle in to evacuate him anytime soon. So we would make do. If we *did* have to leave him later, we would try to find him a place to hide until friendly help could reach him.

We moved along the course the lieutenant had ordered. Before we started moving, we stopped firing at the IF force to make it that much more difficult for them to trace us. There was still a fair amount of gunfire, but it was all coming from the other direction, and after the first thirty seconds, it was all aimed at where we had been, not where we were.

*   *   *

TWELVE MINUTES LATER WE TURNED BACK TO-
ward the IFers, working to get close to the tail end of
the main body. This was going to be riskier. It wasn't
just that the enemy would be expecting another attack.
There was also a chance that we might get pinned between the main force and the rear guard, but maybe that
angle of attack was one the enemy wouldn't expect, so
we might get away with it. Odds and evens.

The lieutenant detailed one of the men from Chouvana's squad to stay with Tenzik, and move him toward
our next rendezvous point. We gave them a head start,
then moved in toward the next attack point the lieutenant
had chosen.

This ambush went pretty much like our first. We
didn't stick around as long this time—only thirty seconds elapsed between our first shots and the order to
withdraw—and we pulled away without suffering any
additional casualties.

The other spec op team hit the IF regiment from the
other side, also near the tail end of the main force, almost simultaneously. The timing and location could
hardly have been more precise had we coordinated them.
The enemy didn't know which way to turn, and they
had to worry that there might be a considerable force on
their flanks. I mentally blessed whoever was doing the
thinking in that other team as we pulled back.

We headed back north, paralleling the IF route about
two-thirds of a mile out, working to get near the front
of the column before we hit again. The lieutenant sent
Tenzik and his escort off again, almost due east, farther
from the operation. *Should have done that before,* I
thought. Tenzik was still conscious, but groggy from the

painkillers, unsteady on his feet. The bleeding had stopped. That was encouraging.

Our people on the far side of the enemy struck again ten minutes before we got into position for our next attack. Pretty soon the IF commander was going to have to take stronger steps: detach a company or two to try to pin us down or isolate us, or increase the size of his flanking patrols, maybe bring them closer to the main body. Or the regiment had to laager up, go into defensive positions, and quit trying to move. *Something.* It can be bad for morale to keep getting hit without doing anything effective to counter it. We might only be a fly buzzing around their heads, but we were no less pesky . . . and far more dangerous. We hoped to make them stop, at least for a time, to give our line battalions time to get into the capital.

Our third attack was against the flanking platoon on the right. We came up on them from behind, took out the trailing fire team, then launched grenades at the rest of the platoon. Then, instead of moving right, away from the enemy, the lieutenant took us left, between the flankers and the main body of the regiment, and we kept going north. Once more the lieutenant chose the riskier alternative, sticking us in a position where we had IF troops on two sides of us.

This time we waited only five minutes before striking again, this time at the point company in the main force's line of march. One volley of grenades, fifteen seconds of rifle fire. Then we moved east past the flanking platoon—except it looked now as if that platoon had been reinforced, doubled in size.

"We have to disengage," the lieutenant said after ordering a cease-fire on the circuit that connected him to the three sergeants in the team. "Pull off far enough to take a few minutes to rest."

That was fine with me. I was starting to drag, and Nuyi and the biraunta had to be feeling it even more than I was. We had been moving pretty fast. When you're carrying half your weight in gear and ammunition, you don't want to run marathons.

THE IFERS WERE SHOOTING AT SHADOWS, ghosts. We had disengaged, and the other spec ops team couldn't have been responsible for almost continuous attacks on the enemy. But the IF regiment *was* firing, here and there. It was not a full-scale thing, but there was constant shooting from one sector or another of the enemy, and the column had apparently quit moving forward.

"We've done at least part of our job," I whispered to Tonio when the team had gone to ground in an area with sufficient undergrowth to conceal us—and after I had a few seconds to catch up on my breathing. We were a mile and a half from the enemy's flanking unit, maybe two miles from their main force, and we had planted snoops out far enough to tell us if they turned in our direction.

"Just part," Tonio replied. "We've got to keep them occupied for at least another two hours, and that's if our people don't waste time getting into the city."

The divotect had named the capital of Dintsen Miorawinn. I don't know what the Ilion occupation troops called it. As I remembered Miorawinn, it had been a rural sort of place, more a collection of linked villages than a city. The spaceport, such as it was, had been in the center—a terminal, a repair hangar, and a single paved landing strip—with half a dozen small communities spread around it, always at some distance from the port and each other. Divotect like to have plenty of elbow room and extensive gardens around their homes. Of course, I hadn't seen that much of Miorawinn. My battalion had landed there, late one afternoon, and we had left the next morning, working our way north to a divotect army training base.

Leaving Dintsen, we hadn't gone through Miorawinn. The invaders had conquered that in less than twenty-four hours. Those of us from Earth who survived our three-day fight were taken out directly from where we had been fighting, under fire, losing several shuttles and fighters in the process.

"Any word on their progress?" I asked. I hadn't been doing much monitoring of the command channels while we were operating.

"Nothing too specific." Tonio shrugged. "Heavy fighting, slow progress is the best I've been able to glean. But they still seem to be moving. The lieutenant is listening now, trying to see if he can pick anything up."

Tonio didn't have to say that the lieutenant wasn't going to *call* anyone to ask. We were observing strict electronic silence. That was one reason why we couldn't call for a shuttle to evacuate Tenzik. The other reason was that we knew no shuttle would be sent in with so much going on in the area. Not for one man—and maybe not if half the team was down.

JONNIE TENZIK HAD FINALLY LOST CONSCIOUS-ness, which was probably all for the better for him. He had been treated to the extent we were able to provide; our medical training went beyond basic first aid, though none of us was qualified as a full field medtech. Tonio said that Tenzik had stabilized, that he should be all right in time, but that the sooner we got him to the real doctors and their medtanks, the faster he would recover.

We had been resting for fifteen minutes. The team was arranged in a moderately tight circle around Tenzik, Tonio, and the lieutenant, with each man lying on the ground facing out, rifle at the ready, alert to anything that might show in his sector. I was in the middle of my squad. Chouvana was in the middle of his.

Take a drink of water—a sip or two at a time—to keep from getting dehydrated. Try to get your breathing and heart rate under control. Give your feet and legs a chance to rest, stretch the legs and massage the thighs and calves to help prevent cramps. Make sure you have a full magazine or power pack in your rifle. Scan the forest constantly, looking for any threat.

It's a different kind of waiting. Watching. Knowing that combat might come at any second. The snoops might or might not give us any warning. There weren't enough to give us full coverage around 360 degrees.

The lieutenant made a soft whistling noise, an arranged three-toned sequence, calling for Chouvana and me. We crawled back from our positions in the perimeter, and we clustered close together, near where Tenzik lay. When the lieutenant lifted the faceplate of his helmet, Chouvana, Tonio, and I did the same.

"I've managed to pick up a little information," the lieutenant whispered. "The enemy regiment just started moving again, but they're moving more slowly than before and they have broken into two separate main columns, with stronger flanking patrols on the outside— front, rear, and both flanks. On the other hand, the IF force defending the capital has fallen back to prepared defensive positions just outside the old divotect communities, and our people haven't been able to move forward in the past twenty minutes. The fleet is sending in fighters to try to break the enemy line. They'll be hitting in ten or twelve minutes—if they get through the enemy fighter screen. If possible, two or three of those fighters will target the IFers we've been harassing, but that is . . . less certain."

"What do *we* do?" I asked. "Sit here and stay out of the way, or move back in and hit these buzzards again?"

"We move, get in front of them, and *then* wait to see if the fighters hit them from the air. Once we know whether they do, we hit their point company, try to stop them again."

"Either way?" Chouvana asked. "I mean, if the fighters hit from the air or if they don't?"

"Either way," the lieutenant agreed. "If the fighters come in and slow them, we can wait a few minutes longer to extend the delay—perhaps. I'll make a final call when we see what the circumstances are. We'll leave Private Tenzik here with Lance Corporal Koi." Koi was the only biraunta in Chouvana's pick-up squad. If Koi was the only one staying with Tenzik, they would have to stay put. Koi wasn't strong enough to carry Tenzik. "Get back to your men. We leave in three minutes."

I GATHERED MY SQUAD TO BRIEF THEM. THE first thing I did was tell them all to get another drink of water and eat part of an energy bar. They could do that and listen at the same time. It didn't take long for me to repeat what the lieutenant had said.

"That's all I know, so you can probably save any questions. I doubt that I've got the answers," I said when

I was done. Then I pulled out my canteen and took a drink. I had wolfed down an energy bar while I was moving back from the conference.

They saved their questions.

The lieutenant was prompt, ordering us "up and out" exactly three minutes after he had said it would be that long. Once more my squad took the lead, with Tonio and the lieutenant between us and what remained of Chouvana's squad. The route was rather circuitous, since the last thing we wanted was contact with the enemy. In special operations you want to pick the time and place of any encounter. If you let the enemy choose, you've already failed at an important part of your assignment and reduced your odds of success.

We moved northeast, then north, with Iyi and Oyo out in front—as usual. They were *good* as scouts, and the duty seemed to satisfy them. The lieutenant forced our pace, since he wanted us to be in front of the enemy regiment before our aerospace fighters hit them—*if* they did. Either way we would hear the fighters, unless they were unable to make it through the enemy fighters above the atmosphere. We were close enough to Miorawinn to hear explosions. The warheads on the air-to-surface missiles our fighters carried made quite a racket.

We stayed as alert to any possible trouble as we could, knowing that the more speed, the less stealth. I didn't expect to run into trouble on this little move—we were doing our best to stay away from where we thought the enemy was—but there was always a chance that they would have patrols out that far. You never know.

The lieutenant signaled for our second turn, the one designed to put us in front of the enemy regiment. *Then* we did start moving a lot slower ourselves, and paying a lot more attention to where we put our feet with each step. The enemy was most likely to have small patrols in front of the larger point units, which we now figured to be a full company in front of each column.

I couldn't help frequent glances at the timeline on my head-up display. We were near the time frame for the fighters to hit wherever they were going to hit. I glanced upward a couple of times, too, but the forest canopy was too thick for me to see anything—not that I would have seen fighters coming in at night anyway. They're designed to be virtually invisible—to visual, radar, or electronic "eyes"—in the dark.

Looking at the time and sky was a reflection of nerves. Each time I looked for the sky I couldn't see or the timeline I could, I wasn't looking out into the forest at ground level, where any threat would materialize. I told myself to pay attention, and I did, for the most part. My lapses weren't major, but—if nothing else—I was setting a poor example for my men. Whether they noticed was beside the point.

By the time I had forced my mind fully to what it was supposed to be doing, we had reached the location the lieutenant had chosen for us to set up our next ambush. We went to ground by fire team to wait. Iyi and Oyo had come out of the trees and whispered their report before joining the line on the ground. There were no enemy troops within three hundred yards. That was as far as they had looked.

Our troops, the line battalions of the 1st Combined Regiment and the one attached battalion, were more than a mile from us, to the north and east. Beyond them was Miorawinn—and the IF force defending it. The rest of Ranger Battalion was scattered all over the place. Most of the spec ops teams were still harassing enemy units in other locations to make it more difficult for the enemy to reinforce Miorawinn.

THE LIEUTENANT'S TIMING WAS IMPECCABLE. I had scarcely squirmed into a comfortable firing position when we heard the sonic booms of aircraft stooping to the attack, with the first explosions coming fifteen seconds later. Those explosions were far enough away that I knew it was the enemy line outside Miorawinn that was being hit—the primary target, after all, much as I would have preferred to have our fly guys hitting the enemy who were closer to me personally. As a backdrop to the explosions, there was the staccato sound of rapid-fire cannon being fired—the secondary armament of the aerospace fighters—as they strafed the enemy.

I crawled over to the lieutenant to pass along the report my biraunta had brought in. He nodded, and I went back to my place.

There had been several series of rocket explosions by then. They seemed to come two or three in close succession, followed by a gap of ten or fifteen seconds. Then I heard one explosion that was different. For one thing, it was much louder than any of the others. For another, the blast was overhead, not on the ground.

Scratch one bird, I thought, wondering if it had been ours or theirs. I expected that it was one of ours, probably brought down by a surface-to-air missile. *Keep hitting them,* I urged silently. Then I wondered how many fighters our operational commanders had committed to the strike. How many do you send in for ground support? How many do you keep to protect the ships?

I'm glad I'm not the one who has to make those decisions.

*   *   *

AN AIR ATTACK LIKE THAT, WITH THE FIGHTERS
coming in more or less at once, doesn't last long. I don't
think the fighters carry more than six or eight missiles
apiece, and they can use up their 20mm shells in a minute if the pilot has a heavy finger on the trigger. I was
beginning to think that the fighters weren't going to have
anything left to hit the IF regiment we were in front of
before they did come our way.

I heard one or two fighters screaming through heavy
air first, an almost deafening sound. Then I heard rockets
racing, a higher-pitched, more intense sound. Finally I
heard the start of the sound of strafing cannon before
the explosions came.

I could see the explosions, orange flame through the
trees, illuminating smoke and forest five hundred or six
hundred yards away. Four blasts. Then four more a few
seconds later. Several fires started burning darkly and
smoking heavily.

I thought I heard screams as well. As far off as the
enemy was, that almost *had* to be my imagination.

"Let's go!" the lieutenant said. "Drak, your squad on
the left. Chouvana, the right. Straight for them."

"How far?" I asked on my direct link. I was already
on my feet, waving my men into position, holding up
just enough to let Chouvana move his people across to
our right.

"One hundred fifty yards from their point. Back to
electronic silence."

The air assault on the enemy was over. We could hear
the fighters burning for orbit, taking full power from
both rockets and jets—getting the hell out of harm's way
while they could. Or heading toward a different danger.

I had no idea what kind of opposition they faced up around the fleet.

It doesn't matter how good the soldier, that kind of attack from the sky is going to leave anyone stunned. He's going to keep his head down until he's certain it's over. I assumed that the lieutenant was counting on that to let us get close enough to make our attack before the enemy realized they had trouble on the ground again.

IF WE HIT THEM JUST WHEN THEY'RE STARTING to get up, we'll have the maximum effect, I thought. Their nerves would be stretched tight, and it might not take too much to spook them . . . with a little luck.

We were moving very slowly now, taking care to keep as much cover as possible between us and the enemy van, zigzagging from tree to tree, ducking under branches, skirting the rare undergrowth as closely as possible. I stayed so low—legs bent, head forward and down, looking to present the smallest target possible— that my back started to ache.

I got a brief blip on my head-up display—an electronic intercept. Someone up ahead, most likely an officer or a noncom, had used his radio. Not *far* ahead, maybe 150 yards. There had to be at least a patrol that close. A few seconds later I heard a report on the command channel saying that our line regiments had renewed their assault on the enemy perimeter around Miorawinn. At about the same time, I heard that distant firefight, muted reports of automatic rifle fire punctuated by the slightly louder blasts of RPGs and rockets.

That was background noise, though. I was aware of it, but past that basic awareness I had to ignore it and keep my mind on what was in front of us. We were

certain to make contact with our portion of the enemy—
perhaps within seconds.

Tonio and the lieutenant were only a step behind the
skirmish line, in the middle. I glanced their way frequently, waiting for a signal. When it came, we were
just over a hundred yards from the position of that last
blip.

Down. Take cover.

We dropped, then moved to cover on our hands and
knees, each man putting a tree between him and the
enemy, lying flat, rifle or grenade launcher protruding
on one side of the trunk or the other. We were just outside the edge of a clearing—back about ten feet from
the last cover—that extended forty to sixty yards before
the trees closed in again. I wasn't certain what the lieutenant had in mind this time, whether it would be a quick
hit-and-run or whether we would attempt to stick it out
for more than a few seconds before making ourselves
scarce again.

Once we were down, I spent almost as much time
watching the lieutenant and Tonio for signals as I did
watching the direction the enemy was in. There were
enough eyes watching the front.

My palms were sweating again, and my heart seemed
to be fluttering. My body knew that combat was close,
and it didn't like the idea. I wiped my hands and my
trousers and took a couple of slow, deep breaths.

I saw a helmet move, eighty yards away, past the far
side of the clearing. Then another helmet, behind the
first. I glanced to either side of the two helmets—and
upper torsos now—that I could see emerging from the
cover of the forest. It took a few seconds, but I spotted
several more of the enemy, visible more by their movement than anything else. They had a skirmish line across

the front, moving slowly as they approached the clearing. *They're expecting trouble,* I thought as I glanced toward the lieutenant again.

He was waiting for me. He went through a short series of hand gestures, then turned and repeated them for Chouvana. Once he had finished the repetition, he held his right arm up above his head, fist clenched, while he looked out toward the enemy. He held that pose for twenty or thirty seconds, until the skirmish line on the enemy point was several steps out into the clearing and the next squads were visible behind them. Then the lieutenant brought his arm down quickly—the "execute" signal—and ordered "Fire!" on his all-hands circuit.

CHAPTER 14

I DON'T THINK THAT ANY OF THE MEN IN THE enemy skirmish line—those who were on point, out in the clearing—survived our first volley. Too many rifles targeted them, and we were too close to miss. After five seconds we lifted our aim to target the enemy beyond the far side of the clearing.

The grenadiers had worked deeper from the start, arcing their grenades into the forest beyond the clearing out to their maximum effective range—more than two hundred yards—and working a wide angle to spread the damage. Theoretically, our RPGs have a killing radius of thirty yards before the shrapnel loses enough momentum to keep it from penetrating sufficiently, but in practice you can't count on half that. Some shrapnel gets kicked upward after the nose of the projectile hits the dirt, and trees and other obstacles stop a lot of the bits that might otherwise find flesh. The minimal body armor we wear actually works sometimes, and tonatin body armor was at least as good as ours.

We started taking return fire, but in the first ten or fifteen seconds it was all from rifles, and most of that went over our heads or into tree trunks. Then there were a few grenade blasts, well behind us. It wouldn't take the IFers long to find our range, though. I glanced toward the lieutenant, but he was concentrating on the enemy, firing his rifle as ardently as any of us. While we were engaged, any orders would come over the radio, so I didn't let my gaze linger on him.

Time goes absolutely crazy in a firefight. You lose all track. A minute can feel like eternity. If the fight goes on much longer than a minute, time hardly seems to exist at all, becoming an infinite *now*.

"Pull back and move right!" the lieutenant ordered. "Second squad first. Stay low." His voice was little more than a hissing whisper on the all-hands channel.

"Wait for the others to pull out," I told my squad on our channel. I looked over to see Chouvana's squad squirming back, crawling in reverse—an extremely slow procedure—for twenty yards before they turned and moved to the right. Tonio and the lieutenant moved with them, a little behind. I waited until Tonio turned and gestured for us to follow.

"Let's go. Keep your heads and butts low."

Souvana, Nuyi, and I held back, putting out more fire while the rest of the squad started the slow backward crawl. By this time the enemy had to have people out trying to flank us—probably on both sides—to box us in for an easy kill. It wouldn't take long for our position to become untenable.

"You next, Nuyi," I said when the rest had turned. "Souvana, follow me, close. Stop firing when you start moving."

The porracci corporal glanced my way but just clicked his transmitter to acknowledge the order. I gave Nuyi a four-second head start, then started backing away from my firing position—after slipping a fresh magazine into my rifle.

Souvana quit firing and started moving as soon as I did. I felt an itch at the back of my neck, a worry that we had stayed too long. I hadn't gone ten yards in reverse before I decided that I wanted the extra speed moving forward instead would give me, and I turned. Souvana and I were on hands and knees then, crabbing our way forward. The porracci might be gung-ho as all get-out, but he was obviously feeling the danger of our situation as clearly as I was. All that "better part of valor" crap.

Perhaps three seconds later, two grenades exploded in the area where my squad had been. Souvana and I were pelted with dirt and debris, but no shrapnel. It wasn't until later that I managed to realize we had moved just in time.

I heard gunfire in front of us. Chouvana's squad had taken positions again and were firing on the enemy. Apparently they had spotted a couple of IF squads moving to flank us on our right. The bulk of my squad joined in as soon as they saw where the enemy was. By the time Nuyi, Souvana, and I got close enough to contribute, the lieutenant ordered the men to cease firing, and we moved again—in a different direction.

WE NEEDED THREE-QUARTERS OF AN HOUR TO disengage. Those forty-five minutes saw half a dozen brief exchanges of fire. It was in the next-to-last round that the lieutenant took a bullet through his left cheek. The bullet somehow came in under his helmet, broke about a third of his teeth passing though his mouth, and scored his lower lip as it exited, cracking his faceplate and flipping it up. It nearly knocked his helmet completely off. The lieutenant spat out blood and teeth, then slapped a bandage on his cheek, poking it into the hole with his finger. He spat again and adjusted his helmet. Tonio tried to help but the lieutenant waved him off, then gestured for us to move again.

A few others in the team suffered scratches or skin burns from passing slugs or shrapnel in the series of exchanges, but nothing more. We were damned lucky under the circumstances.

I couldn't see that the wound slowed the lieutenant, except that every minute or two he would lift his cracked faceplate far enough to spit blood. We moved, got into another short firefight, disengaged, and moved again. When orders had to be given orally, Tonio gave them, relaying hand signals the lieutenant gave him, or whispers. That was the only concession the lieutenant gave to his wound. It was another half hour before we stopped for a break. Only then did the lieutenant accept any help. Fang and Claw went to him and fussed over the wound for a couple of minutes before the lieutenant chased them back to me.

The lieutenant and Tonio conferred. Then the lieutenant crawled over to Chouvana, and Tonio came to me.

"We can't stay here," Tonio whispered after he raised his faceplate and leaned close. "We're still in the middle, and we'll play hell getting out. Our guys are three-quarters of a mile that way." He pointed northeast. "The regiment we've been harassing is spreading out to either side, ready to advance on our line battalions along the entire front."

"Have our people managed to break through the enemy perimeter around Miorawinn yet?"

Tonio shrugged. "Apparently they've punched a couple of holes in the IFer line, but I don't think they've been able to exploit those gaps."

"How's the lieutenant doing?"

Another shrug. "Right now, more mad than hurting. He's having trouble talking, but most of what I've heard him say the translator can't, or won't, interpret. I'll keep an eye on him. He's still spitting blood." That wasn't good. His cheek had been patched long enough that the medical nanoagents in the bandage should have sealed the bullet wound. Maybe he was just bleeding around the teeth he had lost.

"So which way do we head now? Just try to join up with the nearest of our line battalions?"

"Not yet. The lieutenant wants to continue harassing the enemy relief column as long as we can—until our people can exploit the holes they've punched in the perimeter around Miorawinn." He glanced over toward the lieutenant and Chouvana. "As soon as they get done, we're going to move again, that way." Tonio pointed north. "There's a rocky hill about five hundred yards off. From the overhead view, there should be enough cover to let us create a little havoc when the IFers try to pass it. If we can get to it before they box us in."

"As long as that hill has a back door. The IFers can leave enough people to keep us occupied and move the rest of their force on past us if we don't have a way out."

Tonio grunted, then started crawling toward the center of the perimeter we had formed when we halted.

BY THE TIME WE GOT TO THE BOTTOM OF THAT hill—more a pile of boulders—the sky was starting to lighten in the east. Dawn wasn't far off. The hill really wasn't much. It rose no more than eighty feet over the surrounding ground. It was rocky enough to provide a solid break in the forest, which meant that there was a ring of underbrush and vines rooted in the last pockets of soil that had managed to wedge in around the base and climb the rock, making a dense screen of sorts.

We circled northeast before starting to crawl through the mess at the edge. We had to cut our way through. That was encouraging. If it slowed us up, it would slow the IFers. After we were through, Iyi and Oyo stayed behind to disguise the marks of our passage while the rest of us climbed higher and started moving clockwise around the mound to get into position to hit the IF regiment again as it approached.

They'll have to break to go around this hill, I thought once I had a solid firing position. *Most of them will probably go there, to the right.* South. *Probably only their flankers will go around the other way.*

I was guessing, of course. I wasn't certain where all the elements of the enemy regiment were. I got out my map. There were a few blips representing recent enemy positions, well scattered—from two hundred to nine hundred yards away—officers or noncoms giving orders, most likely. There were a lot more enemy blips in the other direction. The IF units on the Miorawinn perimeter were showing no hesitancy about using electronics.

Our field of vision was restricted. We were high enough that the crowns of the trees surrounding the mound blocked off a lot of ground. We did have a few clear fire lanes—for fifty yards, or a hundred. Tonio and the lieutenant chose the area we settled in for those. There were also a few holes in the forest canopy that gave us peeks at the ground. But it wouldn't take a whole lot of maneuvering for the enemy to go around us and keep out of the way. If they had any idea that we had taken up residence on the hill, they would probably do just that. I would have done it on general principles.

The only thing that might keep the enemy commander from making a wide detour was if he were in a great hurry to attack our line battalions—and we assumed that he was. The whole point of our operations against the IFer regiment was to slow them down, and maybe they would be feeling the pinch of the time they had lost. If so, the most direct route they could follow split right around the rock pile we were sitting on.

I spotted an enemy patrol crossing one of the open lines of sight—six tonatin moving slowly, rifles at the ready, as if they expected an ambush at every step. We let them go past unmolested. The soldiers on point are generally out there in the hope that they will trip any ambush; that the ambushers will be too impatient to wait for their main force. You risk a few men to try to avoid heavier casualties. That works well . . . except for the few men being offered up front.

Three minutes later, a larger force started moving past on the south. The sun had come over the horizon. There was daylight hitting the forest canopy, streaming down into the open spaces, illuminating the enemy briefly. I glanced toward Tonio and the lieutenant, looking for a signal. But it did not come. This was just the rest of the enemy point—one platoon, or maybe the remnants of two platoons.

Okay, now we're taking chances, I thought. We had let at least seventy of the enemy move past us, within rifle range. There might be more on the north, and there would certainly be more farther south, past the stretch where we could observe. If they suspected that we were around, there might already be a full company of IFers closing the circle around us.

I didn't like the feeling, but I sucked in a deep breath and held it for a moment to help quiet the new fluttering in my gut.

I didn't have long to wait, though. The next time we saw the enemy, it was clear that their main force had finally reached us. I started tracking the forward element, expecting the order to open fire to come any second.

Tonio gave the order.

THE SIDE THAT INITIATES A FIGHT LIKE THAT has a momentary advantage: surprise. That surprise might not last long, but even if it only lasts for the first three seconds, it can tell. Men on the other side go down before they know they're under attack. Then it can take from a few seconds to several minutes for the enemy to *effectively* react to the ambush.

I didn't count on surprise carrying us for long. Surprise isn't the Holy Grail, no matter what the training manuals say. We were too badly outnumbered to have a chance of standing off the enemy if they put their minds to stomping us. The lieutenant hadn't said anything about hitting the enemy, then trying to escape before they could come after us. We certainly hadn't made preparations for an exit. And we couldn't count on air support from our people . . . or rule out an air strike by IF aerospace fighters.

There was a lot of room to hide in the rotten rock of that hill, though, crevices that could have hidden fifty men, a couple of holes—not quite caves—that could have sheltered the number we actually had. But it wasn't enough. The IFers could trap us there and finish us off at their leisure.

"Try to make every bullet count," I told my squad. After the initial volleys of automatic fire, we were reduced to either spraying the forest blindly or waiting for some hint of a target. The IFers did not stay out in the open, where we could pick them off. And, despite the load we had started with, we did not have an endless supply of ammunition.

The enemy force did not completely ignore us. We took return fire—a lot more than we were putting out after the first thirty seconds. But I didn't think that the enemy was giving us their full attention. My guess was that we weren't being targeted by more than a company of IFers. We had secure spots, high, with rock all around, and the enemy would need time to get close enough to start dropping RPGs on top of us.

"Start working your way up higher," Tonio instructed. "Make it as hard for them as you can, but don't expose yourself." Yeah, that was a nice piece of advice, about as helpful as "You'll be court-martialed for disobeying orders if you let yourself get killed" would be. "Dragon, you start your squad up first. Chouvana, have your people cover them, then we'll reverse it." Fire and maneuver—basic drill.

"You heard the man," I said on my squad channel. "Iyi and Oyo first. Wilkins and Nuyi next. Souvana, we'll get up to the next level, then cover your fire team while you move past us."

I started moving as soon as Wilkins and Nuyi did. We got into the next set of decent cover, maybe fifteen feet higher, and took over the firing while Souvana's fire team worked their way above us. Then we reversed positions again. Finally we were in the highest positions we could find with decent cover, both from enemies on the ground and from a possible IF air strike. That gave us a little breathing room, but made it harder for us to harass the enemy.

"It's okay," Tonio told me when I pointed that out. He had come to ask how my squad was faring and how much ammo we had left. "Our guys have punched through the IF perimeter around Miorawinn. We got a couple of batteries of rocket artillery close enough to pound their positions, and the line battalions followed through the gap. The fighting is in close now."

"Does that mean we can get the hell off this rock?" I asked.

He shook his head, then said, "Not yet."

"When?"

"I don't have any idea. Maybe not until tonight. If then."

"You mean we've got to hold out for fourteen hours or more?"

"If necessary. Darkness will make it easier to get through whatever the enemy has left us. Just make sure your men don't waste ammo. There's no chance of re-supply. Unless some fool stands up down below and begs to be shot, I'd just as soon we didn't do any shooting at all. Maybe they'll forget about us."

"Yeah, and maybe the tooth fairy will make the lieutenant rich for all the teeth he lost."

Tonio gave me a hard stare, then started working his way over to the other end of the line, where Chouvana was. I passed the latest on to my men, and we waited.

ONCE WE QUIT SHOOTING AT THE IF FORCE, they appeared content to quit shooting at us. I was sure they hadn't forgotten about us, but we weren't their first priority. We settled into a watch routine, one man in each fire team keeping an eye on the area around us while the rest tried to get what rest they could.

Rest, not sleep. Even Nuyi was too nervous to sleep.

It wasn't just nerves. We were sitting up in a lot of rock, and as the sun climbed higher, that rock started getting hot enough to fry potatoes—or brains. The temperature climbed above a hundred degrees Fahrenheit before ten o'clock. The only way to fight the heat was to find what little shade there was and to stay as nearly motionless as possible.

Nuyi seemed to be the only one who wasn't bothered by the heat. Divotect are partially exothermic, their body temperature adjusting to ambient conditions. If anything, they tend to get more active as the temperature climbs. "Just how hot does it have to be before you get uncomfortable?" I asked him.

He hesitated, then said, "I wouldn't care to try swimming in boiling water." He made a clicking sound with his teeth that was the divotect equivalent of laughter. "I'm really not certain. I've never been that hot, and I have been in weather hotter than this. Maybe one hundred and thirty degrees by your reckoning. There was nowhere on my home world that got hotter than that."

After making the rounds and talking to each of my men, I went back to listening to reports to and from operations. The battle was a tangled mess. Part of me felt guilty for not being part of it—while another part reveled at *not* being there. I could think of a lot of places I would have rather been.

We saw two fighters collide, less than three thousand feet up, at about eleven o'clock. No ejection pods blew out of either fighter—one of ours and one of theirs—

and there was no chance that either pilot survived.

Two of our rocket artillery batteries on the ground were taken out by enemy fighters; that was one of the reports I overheard. On the plus side, our people were inside Miorawinn, and there was close-in fighting in several locations. Also, there were civilian casualties—a considerable number of them. One of the divotect villages that comprised Miorawinn was burning, and there was no one to fight the fires.

The IF regiment we had been harassing finally joined the fighting to our east. A number of other special operations teams had continued to give them hell, using hit-and-run tactics to keep the enemy force from contributing as much to the battle as they might have.

We continued to sit it out. And sweat. I quit checking the temperature on my head-up display after it hit 112 degrees.

The lieutenant was doing a little better, but he still needed medical attention. His cheek and teeth had stopped bleeding, but the hole in the side of his face was still there, giving him an uncomfortable time even if he was no longer in real pain.

Sometime around midafternoon, I dozed off into something between sleep and delirium despite the heat. It was more draining than restorative, though, and when Tonio woke me, not long before sunset, I felt worse than I had before I went to sleep. I needed a moment to get alert enough to understand what he was saying.

"We've got to be ready to get out of here as soon as it's dark. There's a lull in the main fighting. We need to get away before the IFers come back looking for us."

CHAPTER 15

THE BULK OF THE FIGHTING HAD DRIFTED FAR-
ther from us, east and south. It wasn't a matter of advance and retreat, just the flow of movement here and
there until there was little left that resembled coherent
lines. The common goal on both sides seemed to be to
avoid getting pinned down, to remain able to move
freely.

We didn't know if there were any IF troops keeping
watch on the hill, but we knew that there had been no
electronic intercepts nearby in five hours. At least the
bulk of the regiment we had been harassing had moved
four or five miles away. That was encouraging, but when
we formed up to try to slip off the hill and back into the
forest, we did not assume that it was going to be a peace-
ful walk in the woods. There *could* be a significant enemy force waiting, maintaining electronic silence, ready
to spring on us the instant we gave them a target. Even
if the enemy wasn't lurking about the base of the hill,
they might have left surprises—land mines or other
booby traps.

Mines were the most likely danger—almost a certainty—but I warned my men to be ready for anything. And everything.

The lieutenant did not wait long after sunset to get us started. It wasn't full dark when we started picking our way down the side of the hill—working our way over to the east slope. I could still feel heat radiating from all the rocks. That would help conceal us, throw off any infrared detection.

My squad took the lead. We were still fully manned, so that was pretty natural. Chouvana was missing Lance Corporal Koi and Private Tenzik from his pick-up squad. Assuming we got off the hill without difficulty, we were going to head back toward where we had left them.

When we got near the bottom of the hill, we took covering positions while Iyi and Oyo cut us a new path through the vines and stuff that ringed the rock outcropping. Since there were only a limited number of routes that left us cover and a decent chance of cutting through without observation, this was one of the points where the enemy might have decided to leave any surprises, animate or otherwise.

It was thirty minutes before Oyo came back to tell us that the path had been opened. "We found a land mine, out fifteen yards from the last rock, near the other side of the thicket," he said. "A trip wire across the logical path. My brother was able to disarm it. There is no sign of enemy troops waiting for us."

IT WAS TWENTY DEGREES COOLER ONCE WE GOT away from the heat reservoir of those rocks. We moved south, only gradually angling onto a course that would take us to where we had left Koi with the wounded Tenzik. We were a little more than halfway there when

Tonio had me send Iyi and Oyo ahead, and we were within five hundred yards of the location when Iyi and Oyo came back.

"They are both dead," Iyi reported. He was trembling almost out of control, his tail whipping around as if he had no control over it. "We think there may be mines planted along the approaches, but didn't try to find and disarm them. We went in high and dropped to the ground where they were."

"We can do them no good," Oyo added. "There is no need to risk more of us to go to them." He seemed even more agitated than his brother.

"Give me the rest of it," I said.

"They were butchered," Iyi said. "Private Tenzik had a most ugly death."

I relayed the information to Tonio and the lieutenant, with Iyi and Oyo standing by in case there were questions.

"They are our people," the lieutenant said, his voice a hoarse whisper. "Pack brothers." Talking was clearly difficult for him. "We will go to them. Clear a safe path in for us."

I COULD FEEL BLOOD RISING TO MY FACE WHEN I finally stood over the bodies of Jonnie Tenzik and the biraunta lance corporal. Koi's body showed at least two dozen bullet wounds. He had died as a soldier is meant to die in combat. But Tenzik. . . .

Fred Wilkins threw up—noisily and at length. Fang also threw up, but more quietly, with Claw holding his shoulders, supporting him. I felt like heaving my guts myself.

Butchered was the right word for the way Jonnie Tenzik died. He didn't show any new bullet or shrapnel wounds, but someone had taken a knife and cut his throat—all the way around. They had cut deep, severing everything, down to the bone. Only the spinal cord kept Tenzik's head attached to his body.

I DON'T KNOW WHY TENZIK WAS MUTILATED and Koi wasn't. Maybe it was just because he couldn't fight back, because he was still alive when Koi was killed and the IFers overran the position. Maybe it was because humans and tonatin resemble each other more closely than either resembles any of the other species. I wasn't sure how much of what we had been told about the tonatin was true and how much was propaganda, but right then I was willing to accept the worst about them. Whatever the reason for what they had done to Jonnie Tenzik, it was . . . unacceptable. I could taste blood in my mouth and realized that I had bitten the inside of my cheek in my reaction to what I had seen. The knot in my stomach caught fire, and I could feel the heat of anger spread from there.

We buried them both, shallow, and noted the exact location so that the bodies could be retrieved later and returned to their homes. If that was practical. At that point we couldn't be certain that any of us would get off the planet.

Then we moved east. We had no specific orders. We did not risk giving away our position by radioing for instructions. Spec ops teams are trained to use their own initiative. Until we could safely contact operations—or were desperate for help—we would look for our own ways of striking against the enemy until new instructions came.

Make no mistake about it, after seeing Koi and—especially—Tenzik, we wanted blood. Revenge. We wanted a chance to work out the sick feeling in our guts. It's a good thing we didn't happen across any enemy in the first hour or so after we finished the burial detail. Emotion would have gotten in the way of logic. Hard telling what we would have done . . . or what mistakes we might have made.

We moved through the forest, aiming for one of the concentrations of enemy troops we could mark from their electronic emissions, taking great care to watch for mines or booby traps. The lieutenant said we would move in, see what the situation was, then do whatever seemed practical. As time passed, the blood fury we had felt mutated into something colder, less emotional. A determination: We would do whatever we could to hurt the enemy, badly, no matter the cost.

Emotion made it easier to keep going, even though we were tired. At that, we were probably in better shape than most of the men in the line battalions—or in any of the enemy units. We, at least, had had a little time to sleep during our hiatus aboard *Tarsus*. I doubted that few men on the ground, in either army, had managed to get much sleep since the landings.

More than anything else, that was probably why both armies had done what they could to disengage during the afternoon, why there was a lull in the fighting. Soldiers can't go forever without sleep. They turn into zombies. And zombies are easy to kill.

ZOMBIE WAS ONE OF MANY WORDS THE TRANS-lation programs had trouble with. I had used it during training, and apparently there was no precise way for ghuroh translator buttons to interpret it. I had tried explaining the concept to Fang and Claw and had found that my own knowledge of the word wasn't as complete as I had thought. I had brought Tonio into the discussion when it turned from the practical meaning of the term to the religious meaning it had originally had in parts of Earth. Finally we had managed to get the background across to Fang and Claw. At least they *said* that they understood what we meant.

After a few other humans had found it difficult to convey that same term to ghuroh, it was added to the database and programmed into the ghuroh translator buttons. There had been a lot of words like that, colloquialisms, from any language to any language, back on Dancer. Most of those terms had been added to the databases and incorporated in the programs of the translator buttons—though every now and then some new deficiency became apparent.

We were still learning.

THE LIEUTENANT KEPT US MOVING AT OUR BEST pace for two and a half hours after we buried Koi and Tenzik. Then we moved away from the trail we had been following and set up a perimeter in the heavier growth along a creek, where we could refill our canteens. "We need to take time to rest," the lieutenant told the three sergeants. Maybe the lieutenant understood the concept of soldiers turning into zombies—sluggish physically and mentally, less able to react quickly or intelligently. "An hour, I think." He sounded tired. "Maybe two hours," he added after a pause. "We need to give everyone a little time to sleep."

Sleep. Just the mention of the word forced a yawn

from my throat and made my eyes start to water. "Half and half?" I asked when I got the yawn under control. My faceplate was tilted up so I could wipe the tears from the corners of my eyes without difficulty, though they started to burn a little.

The lieutenant's hesitation before he said yes seemed far too long. I guess he needed sleep worse than the rest of us. Maybe he wasn't in any real pain—the analgesics in the bandaging on his cheek should have prevented that—but you can't completely escape the effects of a wound and the loss of blood. He couldn't be at anything near peak efficiency.

We split the fire teams so everyone would know who was on sentry duty when. Tonio and the lieutenant would split the watch between them so one or the other would always be awake. Chouvana and I would do the same. Chouvana offered me the first chance to sleep, and I didn't bother arguing. "Wake me when my hour is over," I told him.

It might have taken me all of twenty seconds to fall asleep.

AN HOUR OF SLEEP, OF OBLIVION, ISN'T enough to do much more than make you feel groggy as hell when you wake. Sometimes I think it's worse than no sleep at all. Still, when you're in the field and don't know how long it will be before your next opportunity, you sleep when you can—if it's an hour or five minutes.

Chouvana woke me, and waited to make certain I was awake before he crawled back to his spot on the perimeter and curled up to take his own turn at sleep. I used a lot of my drinking water, splashing it in my eyes before I took a long drink. I could afford to be extravagant

with water while we were lying next to a clear stream
with an uncontaminated flow of the stuff. I rubbed my
face vigorously, then took my helmet off long enough
to douse my head completely with water. Then I put my
helmet back on and checked to make sure the rest of my
squad had switched over, that everyone who was supposed to be awake was.

Staying awake was still difficult for me, so I assumed
it would be for the others. I did what I could to check
on the others, watching them as much as I watched the
forest. That's part of a squad leader's job. I also listened
to the command channels. There didn't seem to be much
going on anywhere on Dintsen. There was nothing so
formal as a truce, but the effect was almost there.

An hour asleep, an hour awake. The lieutenant had
the second watch. He woke Tonio precisely at the end
of an hour. We roused everyone else.

"We're going to move," Tonio told Chouvana and me.
He made the assignments, and put Chouvana's squad up
front for a change.

We got up and got started. But we hadn't gotten far
before the lieutenant stopped us. We went to the ground
where we were, facing either way along the line, waiting.

"We have orders," Tonio said after about a minute
and a half. I guess the lieutenant had him listening in.
"We head northwest, toward a clearing a bit over four
miles from here." He gave me the coordinates. "For resupply and so forth. Some of the other teams are also
being directed there. There'll be medtechs, and I suspect
that wounded will be evacuated if they can't be treated
on site." We both glanced toward the lieutenant, fur-
tively, as if we didn't want to be caught.

*   *   *

MOST OF THE OTHER TEAMS AT THE RENDEZ-
vous were from C and D Companies of Ranger Battalion, the units that had been concentrated in the area
during the original landings. Only a few teams from A
and B Companies had been this far south, or had been
reassigned after the first night on Dintsen. By the time
we got to the rendezvous, there were already more than
forty men there, and within the next hour the total more
than doubled. That was when two shuttles came in. We
had formed a perimeter around the clearing to give the
shuttles protection against the threat of attack. Two abar-
and fighters escorted the shuttles in.

Our lieutenant was hesitant about seeking treatment,
but Tonio insisted. We assigned Fang and Claw to ac-
company the lieutenant, then Tonio had me go along to
pick up any orders there might be for us . . . in case the
lieutenant was held for evacuation, which seemed likely.
"See what news you can pick up," Tonio whispered before we left the perimeter. "Ask around." I nodded. I
would have done that in any case.

It was clear that our lieutenant was not the most badly
wounded soldier in the clearing. More than 10 percent
of the men who had made it to the rendezvous had
wounds, and some of them were a *lot* worse off than
our lieutenant. Every medtank was filled.

Medtanks. I'm not really sure why they're called
tanks. That calls to mind an image of something substantial, like a barrel or a crate filled with liquid . . .
something. They are more like plastic bags. The fluid is
there, but it's only a thin film between the surface of the
bag and the patient. At the head of the bag is a small
case with monitoring instruments and the tubes to pro-

vide fluids and the repair nanoagents that do most of the work of healing wounds and sustaining the patient. A wounded man can be kept alive in a tank while waiting for a surgeon to remove any large foreign objects—like bullets and shrapnel—and handle crises that a tank can't handle quickly. Then the patient can be returned to the tank to speed the process of recovery.

The one surgeon who had come down with the medical team went to work within minutes, and he had cases lined up waiting. There had been men killed as well, too many—always too many. Two of the wounded soldiers in the clearing died before they could get help.

Fang and Claw stayed with the lieutenant while he waited for treatment. I wandered around the hub of activity near the shuttles, looking for whoever was in charge, stopping to listen to men talking along the way, asking questions when I came across someone I knew. None of the stories I heard was encouraging. Sure, we had done a lot of damage to the IFers, but we had suffered a lot of casualties. I tried not to take the stories literally. Soldiers tend to exaggerate, both the good and the bad. Hell, the fact that we were able to put two shuttles on the ground and hold them there without coming under attack was fairly positive news. We weren't in such bad shape that the enemy had control of the air, or had ground forces close enough to hit us.

I found the command post that the human captain in charge of the operation had set up, reported, and asked if there were orders for our team—and when and where we were to go to pick up ammunition and supplies. The captain consulted his sergeant, then gave me directions to the resupply operation and said that orders would be "forthcoming" later but that we could expect to remain in position until the shuttles lifted off. He couldn't—or wouldn't—estimate when that might be.

With the captain's permission, I used my radio to call Tonio and give him the information—that was another mark of how secure our bosses were of our position. No attempt was made to impose electronic silence on us. The team was to leave its spot in the perimeter and head in to the shuttles. We had fifteen minutes to get what we needed and return to our positions so that the next team could go. The perimeter could not be abandoned with shuttles on the ground.

I went to collect Fang and Claw so they could get what they needed, and told the lieutenant what our immediate orders were. A medtech had taken a preliminary look at the lieutenant—triage—and he was waiting for treatment. "They want to evacuate me," the lieutenant said, "but I have asked to be treated here so I don't have to leave the team." He could speak more clearly now, with the hole in his cheek patched better than we had been able to do in the field.

"They *will* take him," Claw whispered after we were away from the lieutenant. "I was there while the medtech made his examination. There is considerable damage inside his mouth. Bits of tooth imbedded in the cheek and in the roof of his mouth have been isolated by his implanted medical system, but they must be extracted by a surgeon. And the bullet wound is not healing as it should."

"He has not been able to eat solid food since he was wounded," Fang added. "A ghuroh who cannot eat cannot fight." That sounded like some kind of ghuroh cliché.

"He does not like to be separated from the pack. No

ghuroh would," Claw said. "That must pain him more than his wound."

"He needs to let the medicos get him fit," I said. "He'll do himself and the team a lot better if he's healthy."

WE REPLENISHED OUR AMMUNITION, FOOD SUP-plies, and first-aid pouches. The quartermaster section was doing a good job making sure that each species had their own food and the right ammo. Then we went back to the perimeter, ate, and settled in on half-and-half watches—50 percent of the men on duty, the rest sleeping, switching off every hour.

Sleeping like that, a little at a time, isn't nearly as helpful as getting it all at once, but we couldn't make half the men stay awake all those extra hours. We couldn't tell how long we had, or how much longer it might be afterward before any of us had another chance to sleep.

No one seemed to be in any hurry to send us back out into the woods. Maybe no one had any idea what to do with us. We managed three full sleep rotations in the team. I was still a bit groggy, yawning frequently, but I was in better shape than I had been at the start. My last turn, I had actually needed three or four minutes to fall asleep.

Dawn came, and the sun climbed into view. There was still one shuttle on the ground. The other had taken off two hours earlier, evacuating the more seriously wounded. The lieutenant was gone, despite his protests. Tonio was in command of the team.

There had been some additional reorganization. Three new guys had been added to Chouvana's squad. Holden

McGuire was a lance corporal who had been in the first class that had graduated from ranger school after my own—years back. The two other newcomers were porracci privates, Trievauna and Zauvana. There was a bit of ritual growling and posturing between them and their new squad leader, but they accepted their positions without causing difficulties.

"You figure we'll be moving out soon?" I asked Tonio shortly after the three new men arrived.

Tonio shook his head. "I don't have the faintest idea. Nobody's said anything."

"How 'bout that second shuttle? Any news on how long they're going to let it sit out there?"

"Do I look like a freakin' encyclopedia?" Tonio asked. He sounded annoyed—which was unusual for him. I let well enough be and went back to my squad.

IT WAS MIDMORNING BEFORE THE SECOND shuttle took off. There had been no orders for any of the special operations teams around the clearing. A couple more squads had come in earlier that morning, not long before the first shuttle left. We waited, staying in our perimeter—about eighty men altogether, under the loose command of a porracci senior lieutenant. The human captain had left on the first shuttle. Somebody always *has* to be in command; that's the way the military thinks.

"Maybe we're just supposed to keep this LZ secure," I told Fred Wilkins when he asked me what the hell we were supposed to be doing. "Maybe they're going to bring more casualties here to evac. Maybe the brass is going to come down to look around. How the hell should I know?"

"No need to snap my head off," Wilkins said. "I was just asking."

I sucked in a deep breath and held it for an instant. Okay, I wasn't crazy about Wilkins, but this was one time he was right. "Sorry, Fred. It's getting to me, too, but nobody has said anything. Until we get orders, we sit and wait. We'll take our turns on watch and sleep while we can."

There were a few work details before the second shuttle left. The porracci SL had each team string electronic snoops and command-detonated mines beyond the perimeter. The shuttles had left abundant supplies of snoops and explosives, leaving plenty after everyone had packed as much as they could carry. Taking that much care of the approaches lent some weight to the possibility that we might stay put and hold the clearing. It might not be "proper" use for spec ops soldiers, but you use what you've got.

It was after four o'clock that afternoon before we learned that we weren't going to be sitting around doing nothing much longer. The porracci lieutenant and two squads would "hold" the clearing. The rest of us were being sent out, moved toward the enemy, beginning within minutes after we got the news. We would break up into our teams and squads and take different routes, but we were all going to be thrown back into the battle.

The fighting had started to ratchet back up.

OUR TEAM DREW ONE OF THE LONGER ROUTES, curving west before heading south and then east, so we were one of the first groups dispatched. Our target was a small enemy encampment away from the main fighting—a place where they were trying to rest troops a company or so at a time, treat their wounded, and protect a supply depot. That was the intelligence we were given.

We were to destroy any supplies, especially ammunition, and generally raise as much hell as we could, striking and moving over and over until we got the job done ... or until things got too hot for us to stick around. Another squad was being sent toward the same site. They would hit from the other side, initially, then do what they could to increase the enemy's confusion level, mostly lying in wait for any enemy units coming in or going out. I just hoped it wouldn't add to *our* confusion as well. We might not be able to do much coordinating, and friendly fire can kill you as quickly as unfriendly fire.

It was half an hour before midnight when we got into position. Iyi and Oyo had scouted the area in front of us, spotting a pair of enemy snoops and several land mines. We couldn't do anything about the snoops until we were engaging the enemy. By the time you can reach a snoop to deactivate it, it's already told the enemy you're there. If you shoot it from a distance, the result is the same: The enemy knows you're there. The mines—well, knowing where they were would let us avoid them while we were sneaking around, and once the shooting started, we could take them out with grenades or rifle fire.

I went forward as far as I dared to have a look at the enemy camp. It's not that anyone doubted the report Iyi and Oyo had given—they had shown how good they were—but Tonio wanted me to have a look, to try to get a better idea of the enemy's numbers and positions.

The estimate that the enemy strength was a company—about two hundred men—seemed close, not counting the casualties who were in two open-sided tents near the center of the camp—maybe thirty or forty wounded, with half a dozen medtechs or orderlies taking care of them. It looked as if only about half of the un-wounded IFers were on the perimeter. The rest were around the medical station, some of them apparently sleeping. They didn't look as if they were expecting trouble. There were also several stacks of crates in the center of the camp—the sort of boxes that ammunition would likely be stored in.

I crawled back to describe the layout for Tonio and Chouvana, sketching the arrangements in the dirt. Tonio asked a couple of questions, and I answered them as best I could. Then he stared for a couple of minutes at the diagram I had drawn. Occasionally his hand moved over the chart without touching it.

"Okay, here's what we'll do," he said then. He drew lines around mine, showing where we would hit and where we would move afterward, laying out assignments for each fire team in both squads. Chouvana would be on the right. I would be on the left, and somewhat closer to the enemy at the start. Chouvana's squad would open the attack. If the enemy sent men toward them, we would hit from the side. If they didn't, we'd strike directly at the perimeter in front of us.

After the first exchange, we'd move farther left, around the enemy perimeter. Chouvana would move farther right, and we would both hit them again. By that time the squad operating on the far side of the camp should have hit—at least once. Then our two squads would move back toward each other, with Chouvana's people doing most of the moving, trying to draw some of the enemy into another ambush. After that . . . well, that would depend on what the enemy had been up to.

*   *   *

THERE'S ONLY ONE GOOD THING ABOUT LACK of sleep. When the brain is groggy, fear has a harder time laying hold of you and strangling your insides. When you're well rested—and we had had enough sleep during the day to push that brain-numbing exhaustion to arm's length—the fear is there on the end of your nose, almost. You have to face it, fight it. Once the fighting starts, the fear can get lost in the needs of the moment, but while you're waiting for the fight, moving toward it or sitting somewhere with the fight moving toward you, that's when fear can grab you by the throat and threaten to choke the air out of you.

I was sweating fiercely, and I could feel my heart pounding as if it wanted to get the hell out of my body while it could. I fought my nerves the way I always do, forcing myself to pay attention to the terrain, checking the men I was responsible for; watching, listening. Tighten the focus until there's no room for anything else.

We worked our way slowly toward the enemy camp, with the men on point—Iyi and Oyo for my squad— looking for more snoops or mines. This was a time for us to take considerable care for where we put our feet, to watch for that infamous snapping twig. A snoop's microphone might pick that up at a distance of thirty yards or more, if there wasn't much other sound to mask it.

I kept my eyes, and the muzzle of my rifle, moving back and forth across the line of march, ready to start firing instantly if that became necessary. It's almost a snake dance, hypnotic, with every man moving that way, not in step. At any given second some rifles will be looking left while others point right. Part of your attention is always on the man in front of you. When he stops, even if it's only for a second, you stop as well, *instantly,* and watch for his next move. When he changes course, you also change course, trying to turn at *exactly* the same point, semiconsciously working to step in his footprints.

This was a relatively open area of forest—not rain forest, even though we were in the tropics. The trees did not crowd each other so closely that there was no sunlight left for growth on the ground, so there were bushes, and occasional patches of reeds and grass between the trees. Not that there was anything like sunlight at the moment. It was dark, and the trees and cloud cover meant that there was little moonlight or starlight. We had to rely completely on the night-vision systems built into our helmet faceplates. With night vision, the world gets painted in shades of green and gray by the combination of infrared sensors and available light multipliers. It gets more difficult to determine distances, and you lose some of the depth of field, making the background look flat and bunched together. It takes practice to work efficiently like that, but the night gives us a little edge. We might not be able to see *quite* as well as we can in the daylight, but that means that it's that much harder for any enemy to see—and target—us. Infantrymen love the night.

At times there was little room to move on the ground without disturbing the greenery, and you want to avoid causing unnatural motion in the branches and so forth. That can give you away. Our progress was almost agonizingly slow, but we wanted to hold the element of surprise as long as we could. The first indication the enemy should have of our presence was the first burst of gunfire that hit them.

Our two squads had separated almost at once after Tonio laid our what we were going to do. Tonio stayed with my squad, and when our fire teams separated, he went with Souvana. We moved on our different courses, keeping track of each other by the blips on our head-up displays once the squads and fire teams were out of each other's sight.

Iyi gave a hand signal when we were forty yards from the nearest of the snoops he and his brother had spotted. We moved to our left, and my biraunta went back up into the trees to look for additional snoops. They found one by the very-low-level electronic emissions it made, but the snoop was far enough over to let us snake our way through a slight depression between it and the others. As long as we stayed flat on our stomachs, there was a good chance we could get past the snoops without setting them off. With a little luck we might even get completely inside the ring of snoops and land mines the IFers had planted to warn them of any attack.

That was exactly what we wanted.

AT THE END, I WAS MOVING FORWARD AN INCH at a time, sliding toward a position with decent cover from a rather thick tree trunk. An arthritic tortoise could have raced past me. The tree I was aiming for was 140 yards from the nearest point of the enemy perimeter. When I got there, I had a clear field of fire across ten yards of that perimeter—without moving more than the barrel of my rifle. Once I settled in, I looked to my left and right, picking out where the rest of my fire team was. That was as much as I could see. Even Souvana's fire team was too far off—and too well hidden—for me to see them.

Once I was certain that everyone on my fire team was in place, all I could do was wait. Unless the enemy opened fire or moved toward us, Chouvana's people were to start our attack. I double-checked my rifle to make certain there was a round in the chamber and that the safety was off. I opened the flap on one of my ammo pouches so I could save a fraction of a second when the time came to put a new magazine in my rifle. I adjusted my position minutely, trying for any slight improvement I could find without making a ruckus that might draw enemy attention.

Wait. The wait was actually less than three minutes, but it seemed infinitely longer before I heard the rattle of several rifles firing on full auto, and the throatier tharumps of RPGs being launched. Immediately I gave my squad the order to fire, and opened up myself. I had been tracking two tonatin on the enemy perimeter, and my first burst caught both of them before they had a chance to react.

I had warned my squad to keep their fire low. First of all, there was that other spec op squad operating on the far side of the enemy camp, and we didn't want to inflict friendly-fire casualties. Almost as importantly, we wanted to do everything we reasonably could to avoid hitting any of the wounded enemy soldiers in the center of the camp. *Reasonably.* We didn't target them, or the medical people, but we would not give active enemy troops a free pass just because there might be wounded men in the line of fire behind them. Maybe it was too fine a distinction, but that was where I drew my own line.

As soon as I saw my first targets go down, I took the next section of the enemy perimeter under fire, then looked beyond the line toward the troops who had been sleeping near the tents with the wounded—slightly to the right, from my perspective. Chouvana's grenadiers had dropped RPGs in the clearing, targeting the sleeping men. Getting their attention, you might say.

There was considerable activity in the clearing, and it probably wasn't as disorganized as it looked. It wouldn't be long before they started concentrating their fire on us, or even put soldiers out to try to track us down. *Another twenty seconds here,* I told myself. *Then we'll start shifting to the left.* If we stayed put much longer, we could expect to have enemy grenades raining on us.

Twenty seconds were long enough for me to empty the double-drum magazine I had started with. I was putting a fresh clip in my rifle when I gave my squad the order to move. I pulled back from the cover of my tree and got up on hands and knees to scurry along with the rest of my men.

Fred Wilkins was four yards ahead of me as we started our move. He got up too high, trying to make the move faster. I was looking right at him when a burst of enemy gunfire blew his helmet away . . . along with half of his head. There was no need to check on his condition. He had to be dead before he hit the ground. If you've got to go, I guess it's better if you don't know what's going on and get to skip the painful part of dying.

I *did* strip off his web belt with its ammunition pouches as I crawled past him. I might need those bullets.

THE SQUAD ON THE FAR SIDE OF THE CLEARING struck while I was getting my people down in their next positions. We opened fire five seconds later. Chouvana's squad opened fire about ten seconds after we did. The enemy returned fire in every direction, including some where there weren't any of our people. Iyi took a flesh wound, a crease along his right shoulder that burned fur and scored the skin, but it wasn't enough to keep him from continuing. Jaibie took a pair of bullets through the thin membrane of his left wing, but abarand don't have nerve endings through much of those membranes, so he didn't feel the "wounds." It wasn't until later that he even noticed.

We moved twenty yards closer to the enemy perimeter, angling left. This time we held our fire and just took cover, hoping we hadn't been spotted. We waited while Chouvana's squad continued attacking—moving clockwise around the perimeter, toward us. If they got far enough, they would pass behind us, sixty or seventy yards farther from the clearing than we were, trying to draw an enemy patrol close enough for my squad to take them out.

This time, once I was in position I didn't move at all. We didn't want so much as the rustle of a single leaf to show the enemy where we were. The extra squad on the far side hit again. They seemed to be moving clockwise around the clearing as well. *Indians circling the wagon train* ran through my head, something from some adventure vid I might have seen as a kid on Earth.

Chouvana's squad took heavy fire this time, from rifles and grenades. They lost two men during their move, and I learned later that they had lost one during the first exchange of gunfire. But they moved farther from the enemy, as planned, and that gave them more cover. *Get ready,* I thought, glancing around at where my people were. I had spotted a patrol moving out from the IF perimeter, about a platoon in strength. The enemy was putting a fourth of their available manpower into this, which meant that the rest of their perimeter would be that much weaker.

The squad on the far side hit that perimeter again, harder than before, concentrating their fire on one small segment, as if they were trying to break the line. I saw more of the enemy moving to that side. They were really disorganized, throwing men one way and the other in response to the most recent assault. *If only we had a couple of full platoons,* I thought, *we could take them down completely.*

The enemy platoon looked as if it would pass forty yards to our right. We weren't lined up quite properly to spread out against their flank, and there was no way we could move at this point. I decided to give the order to open up on them while we still had a bit of an angle, before we would have to fire over each other's heads at the IFers. I marked a spot, and watched as the enemy approached it. They were looking ahead, intent on Chouvana's people.

"Now!" I shouted when the first IFer crossed the spot I had marked. "Give them everything you've got." I was using my squad frequency, so everyone got the message. There were nine of us and about fifty tonatin, but the brief advantage that surprise gave us was enough. Besides, Chouvana's squad stopped, turned, and added their firepower to ours within two or three seconds.

Rifles and grenade launchers. We put so much hell into an area forty yards long and twenty yards wide that it was a miracle that any of the enemy survived. Some did. In less than a minute those tonatin who were able to move were headed back in the other direction as fast as their bowed legs could carry them. Seven, maybe eight men. None got back to his original perimeter.

"Let's finish this job!" Tonio said on a channel that

connected him to both Chouvana and me. "That other squad is going to move in as well."

I relayed the message to my squad. We started moving forward—fire and maneuver, with one fire team covering the other—from cover to cover, zigging and zagging, hunched over as far as we could, diving to the ground after two or three running strides, crawling, rolling to one side or the other, anything to confuse the enemy and throw off their aim.

Even with our team and the squad operating on the other side of the clearing, the IFers still outnumbered us, but—discounting the wounded and the medical team—their advantage wasn't much more than four to three now. It wasn't enough.

I was forty yards short of the enemy perimeter when they decided they had enough and surrendered. Including the wounded and the medical team, we took seventy-odd prisoners once we rounded up those who had been wounded while they were chasing Chouvana's squad into our ambush. We counted sixty enemy bodies, but didn't go looking for more of them in the forest.

And five bodies of our own: Wilkins, the three men from Chouvana's squad, and one man from the squad that had been working the far side of the enemy perimeter.

CHAPTER 16

THE NEXT FIVE DAYS ARE SOMETHING OF A blur in my memory. We took part in a number of small engagements—ambushes, mostly. Members of my squad suffered a few minor wounds, but nothing that kept anyone out of action for more than six hours. We also went on three missions to knock out suspected enemy munitions and supply caches. Those were almost boring. We didn't fire a single shot on any of those jobs. We infiltrated insufficient defenses, planted our explosives, set the timers, and got well away before the bombs went off. Textbook special operations exercises.

Twice in that time we were moved by shuttle from one area to another. Chouvana's squad got detached from us and was used elsewhere. We picked up the second squad from our platoon for one of our operations; then they were sent off on something else, and Tonio Xeres went with them, and through the rest of the period it was just me and my men.

All in all, we had too little sleep and too much tension. When we weren't actually on a mission, there was a lot of arguing. If we hadn't all been so damned tired most of the time, I figure we'd have had a dozen fights within the squad. Everyone had a short fuse.

It wasn't just the spec ops teams of Ranger Battalion who were short on sleep and overloaded with anxiety. That was pretty much the way of it for all the soldiers on Dintsen, on both sides. The line units were pretty much up against it one way or another all of the time. We were in and out of danger spots, and the yo-yo effect added to the tension. I guess it was just as bad for the pilots of the aerospace fighters and the crews of the ships. The fighting wasn't all on the ground, though those of us who spent our time kissing mud never really had any idea what was going on overhead—except that, each day, there were fewer friendly fighters to support our operations.

We won a few battles; the enemy won a few. We all expended ammunition and suffered casualties. If what we were told by the brass was true—and I can't guarantee that—the IF force was losing a lot more men killed and wounded than we were. We took several hundred prisoners. Since we couldn't spare men to guard them on the ground, they were shuttled up to one of the ships, locked off in a section of it with the gastight hatches welded shut to make certain they couldn't take over the ship. We were told that the enemy wasn't taking prisoners. Later I learned that wasn't entirely true, but there weren't many.

Neither side received reinforcements, though the Ilion Federation *tried* to bring in a couple of battalions. Our fleet managed to turn the enemy ships back, with losses on both sides. From what I was able to glean from the command channel, we weren't expecting help. Dintsen was the 1st Combined Regiment's to win or lose. I was getting close to not caring which way it went—as long as it went quickly.

AFTER OUR LAST MISSION TO BLOW UP A SUS- pected enemy munitions cache, we met a shuttle and were lifted back to the clearing where we had gathered almost a week before. The area had turned into a semipermanent headquarters for our forces on Dintsen, since the fighting had moved generally south and east of Miorawinn. There were more of our people there this time— including nearly all of B Company of Ranger Battalion. Only two squads from fourth platoon were missing . . . other than the dead, and those wounded who had not been returned to duty yet.

Lieutenant Fusik met us when we came off the shuttle, listened to my report, said "Well done," then told us to get a hot meal—there was a field kitchen operating finally—and sack out for a few hours. He showed us where the rest of the company was bivouacked. Then the lieutenant went one way and we headed in another. We were all dragging. I told everyone that we could eat first, but after that, we would clean our weapons before anyone sacked out.

I'm not exactly sure what happened next. We were walking toward the company area, strung out over fifteen or twenty yards. *Apparently* Corporal Souvana said something to Lance Corporal Kiervauna. Kiervauna said something back and turned away. I didn't hear the exchange, but the word that Souvana shouted next was loud enough for me to hear, loud enough to make me turn to see what was going on, but my translator button did not interpret the word—some porracci cussword, I guess.

Kiervauna kept walking, and Souvana ran after him—
almost *jumped* toward him. At first I thought that Kiervauna wasn't aware of what his fire team leader was
doing, but just before Souvana could grab Kiervauna's
neck, Kiervauna spun on one foot and brought his rifle
butt around, catching the corporal square in the gut—
hard. If it had been me on the receiving end of that, I
would have been on the ground, helpless. Souvana
gasped as the breath was knocked out of him, and he
nearly doubled up, grabbing at his stomach as if that
might help, but he wasn't down for the count the way I
would have been.

I was tired, mentally sluggish. For an instant I
couldn't believe what I had seen. I thought I was having
some sort of hallucination. Kiervauna had always been
totally submissive to the more dominant Souvana. Kiervauna had always done exactly what Souvana said and
had been downright meek in their dealings. But I had
never seen such a look of fury on his face as he had at
that moment, and I saw it up close.

I got between the two porracci to keep Kiervauna
from doing more damage. Souvana straightened up
much faster than I would have been able to after a blow
like he took, and started forward. Luckily for Kiervauna—and for me—Fang and Claw had been close.
Each of the ghuroh grabbed one of Souvana's arms
when he lunged for Kiervauna and held him back, wedg-
ing him between them.

"Damn it! That's enough!" I shouted. I had to clip
Kiervauna across the throat with the side of my hand to
keep him from simply pushing me out of the way. "Back
off, Kiervauna. That's not the way we do it here." I felt
Kiervauna ease off. He quit pressing so hard against me.
I couldn't have held him off much longer. I pushed and

he backed off a couple of steps, but he kept looking over my shoulder at Souvana.

I turned so I could see both of them. Souvana was still struggling with Fang and Claw, trying to get loose, but the two ghuroh were able to hold him. I kept one hand extended toward Kiervauna's chest in case he decided to go after Souvana again.

"Back off, Souvana," I said. "Settle down." The rest of the squad had moved in by this time. Jaibie and Nuyi edged close to Kiervauna; Nuyi was speaking softly to the porracci, trying to calm him. Iyi and Oyo stood at one side of the group, equally distant from the two porracci. I didn't expect them to get involved, not the way biraunta feel about porracci. But they were close, just in case.

"Cool down, both of you," I said, turning from one porracci to the other. "This is the Combined Regiment. We don't handle things the way you do in your army. Control yourselves."

I started to wonder who else might have noticed the incident. I didn't want to have to play this by the book. That would mean a court-martial for Kiervauna—striking a superior is the kind of offense that can bring jail time, or worse, in any army. I didn't want that kind of grief in the squad, that kind of blot on our record—and I damned sure didn't want the annoyance of the red tape and testimony a court-martial would require. Luckily, no officers came running to ask what was going on. Nobody outside the squad seemed to be paying any attention.

Souvana was slow to back down, to quit putting pressure on the ghuroh who were holding him back—and Fang and Claw were the only ones in the squad who *could* have held Souvana. He continued to stare past me, at Kiervauna, who wasn't flinching as he had every other time Souvana had looked crossways at him.

"This ends here," I told Souvana, moving closer until we were almost nose to nose. "The alternative is we split you up, ship you both to other platoons, other companies. If that happens, I'll make sure both your new commanders know why. I don't want that to happen. Until now, we've worked well together. We're all tired, not thinking straight. Right now we do what the lieutenant said—eat and then sleep. After we clean our weapons. Later, we'll hash this out, just the three of us." I turned my back on Souvana and took a couple of steps toward our other porracci.

"Kiervauna, you stay away from Souvana. Don't try to pick up where you left off." I turned around again, this time about equally distant from the two.

"Souvana, you will not touch Kiervauna." I spaced those words out, emphasizing them. Maybe Souvana's translator button wouldn't put all the feeling into the words I did, but he would see, know. "If you do, I'll have you up on charges.

"Kiervauna, you're on thin ice." I didn't think then that he might not understand that phrase, and I don't know how his translator button interpreted it. "I don't want to have to bring you up on charges for this, and I'll try to find a way to avoid that—unless you do anything else."

I looked from one to the other then. "Understand?" I demanded—twice, once while facing each of them.

Kiervauna was quick to say, "I understand, Sergeant. I will do what you say."

Souvana glared at Kiervauna for twenty seconds before transferring that look to me. He grunted, nodded, then said, "I will obey," extremely softly.

"Okay. Now let's get to the food. We're wasting our

own time here, and we don't know how much of that we're going to have before they send us out again."

HOT FOOD AND COFFEE. A CHANCE TO WASH up and put on clean clothes after we cleaned our weapons and drew ammunition. Then we rolled out our sleeping cloths—more insulated tarpaulins than blankets—and lay on them to get some sleep. Nobody had said anything about posting sentries or contributing to a guard force, so I didn't ask questions. If they wanted us, someone would let me know.

I set things up so that Souvana and Kiervauna were at opposite ends of the squad, as far from each other as we could manage without exiling one or both of them completely. If I did that and anyone noticed, I would have to make explanations, and those would either have to be the truth or a fabrication so sticky it could entangle us all.

Even though I was upset about the incident, I didn't need much time at all to fall asleep. The situation between my porracci would wait. Sleep might not. I dropped off quickly and went deep, into total oblivion.

I only woke once on my own, to momentary confusion. There was a fragment of a dream fading rapidly. I had been on Earth, still a teenager, before I joined the army and my parents basically disowned me. There was a girl named Kelly. I couldn't recall her last name after I woke, but I could still picture her in my mind. We had gone together for a few months. I had been more serious about the relationship than she had. The dream-thought that had wakened me was *If we hadn't broken up, I wouldn't have joined the army.* Somehow that had scared my sleeping mind. I don't know why. As I sank back into my exhausted sleep I remember thinking, *Maybe that's why I've never been able to get hooked on anyone else.*

It was nearly sunset before I was awakened by Junior Lieutenant Taivana, B Company's executive officer. For a few seconds after I opened my eyes and saw our porracci officer, I felt a knot in my stomach, the fear that he had somehow learned of the earlier incident. I got to my feet as quickly as I could.

"Your squad will alternate with first platoon's third squad on the perimeter tonight," the lieutenant said. "Your first three-hour shift will begin in exactly seventy-four minutes." He pointed out the section of the perimeter we would be responsible for. "Wake your men and give them time to take care of the necessities and eat a meal first."

"Yes, sir." I gave him a quick salute, not especially crisp or military. He returned it in a more proper fashion, then strode away.

I looked over my sleeping men. Well, Iyi and Oyo were awake, sitting with their arms wrapped around their knees, watching me. The rest of the squad was sleeping, though. My two porracci. I looked at each of them and shook my head. I had to have a talk with them before much more time elapsed. It wasn't enough that we hadn't completely ironed out all the prejudices among the species. The porracci had to complicate things by fighting among themselves.

"First squad!" I said, not quite in a shout. "Everybody up!" It took a little more than that, but everyone was moving and had their eyes open in less than a minute. "Ten minutes for latrine call. Then we eat. After that we play soldier again, duty on the perimeter. Let's get moving. The vacation is over."

Once everyone in the squad was on his feet, I called the two porracci over. "Let's go over there," I said, pointing to an empty area away from where the rest of the squad was heading. "We've got a few things to get straight."

Neither of them replied, but they went where I told them to, careful to stay out of arm's reach of each other. When we were far enough off that I was sure no one else would hear what I had to say, I said, "Sit," and pointed at the ground—two spots, six feet apart. They obeyed, Kiervauna as quickly as if his legs had been kicked out from under him, Souvana more slowly, his eyes never leaving mine, letting me know that he still considered himself my physical superior. I didn't flinch from his stare. Either of the porracci could have decked me in a hurry, but I didn't think either would try, and I was upset enough that I didn't care if they did. If one or the other did make a move, I'd drop him fast, and not worry whether I was fighting "fair."

I still wasn't certain how to handle this. My brain was racing, but it seemed to be going in three directions at once. I was still a little foggy, not fully alert. Even though I had managed about seven hours of sleep, I was tired and not thinking at my best. I stood almost between Souvana and Kiervauna, just enough to the side that I could see both of them without moving my head too much.

"I don't know what set off that scene this morning, and frankly, I don't want to. I don't know what either of you said. Let's keep it like that. If I knew more than what I saw, I might be forced to take official action, and I don't want to have to do that. *If* I can avoid it without risking more trouble in the squad. If we have to put this on the record, it's not going to do either one of you any good. You understand that?"

I looked from one to the other until both nodded—Kiervauna quickly, Souvana more reluctantly. Predictably. I tried to hold in a sigh. Souvana wasn't going to let go any faster than he absolutely had to, wasn't going to give an inch I didn't force from him.

"This squad has worked well together since we landed. We know this can work, that the different species can function together as a team. Then we have this happen between two porracci. You both know the rules this regiment operates under. We do not settle things through the porracci custom of challenge and combat." I hate having to spiel on like that, but I was still angry, and I'm sure it came through in my voice.

"Lance Corporal Kiervauna, you will apologize to Corporal Souvana for your unwarranted attack on him. There will be no repetition of it, or any other act of insubordination on your part. If there is, I will recommend formal disciplinary action. A court-martial. Do you understand?"

"Yes, Sergeant. I understand," Kiervauna said. He looked at Souvana. "I apologize for my actions, Corporal. I was wrong and will not repeat my mistake."

I turned my attention to Souvana. "Corporal Souvana, you will accept Lance Corporal Kiervauna's apology. You will take no action against him. The alternative remains the same. I will recommend formal disciplinary action, and suggest that your part in this is not without blame. Do you understand me, Corporal?"

Souvana glared at me for a moment, but then nodded and said, "I understand, Sergeant. I will obey." He looked toward Kiervauna—or slightly over his head—and said, "I accept your apology, Lance Corporal."

"Good. We've got this settled. It's over, ended, forgotten." I looked from one to the other and hoped that it really was over. "Now let's get cleaned up and eat. We've got the IFers to worry about again."

THE NIGHT SEEMED AS LONG AS THOSE ON Dancer. There was no enemy activity anywhere near us, but we had to stay alert. If we got lax, we might be in for a lethal surprise if the enemy did come for us. And I had my porracci to worry about. I wasn't overly confident that my little chat with them would take. If there was a next time between the two, it might happen while we were in action or—almost as bad—when one of our officers was close enough to see.

Our rotations on the perimeter lasted through the night and until noon the next day. When we turned our section back over to third squad and went to eat lunch, Lieutenant Fusik and Tonio came over and took me aside.

"We're going back to real spec ops work," Fusik said, almost in a whisper. "Most of the battalion."

"A big push to try to end the whole campaign?" I asked. It was a guess, but . . . well, the idea just came to me and straight out my mouth before I had a chance to think it over. I didn't *really* think that we had reached the point where we could attempt something like that.

"That's the intent," Fusik said, and that lump in my stomach started to grow again. "The Ilions have tried to reinforce their garrison here once already. They know what's going on and they might try again, with more people and ships. Our brass wants to take care of the enemy on the ground first, if possible."

I took a deep breath. *Start thinking about this like it's real,* I told myself, *because it looks like it is.* "Well, if we were supposed to slow the IFers down, keep them from invading somewhere else, I guess maybe we've done our job," I said, looking from the lieutenant to Tonio.

"Half the job, maybe," Fusik said. "Maybe we've crimped their timetable for invading the divotect core worlds, maybe we haven't. But any troops the Ilions send here are troops they're not going to have available for other objectives. Our brass would still like to see us win the fight on Dintsen, now that it seems at least possible."

I couldn't hold back the sour laugh the lieutenant's words roused. He didn't say anything about that, but he gave me a look as sour as my laugh before he continued.

"As soon as it gets dark, we'll be moving out—little by little—operating as platoons and companies, for the most part. We'll have the rest of tonight and as much of tomorrow as we need to get into position. The enemy has consolidated most of its remaining force on Dintsen in an area southeast of the divotect capital. Our line battalions are facing them on the east and south, with only limited forces to either-side. It's going to be up to Ranger Battalion to cover the rest of the enemy perimeter and keep them from retreating or moving back into Miorawinn. The general wants to force a major engagement on territory that offers us some advantage, and try to bring the battle for Dintsen to a conclusion."

"Risk it all on one throw of the dice?" I suggested, knowing that the sarcastic tone was out of line but unable to stop myself.

"The operations staff seems to think that it's at least even odds," the lieutenant said, a little bit of a squint his only visible reaction to my comment. "The Ilions still have us outnumbered, but not nearly as badly as they did at the start. We've hurt them worse than they've hurt us. We've got them crimped in, so we're choosing the ground. We've still got a few batteries of rocket artillery operational. They don't. They also don't seem to have any rangers, or anything similar, on Dintsen." That much made sense. Rangers, special operations troops, wouldn't be the most likely candidates for an army of occupation. "Since we've got no place else to go, we might as well finish the job here."

"Well, I've got nothing else to do," I said.

"Awfully big of you," Tonio mumbled, his voice almost sharp, but the lieutenant didn't seem to mind. Then he laid out our part of the operation for me. It sounded only moderately insane. Maybe we could even pull it off.

CHAPTER 17

NOT EVERYONE IN RANGER BATTALION STAGED for the attack through the clearing where our command post was. Some moved in from other places; a few dropped moderately close to their area of operation by shuttle, where that could be done without compromising missions. But most of us had to walk.

Every platoon was shorthanded after eight days of operations on Dintsen. More than half a dozen spec ops squads (of the original sixty-four) had ceased to exist, their surviving members transferred to fill holes in other squads. No one was giving out exact numbers, but my guess was that we had lost 20 percent of the battalion—dead or too badly wounded to be returned to duty yet. The rumors I heard suggested that the line battalions had suffered even heavier casualties—perhaps as much as 35 percent in 2nd Battalion.

My squad had only had one man killed, and the wounds to other men had been minor. We weren't given a replacement for Wilkins. Too many other squads had lost more men.

During the afternoon we ate two meals, cleaned our

weapons—again—and topped off our loads of ammunition. Once more it was a matter of each man taking
as much as he could carry . . . and then a little more.
Some of us also managed an hour or two of sleep, those
who could set aside fear enough to drop off—and those
who were simply too exhausted for fear to keep them
awake. With any luck we'd get in position early enough
in the morning to get some sleep before what our brass
hoped would be the decisive battle, but there was no
guarantee of that.

FIRST PLATOON OF B COMPANY LEFT THE PE-
rimeter an hour after sunset. Several other units had already departed. I don't know if it would have fooled
anyone, but each unit moved into the perimeter—under
the cover of the trees surrounding the clearing—then
moved forward a few minutes later, to be replaced on
the line by the next unit that was going to leave. Only
a small force was going to be left behind with the medtechs and staff people. A shuttle was on the ground to
take them off if necessary.

My squad was top-heavy. Lieutenant Taivana, wearing his second "hat" as first platoon leader, was with us,
and so was Tonio, our platoon sergeant. I didn't understand why both of them came with my squad, since the
entire platoon was together. Theoretically, one of them
should have taken a position with one of the other
squads, but this was not a theoretical mission. The nervous part of my brain told me that we had both of them
because we were going to catch the worst assignment in
the platoon, maybe in the whole company.

In a way, having the porracci lieutenant along gave
me a partial solution for dealing with the difficulty be-

tween Souvana and Kiervauna. I told Kiervauna to stick
close to Lieutenant Taivana until he heard differently.
And I kept Souvana near the tail end of the squad, using
his fire team at the back. If I could keep the two apart,
they couldn't fight. And as long as Kiervauna was close
to the lieutenant, Souvana wouldn't dare to do anything
even if he had a chance.

Second squad had the point during the first part of our
hike. Tonio stayed close to me, near the front of first
squad. The lieutenant and Kiervauna were between my
two fire teams. Third and fourth squads moved parallel
to us, staying twenty to forty yards to our right, depending on the terrain.

Our course was almost due east once we got a mile
south of the clearing. We were going to go through the
northern part of the divotect capital, through the wooded
area between the villages on that side and the spaceport.
There were still some divotect alive in the capital. Most
were staying low, out of the way. Since most divotect
houses are built partially underground, they were generally barricaded in the lower rooms of their homes. Not
a bad idea. Only a direct rocket hit was likely to create
any danger for them.

Lieutenant Taivana did not consciously push our pace,
but he was used to the speed porracci make on the
march, and Tonio had to remind him that we weren't all
porracci. Taivana slowed the pace then, and he did allow
the biraunta to move through the trees when that was
practical. Oyo and Iyi were the only biraunta left in the
platoon. The few others were either dead or wounded.
We walked for eighty minutes, then rested for ten. After
six hours the lieutenant gave us a longer meal break.

We were within two hundred yards of the nearest divotect village, right about on the edge of Miorawinn,

when we took our meal break. We made no attempt to
go into the village or to contact any of the residents.
Nuyi asked, but I had to tell him no. Our orders were
to steer clear of civilians. It wasn't the time for distractions of that nature, and there was a chance that the
enemy might have left ambushes behind, maybe a squad
hiding in a divotect house, just hoping for a chance to
score a few hits against us.

I used binoculars to examine the village and gave
Nuyi the opportunity to do the same. There were no
people outside—since it was the middle of the night,
there probably wouldn't have been even before the invasion. I could see that some of the buildings had been
damaged. None of the ruins was smoking. It had been
six days since the last fighting near this corner of Miorawinn.

"My people here have suffered terribly," Nuyi whispered when he gave the binoculars back to me. "I wonder how many survive." He knew *some* had. The last
estimate I had heard was that at least a third of the divotect were still alive. Operations phrased it like that
instead of saying that perhaps two-thirds had been murdered by the IFers.

"With any luck, their suffering might be almost over,"
I whispered back. "We can't undo the killings that have
already been done, but maybe we can prevent any
more." Nuyi nodded—somewhat forlornly, I thought—
then went back to his position a few feet away from me.
Our rest period was almost over.

We hiked more than fifteen miles that
night. Considering that each of us carried 50 percent or
more of his body weight in weapons, ammunition, and

gear, that was a significant distance, since we were moving cross-country and steering clear of anything that looked like it might be a well-traveled path. "Easy" paths are more likely to be mined by an enemy.

Once we crossed the boundary of Miorawinn, there was little extremely wild country. Although the villages that comprised the capital were separated from each other by several miles, and the villages were spread out so the average population density was about ten per square mile, some care had been taken to tame the wilderness within the oval area of the capital, to turn it into parklike terrain. There were gullies, some with water running in them. Others were dry, and—for the most part—those had been left natural, with thickets, vines, and thick clusters of reeds. But the flat areas had been tended, with the grass kept relatively short and some of the trees pruned.

It was three hours before dawn when we crossed out of Miorawinn into an area that had been little used by the divotect population or the invaders. The ground was rougher east of the capital, broken at the beginning of thirty miles of foothills leading to a mountain range farther east. There had been some mining operations in those mountains, and some of our spec ops teams had been active there, dealing with the IFers who had been guarding the forced labor of the divotect miners. But the IFers had moved most of their troops closer to the capital in the first two days after our landings.

Our assigned position was six miles east of Miorawinn's northeasternmost village. We were to set up at the edge of the foothills, where they looked out on the open savanna and sparsely forested areas closer to the capital. That was where the IFer main force was, trying to fight their way into the hills, where they would be more difficult to dislodge. If they got into the hills, they might hold on indefinitely—until the Ilion Federation could get reinforcements to Dintsen.

It was less than an hour before dawn when Lieutenant Taivana decided we were where we were supposed to be—on the north slope of the last significant hill before the ground flattened out to the south and west. He brought all four squad leaders together with Tonio near the crest of the hill, just low enough that we wouldn't be silhouetted for anyone to the south to see.

"This will be our center of operations," the lieutenant said. "We've got enough cover below to sneak out and do some damage if we have to, and the ground here is favorable for us to keep the Ilions from breaking through easily."

Other teams would be set up in similar positions all along the northern and eastern sides of the enemy—a thin line to hold the IFers out in the open, where our line battalions could get to them.

"Drak, take your squad and plant mines and snoops along that draw." The lieutenant pointed to a low area between two hills to our left, east, three-quarters of a mile from where we were standing. "As concealed as possible. Set them for dual control." That meant rig trip wires and leave the circuits for command detonation active. "Put snoops farther over on the flank. If they attempt to come at us over that hill beyond the draw, I want to know early enough to stop them."

After I acknowledged the order and started to gather my people, Taivana gave second squad orders to make the same preparations in the pass on the west side of the hill.

*   *   *

MOST OF THE TREES AROUND US WERE SMALL and twisted, something like olive or cork trees from Earth in appearance, though there were several species. One variety had two-inch-long thorns—spikes—sharp, with some sort of toxin that produced red welts that itched ferociously where they scratched me, and it took quite a while for the medical nanoagents in my body to counteract each irritation. It was annoying, a distraction, but not *really* painful. Although the specific effects were different, the rest of the men in my squad were also affected—except Nuyi. The divotect's leathery skin seemed impervious to the needles.

It was almost impossible to pick our way between the trees to avoid scratches and punctures. My helmet and body armor were proof against them, but the needles seemed to work at every inch of exposed skin and picked through the fabric of my shirt and trousers everywhere that wasn't covered by armor. Where the needles couldn't penetrate, they grabbed at packs and harnesses. The only stretch that seemed to be clear of the trees was along the bottom of the draw. The ground was rocky there, a dry creekbed. A double file of men would move along that draw fairly quickly.

I kept our pace slow out of necessity, but even that couldn't prevent all of the catches the thorns made. Even crawling wouldn't have been enough, and that would have made it impossible for us to get our work done before daybreak. I wanted to get the mines and snoops planted before it was light out. That way, maybe we could get far enough away from their locations before we were spotted. You make trade-offs, and hope your choices don't rear up and bite you.

We were almost to the area where the lieutenant wanted the mines planted when we got bit.

* * *

I HAD NUYI ON POINT BECAUSE HE WAS THE least vulnerable to the thorns and because these trees weren't the kind that Oyo and Iyi could get up in. These were only fifteen to twenty feet tall, and there were those spikes. My biraunta were behind Nuyi, followed by Kiervauna. I was next, with Jaibie behind me, then Fang and Claw. Souvana had the rear, which seemed to be to his liking. We had worked our way down into the draw and were finally clear of the thorny trees. I figured to go another hundred yards south before we started planting the land mines.

Souvana shouted "Down!" over the squad frequency just a fraction of a second before we heard gunfire. Fang, Claw, and Jaibie were all hit in that initial volley. They were all alive, but I couldn't tell how badly they were hurt. I twisted around to face the gunfire coming from our left, on the slope of the next hill over, forty feet above our position and slightly north of us—behind us, up among more of those trees.

Fang might have been hurt, but he was still able to use his grenade launcher. Nuyi started popping grenades toward the enemy as well. But that tangle of trees meant that some of the rounds were deflected. Maybe it was just as well we had those trees, because two enemy grenades exploded just far enough from us that they caused no damage.

"Iyi, Oyo, Kiervauna—we've got to get to them," I said. "We'll circle around on both sides. Iyi, Oyo, the two of you go left. Kiervauna and I will go the other way. The rest of you, give us as much covering fire as you can."

I had no idea how large a patrol we were up against.

I assumed it was just a patrol, but that might be five men or fifty. All I knew was that they had us in a bad spot. I radioed the lieutenant, told him our situation, how many wounded I had, and what we were going to try to do.

"Do what you can. I'll start fourth squad around to your left, but it's going to take them too long if you can't help yourselves," the lieutenant said. Not that I expected miracles. I knew how hard it had been for us to get through those trees, and fourth squad was going to have even more ground to cover. I didn't ask about withdrawing, and the lieutenant didn't offer the option. If we were going to do our job, we had to get rid of the IFers who were already there.

Iyi and Oyo had shed their packs and only had rifles and ammunition with them—fewer edges to be caught by the thorns, and less weight to haul. I shed my harness. Kiervauna didn't bother. I led him out on the right, staying as low as possible—crawling on hands and knees much of the time, getting up to sprint a few steps when I saw an opportunity.

Only two minutes had passed since the first shots. I realized that the enemy patrol had to be small. The volume of fire gave me reason to hope that it was only a single fire team, five or six men. It still left us in a bad spot. The enemy was above us and had drawn first blood. Besides, dawn was only minutes away. We had lost most of the slight advantage that darkness might have given us.

I no longer felt the scratches and punctures of those thorns or the way they grabbed at my clothing and web belt. There were more important things on my mind— like staying alive. Kiervauna and I circled around. Once we got to steeper terrain on the slope, the enemy patrol could no longer target us without exposing themselves. I expected them to pull back before we could engage them directly and turn the tables. *We* would have the advantage in those circumstances; I probably would have started my men moving after the first volley. If the IFers moved, it would have to be north or south, along the side of the hill. Trying to climb away from us would expose them too much, and trying to move toward us would have brought them too close. We might have ended up going hand-to-hand.

I gestured for Kiervauna to move farther right, toward the edge of a slab of rock that rose vertically about eight feet in front of us. Up against that rock, we would be out of the line of fire, but that wasn't what we were looking for. I had spotted a way up the slope on the south side of the rock. It might even give us a direct view of the enemy patrol if they were coming our way.

Kiervauna changed course. I noticed that his left arm was bleeding—high, just below the shoulder. It didn't look as if he had been wounded by enemy fire but more as if one of those damned stickers had managed to prick a blood vessel. His fur on that arm was matted down, glistening wet.

Kiervauna was right at the edge of that bare rock face when he suddenly dove sideways and down, rolling. He started firing his rifle up the slope at the same time, even before he came to rest. I backed away from the rock and started firing as well, before I saw what Kiervauna was aiming at, using his direction of fire as a guide to my own. I had already let off a couple dozen rounds before I saw movement above us. At first it was only movement that I noticed, and I fired a burst directly at it before I realized that I had seen the helmet and shoulders of an enemy soldier. By then he was tumbling forward, mortally wounded if not already dead.

The man—tonatin—hit the rock ledge above us and a little to the left, then fell over the edge and bounced to a rest almost at my feet. He rolled half over, then caught against the trunk of one of those trees. I had no compunction about loosing a short burst into him from a distance of four feet to make certain he was dead.

I heard Nuyi yell "Duck!" on the squad channel and I went flat on the ground instantly. As I was looking to see if Kiervauna had heard, two grenades exploded behind the ledge above us, almost too close for comfort. As soon as the blast faded and the last debris stopped raining on me, I was back on my feet, heading past Kiervauna and up the sloped side of the rock. Kiervauna was a little slower getting up, but he wasn't far behind me.

We moved with our rifles spraying short bursts into the trees and grass ahead of us, not worrying about whether we had anyone in sight. If there were enemy soldiers, suppressing their fire was more important than trying to hit them while we were moving. When we *did* see enemy uniforms, we targeted them quickly, but it didn't take long for us to figure out that none of the IFers on that hill was in any shape to fire back.

"Hold your fire," I said on the squad channel. "Iyi? Oyo?"

"We're both here, Sergeant," Iyi said. "We have three enemy bodies in sight."

"Work your way to my location," I said. Then: "Souvana?"

"Yes?"

"How are the men with you?"

There was a pause of thirty seconds before he replied.

"Fang and Claw have minor wounds, not quite superficial. They have treated each other and are . . . mobile. Jaibie is hurt more seriously, but he is alive. It appears that he was hit several times. The wounds have been bandaged and the bleeding is . . . subsiding. Claw gave him an extra dose of painkiller." From the hesitant way Souvana spoke, I suspected that Jaibie's wounds were life-threatening, but I didn't say anything on the squad circuit, in case Jaibie was conscious enough to hear.

"Nuyi?" I asked.

"I am uninjured, Sergeant." He did sound out of breath, but that wasn't unusual for the divotect.

"Fine. I want you to collect all the mines and snoops the others with you have and bring them over here. Souvana, you stay with the wounded. Make sure everything possible is done for Jaibie. Fang, Claw, you stay with them as well. Help out with Jaibie if you can, and keep watch. We'll take care of planting the mines and snoops."

We still had work to do, even though there had been enough shooting to let anyone within two miles know exactly where we were.

CHAPTER 18

I HAD OYO AND IYI TAKE CARE OF PLANTING the snoops. The biraunta were smaller and could work their way through the tangles better than any of the rest of us. Nuyi, Kiervauna, and I planted the mines. Although we had a couple of different models, they were basically similar in design. Each carried either two or two-point-three pounds of high explosives in a shaped charge faced with eighteen or twenty-two ounces of depleted uranium pellets. The mines were designed to spray that shrapnel across a sixty-degree arc through a twenty-degree rise. The "official" kill radius was thirty yards. In practice, the reliable kill radius was somewhat less.

As long as you're careful and know what you're doing, those mines are fairly safe to work with. I showed the others where to set them to cover a long stretch of that open draw between the hills. The first few we armed just for command detonation, though that wasn't exactly what the lieutenant had instructed; he would have made allowance if he had thought about it, I reasoned. If the enemy came through that draw, we wanted as many of them as possible within range of the mines before they started going off, rather than only catching the point men and letting the rest either find a way around or search out the remaining mines to detonate them. The later mines, those farther into the draw, were set for command detonation, but we also stretched trip wires—metal threads about the same diameter as the threads of a spiderweb—across the dry creekbed in the draw, where a boot could set the mines off.

By the time we had all the mines and snoops set and armed, Fang and Claw had fashioned a litter to carry Jaibie back to the command post—CP—Lieutenant Taivana had set up on the north side of the hill. I checked Jaibie before we moved him. He was in serious condition but seemed stable. I had no idea whether he would survive to reach a field hospital. There was no chance of getting a shuttle in to evacuate him, so it might not be until the coming battle was settled before he could get more help than what we could give him ourselves.

It was slow going carrying Jaibie to the CP. We still had all those thorny trees to get past. Souvana and Kiervauna carried the litter. They were, arguably, the strongest men in the squad, especially since Fang and Claw had both been injured—even if not seriously. I stayed close, as much to keep an eye on the porracci as to be handy for Jaibie. Nuyi led the way. The ghuroh were behind me, and Iyi and Oyo were in the rear.

When we got back to the others, Lieutenant Taivana took over Jaibie's treatment, and acted as if he knew what he was doing. He set up an intravenous drip of water—plain canteen water—into the abarand's arm. The medical nanoagents in Jaibie's system could use that to build blood cells. If they could do that fast enough, he had a chance.

Tonio told me where to deploy my squad. "The Ilion army is on the move," Tonio told me. We could be in action within three or four hours."

What happened to that "not until after dark" line they gave us? I wondered, but I knew better than to waste time and breath asking. You can't expect the enemy to stick to the timetable you set.

WITH SO LITTLE TIME LEFT, WE COULDN'T waste any of it sleeping. We dug foxholes where we could in the rocky dirt, piling the soil and rocks in front of our positions for the little extra protection that could afford us. My squad's position was on the southeast "shoulder" of the hill, twenty yards below the crest. The rest of the platoon was spread across the southern face of the hill and onto the southwest shoulder. We were situated so we could cover the easy passes on either side of our hill as well as any direct assault against us.

We ate. We drank water. Some of us made small improvements in our fields of fire, chopping a few low-lying branches down—what we could do without making it obvious where we were—and using the cuttings to help camouflage our positions. There's a trick: You rub dirt over the cut ends of the wood so they don't stick out like proverbial sore thumbs. We got as comfortable as we could . . . and waited.

Third squad had gone to the bottom of the hill and out into the flat to plant more mines. Snoops weren't necessary there—at least not many. If the IFers were coming in daylight, we would see them before they got close enough to "wake" a snoop. If the fight went on after dark, it was more likely that *we* would be moving through that area than that the enemy would.

I moved along my squad to check on the preparations my people had made. Fang and Claw had cleaned their wounds, and neither was willing to admit to more than slight discomfort. Since they were alert and showed no obvious disability, I took them at their word. I didn't have much choice. If the fight got close, we would need every gun we could get.

After I had visited every man in my squad, I climbed over the crest of the hill to where Tonio and the lieutenant were. There was a slight crease in the terrain that let me move without being exposed to anyone watching from the south.

Jaibie was holding on. If he was not visibly improved, at least his condition had not deteriorated. Three pints of water had been pumped into Jaibie's system intravenously, as quickly as his medical nanoagents could convert them to blood. He was no longer bleeding, not externally. The lieutenant admitted that he wasn't sure if there was any internal bleeding but he thought that there wasn't—not the major kind of bleeding that can kill a man. That Jaibie was still unconscious was probably as much the result of the painkillers as the wounds.

"He thinks Jaibie can make it," Tonio told me after the lieutenant went back to his observation post at the crest of the hill. "No guarantees, but if we can hold out until this is over, I think he can, too."

Yeah, *if* we could hold out.

WE COULD SEE THE ILION ARMY WHEN IT MOVED across open sections of the savanna south of us, beginning about two hours after we set up our line in the hills. Like the lieutenant, I spent much of my time scanning the area through binoculars. Even when no enemy units were visible, we could see where our artillery was hitting them, and hear the explosions of the rockets. The nearest enemy units had to be three miles away when I first spotted them.

I didn't know if all our spec ops units had gotten to where they were supposed to be. Some had had a lot farther to travel than we had. I wasn't able to pick anything up on that over the command channel. What little traffic there was came from the line battalions that were attacking on the south and west, pushing the IFers toward the hills. The battalions spearheading the drive were taking heavy casualties.

Twice the IFers tried to counterattack, but neither attempt succeeded. Their general move toward the north-northeast continued, bringing them closer to us. We started hearing the distant rattle of rifles, a slight rattle on the edge of hearing that only slowly became louder and distinct.

Both sides brought aerospace fighters down. Instead of either side being able to use their fighters for close ground support, they ended up fighting each other. We had a pretty good view of the dogfights. I counted six fighters destroyed, blowing up or spiraling down to crash, though the fights were too far away, and too high, for me to be certain how many of the planes were ours and how many belonged to the enemy. No pilots ejected from any of the downed fighters. After five to seven minutes, the remaining aircraft had to burn for orbit to return to their ships—low on fuel or out of ammunition.

Ninety minutes before noon, the nearest enemy elements had moved to within a mile of us, apparently unaware that there was anyone blocking their path. The IFers had no scouts out on our side, and that was obviously a mistake, one I hoped they wouldn't realize before it was too late for them. Their attention was focused entirely on our line battalions.

With binoculars I could see where the front line was to the southeast, maybe three miles away. Our people were barely moving on that side of the battle, skirting the southeastern corner of Miorawinn. Our main effort was on the south, since we wanted the IFers to move more north than east. I couldn't make out exactly where the front was on that side. It might have been three miles, it might have been more.

Of course, it wasn't exactly a *line* at the front, on either the south or the west. You don't have ranks of soldiers moving forward in step. Tactics like that proved suicidal centuries ago. But there were knots here and there, units moving forward as they could, forcing the enemy back—or being forced to stop themselves when the enemy resistance was too much. Back and forth, side to side—fluid—each army maneuvering for the best advantage it could find, trying to avoid getting pinned down. Even on foot, mobility is the key. One of the keys.

FOR AN HOUR OR MORE THE FIGHTING DIDN'T get noticeably closer to us. The enemy did what they could to move men forward again, toward our line battalions, and for a time the enemy units closest to us were moving in the opposite direction, away from us, leapfrogging units that had been directly engaging our line battalions, trying to give those units a breather. That meant that they were moving farther from us. We relaxed a little. Our part in the battle, whatever it might turn out to be, was that much farther off.

I went back to check on Jaibie again, and to talk with

Tonio to see if he had learned anything more. Jaibie was about the same as the last time I had looked, no better but at least no worse. Tonio. . . .

"It's a mess out there," he whispered. "We've been getting updates from Colonel Hansen's staff. "The way things are going, neither army is going to be in shape for much after this fight, no matter how it ends. They're chopping each other to pieces."

I was conscious of blinking, twice, before I thought of anything to say. "If it's that bad, maybe they'll pull us down to hit the IFers from behind?" It was a question, even if it wasn't worded that way. I was afraid that it was a prophecy, and when that came to mind, I wished I hadn't said it. If things *were* bad, they wouldn't let us sit on the sidelines for long.

Tonio was as slow to answer as I had been to ask. "Nobody's said anything, but it's possible." He hesitated again. "If they do, I hope they hold off until nightfall."

I made a vague gesture to the south. "If things are as bad out there as you say, I don't think it can wait for dark. The sun won't set for seven hours or more."

Tonio nodded slowly. "I guess it depends on how soon the brass gets desperate."

HOW SOON PROVED TO BE ABOUT TWO HOURS, but we knew that orders would be coming an hour before that when word was passed to consolidate the wounded from all the spec ops teams at one location three-tenths of a mile east of our position. Our company's third platoon would provide security for the dozen men who were wounded too badly to take part in any action.

Since Jaibie was my man, our squad took him—Sou-

vana and Kiervauna carrying the litter, the rest of us
providing security. Get over to third platoon and back,
as fast as we could; those were the lieutenant's orders.
Several other wounded had already been brought in by
the time we arrived, and more were on their way. We
weren't the only squad that had run into trouble. There
were a couple of medtechs who could provide better
treatment for Jaibie and the others than we could.

I wanted to look for someone who might know more
of what was going on than I did, but the lieutenant had
said to get back as quickly as we could. I've bent orders
before when it suited me, but if action was coming, I
couldn't be late with my squad, couldn't leave the rest
of the platoon shorthanded.

We left Jaibie with the medtechs and started right
back to the platoon. I hurried the pace as much as I could
through those blasted thorns. We had all been stuck and
scratched so many times that it no longer seemed to
matter. It was just one more damned nuisance among all
the others. I itched all over, and the backs of my hands
were covered with the welts the thorns left.

We were fifty yards short of the lieutenant's CP when
I saw Tonio waving for us to hurry, pumping his right
arm up and down frantically. We double-timed the rest
of the distance. The order to move had come.

I TOOK A LONG DRINK OF WATER BEFORE WE STARTED
moving down the south slope of the hill, but by the time
we reached the bottom, my mouth was dry again. At the
same time, my palms were sweating so much that I had
to wipe them dry, and the rest of me . . . well, I was
sweating all over, and not just from the heat. I had felt
fear often enough to recognize it. Crazy ideas run

through your mind, sounding deceptively reasonable. Your feet seem to develop a will of their own, wanting to run in the opposite direction just as fast as they can go. *Fight it. Focus.* You have to learn to use the fear, channel it. But before the fight was when it was difficult. Once the shooting started, the fear would fade to insignificance. At least it always had before.

The lieutenant had been stingy about telling us what we were supposed to do when we closed with the enemy. Maybe the colonel had been just as stingy with the lieutenant. *Get close without being seen. Take what action you can when you get there.* That sort of thing. Pass the decision to the man on the scene. We were special operations, after all; we were supposed to be able to operate like that.

Moving by platoons, and dispersed the way we were, it might be possible to get fairly close to the enemy before they spotted us, particularly if they weren't expecting trouble from our direction. Even though it was broad daylight, we could move with some stealth. We all wore camouflage uniforms, and we stayed in the trees except when we were forced to cross a clearing. Thorns be damned. They couldn't do 10 percent the damage an enemy bullet or grenade could.

Half a mile. We took a short break—three minutes, long enough to take a drink of water while the lieutenant and Tonio tried to get a better line on the nearest enemy positions—lying on the ground, making no unnecessary movements. Then we changed course 10 degrees to our right, and spread out into a skirmish line instead of the two columns we had been in.

Fifteen minutes later, we stopped again. This time Tonio signaled for squad leaders to gather around him and the lieutenant. We crouched or sat on the ground and tipped our faceplates up so we could talk without radios.

"We're about two hundred yards from what's left of an enemy company," the lieutenant whispered. "At the moment, they're not moving. I don't have any firm intelligence on how many effectives they have, or how close other units are. Operations *thinks* they can't number more than one hundred and forty effectives, probably less, but could offer no firm intelligence. We move as close as we can without being seen and open fire once we have targets. Once the shooting starts, listen for my orders. What we do next depends on what happens."

"Are we acting independently or coordinating with the other spec ops units?" I asked.

"Independently," the lieutenant said, "but we will all hit as opportunities arise, and do what we can to support nearby units. Keep the overlay of friendly units on your head-up display at all times. We'll use what the other units do to help determine what we do after this first strike."

It *sounded* good, but I couldn't avoid thinking about the massive confusion that might result, and confusion can get you killed in a hurry. Not that I had any better ideas to offer.

"Yes, sir," I said. That was the only proper reply.

"Get back to your squads," the lieutenant said. "We move in two minutes."

I LAID THE SITUATION OUT FOR MY SQUAD AS quickly as I could, and told them to pay attention to their radios for later orders. Then I took a sip of water, because talking had dried my mouth and throat again. Then the two minutes were up and the lieutenant signaled for us to start moving.

We went at a slow walk, bent forward to present the smallest targets possible, careful where we stepped, trying to keep as many trees as possible between us and where we thought the enemy was. Two hundred yards did not feel like much of a distance. A marksman can bring down a target at twice that range without much trouble. He wouldn't even need to use more than a single bullet. Especially in broad daylight.

The instant anyone on the other side spotted us and realized we were the enemy, the shooting would begin. I hoped the lieutenant wouldn't be *too* optimistic about how close we could advance before we went to ground and started the shooting ourselves. You always want the first shot . . . and the last.

I glanced toward Tonio and the lieutenant, between us and third squad. Second squad was on the left flank, fourth on the right. We were spread across less than 100 yards. And we were 150 yards from where the lieutenant had said the enemy was.

So far I hadn't seen any movement out there. If the Ilion force was down on the ground resting or waiting for orders, that was possible. If they had spotted us, they might be waiting for us to get so close that they couldn't miss. It was also possible that they had started moving again, in some other direction. If they were moving toward us, we would have seen them—or they would have seen us and opened fire. If this. If that. It can drive you crazy.

The prayer in my head was almost unnoticed now, pushed out of mind by the need to be ready to react instantly to anything. *We can't go any farther without risking everything,* I thought, looking toward the lieutenant. *Any second now, somebody is going to spot us. Then all hell will break loose.*

I tried to swallow but couldn't. I couldn't have spit to save my life, and I didn't dare take another drink. I had to keep both hands on my rifle. I was almost in a firing position now, the rifle's butt against my shoulder, the barrel almost parallel to the ground. The safety had been off for a long time, and I had checked to make certain that the selector was on full automatic.

One hundred and thirty yards. The lieutenant gestured for everyone to get lower, to crawl. Hands and knees for ten yards. Then flat on our bellies. For a few seconds we all stayed in place, motionless, searching the ground in front of us and looking for any indication that anyone else in the platoon had spotted anything. I still hadn't seen anyone in front of us, and I should have—*if* there was anyone where we had been told they were. We could hear gunfire, and the occasional blast of an RPG or the larger artillery rockets, but at a distance, background noise, not anything close enough to be aimed at us.

Tonio crawled over to me, got right up close so he could whisper. "Send your biraunta to look for the enemy. We don't see anyone, and there are no unidentified electronic signatures close. We need to know if the enemy is there, or which way they might have gone."

I nodded, and Tonio started crawling back toward the lieutenant while I signaled for Oyo and Iyi to come to me. I repeated Tonio's instructions. "Be careful," I added. "Leave your packs behind so you aren't huge lumps crawling."

They nodded, then started crawling south, toward where we had been told the enemy was. I had come to accept but really hadn't noticed before that their habitual nervous habits disappeared when we were in action. Instead of flickering around constantly, their tails remained calm, trailing behind them instead of sticking up like antennae.

I didn't so much watch their progress as I watched over their heads, anxious to spot any threat to them as early as possible. They were *my* men, and that was all that was important. I edged forward a few inches and got my rifle in firing position. Iyi and Oyo were the ones with their butts hanging out the farthest. I didn't even notice the rest of my squad getting ready to cover them the way I had. I was too intent on the terrain in front of the biraunta.

I had trouble remembering to breathe as Iyi and Oyo edged forward. Once they were twenty yards out, it became difficult to see them in the grass and through the short, gnarled trees without looking specifically for them.

Five minutes. Ten. I had completely lost sight of our scouts. *Good,* I thought. *If I can't see them, the enemy probably can't either.* The best news was that there was no sound from out there—no gunfire close enough to have Iyi or Oyo on either end of it. They weren't making any noise I could hear. No one could be more silent than Oyo and Iyi when they tried.

By the time fifteen minutes had passed I was extremely antsy, wondering what was going on, why they hadn't come back—though I knew it was too soon for them to crawl all of the way to where the enemy was supposed to be and get back, even without taking time to look around to see which way the enemy had gone, if they had left. *It could be another ten minutes, twenty,* I told myself, *maybe longer,* but that didn't do a damned thing for my impatience . . . except maybe aggravate it.

I had to fight the urge to crawl out there to look for them.

I glanced at Tonio, thirty yards from me. He was looking at me. I shrugged. He nodded and looked away. I looked over the barrel of my rifle again, my eyes scanning from side to side, looking for any hint of Iyi and Oyo—or anyone else—heading toward us.

The biraunta had been gone for thirty-six minutes before I spotted movement in the grass, and it was another half minute before I identified Iyi and Oyo crabbing their way toward me on elbows and toes. As soon as I was certain who it was, I turned to signal Tonio that the scouts were on the way back, and I raised up just a little—both to get a better view past them and to let the rest of the patrol know that it was our men coming in.

"The enemy troops have left their positions," Iyi said when he and his brother reached me. "It appears that they moved southwest, though we can't be certain because there has been so much movement back and forth through there. We are certain that there are no enemy soldiers within four hundred yards of our position, anywhere along this course." He gestured in the direction he and Oyo had come from.

"Good work," I told them. I was just turning to crawl over to Tonio and the lieutenant when I saw that both of them were on their way to me. I waited, then repeated what Iyi had told me.

"They must be putting everyone into the lines on the other side," Tonio whispered, more to the lieutenant than to me.

"I believe so," Lieutenant Taivana said. "Then it is even more urgent that we get into the fray as quickly as we can."

"Should we just get up and keep going until we find

them?" Tonio asked, and the lieutenant nodded. Taivana got to his feet and gestured for the platoon to stand erect as well.

I took a deep breath before I stood, not quite certain of the intelligence of providing that much of a target, and I looked around carefully once I had the advantage of those few extra feet of altitude. No, there was no trace of any enemy, and no gunfire suddenly erupted near us. The rest of the men got up, most slowly, looking around as if they were no longer certain which direction the danger might lie in.

Taivana gestured for the other squad leaders, and once we were clustered together, he gave his orders. We would move forward in a double skirmish line, the first two squads out in front, the other two following thirty yards back. "Stagger the lines so everyone has a clear field of fire," he instructed before sending the other squad leaders back to their men.

I took another drink of water, emptying one of my two canteens. It didn't do much for my thirst, but I left the other canteen alone. I couldn't tell how long it would have to last me. I might need that water a lot more later on.

We started moving as soon as all of the squad leaders were back with their men. In the first skirmish line, my men had the left side. I positioned myself in the center of the squad, with Souvana on the far left. Tonio and the lieutenant got in the center of the platoon, about eight feet apart, closer to the first skirmish line than the second.

We didn't move as slowly as we had before, but at something approaching a normal strolling pace. Before, we had expected the enemy to be close. This time we had no idea how far away they were—and the lieutenant was in a hurry to find them. I guess the lieutenant was as capable of getting impatient as anyone.

There might be pure hell waiting for us, but I had reached the point where I figured that the sooner we got to it, the sooner it would be over.

The trees weren't as close together on the flat as they had been in the hills, and fewer of the trees had those nasty thorns. Each time we got to a clearing, the first skirmish line would race across while the second covered them. Then the first line would cover the second as it came across the gap.

The large clearing where the IFer company had been was obvious. That many men have to leave clear traces. It looked as if they had been there for hours. It wasn't just the improvised defense perimeter around the clearing. There were remains of meal packets, other debris. Some of the grass had been flattened down so thoroughly that it wasn't standing back up. In a couple of places the grass had been uprooted, showing bare dirt— and bootprints.

I warned my squad to be particularly careful crossing the abandoned campsite in case the IFers had left booby traps behind. Once we were clear of the area, we remained cautious. Every step we took in that direction brought us closer to the fighting—even if the company we had been looking for wasn't in our line of march any longer. The rest of the battle was not too far away, certainly less than a mile, maybe only half that. The noise of combat had been growing constantly. The battle might be moving toward us faster than we were moving toward it.

Ten minutes, fifteen. *Sixteen.*

I saw a glint of sunlight on dark metal, just a glimpse, so quickly there and gone that it might almost have been my imagination. I raised my right arm, hand clenched in a fist, and whistled softly, shortly, on the platoon frequency. Everyone stopped and went to the ground.

Contact.

The lieutenant and Tonio both looked to me. I pointed toward where I had seen that brief glint, then used fingers and fist to tell them it was 120 yards away. Taivana nodded, then turned to order the men in the second skirmish line forward, using hand signs the way I had. He sent third squad to the left *flank and fourth to the right. They moved slowly, crawling flat on* their stomachs to try to keep the enemy from spotting them, so it took three or four minutes for everyone to get into place.

By that time I had seen or heard more indications that there were people up there, though I hadn't seen anyone directly. I knew they were there, and I wasn't the only one who could read the signs. Branches and leaves were moving in ways they shouldn't have. Patches of green and dark brown appeared too solid. Things like that. It seemed a minor miracle that the enemy hadn't spotted us coming, but I wasn't about to question Providence. I didn't even wonder if this was the single company we had been looking for or a larger segment of their army.

The lieutenant looked both ways along the line, assuring himself that everyone was ready. His voice on the platoon channel startled me. I expected him to continue using hand signs until the action actually started.

"Grenadiers first, then rifles, on my order." There was a pause of no more than ten seconds before he gave that order: "Fire!" The first RPGs were barely out of their launchers before he ordered the rifles to start as well.

Thirty rifles firing on full automatic along a narrow front can chop up the vegetation in a hurry. Grass was cut. Low branches fell from trees. Trunks were pocked and chipped. Grenades started popping off as well, from 120 yards to nearly 200 yards away. Our grenadiers were good about spreading their brand of mayhem. A lot of the cover between us and the enemy disappeared. In a couple of places dry vegetation started to smolder, though I didn't see any open fires.

For maybe fifteen seconds, the shooting was one-way. The enemy needed that long to react and figure out where we were. By then they had already suffered casualties—though we had no way to know how effective our barrage was. Then the enemy turned to face us, and the shooting ran both ways. The fact that we were all flat on our stomachs gave us some advantage. Most of the incoming was over our heads—not an uncommon event, I'm told. But once the enemy started shooting back, we had better targets. We weren't just saturating an area.

"Third squad, start moving around on their flank!" the lieutenant ordered. "Everyone else, continue firing."

I worked my field of fire as methodically as I could, sweeping about forty degrees from left to right and then back, overlapping the men on either side of me, replacing magazines each time the bolt of my rifle stayed back over an empty chamber. I had the stump of a tree at my left shoulder, giving me some cover. Half the platoon had at least a *little* solid cover. Some of the branches and leaves had come down, on and around me, and I could smell freshly cut wood. That sweet smell was somehow able to combat the odor of the liquid "gunpowder" of our rifles and the acrid smoke of the first enemy grenades that hit near us.

"Lieutenant!" The firefight had been going on for three minutes when I yelled that word over my circuit to Taivana.

"What?"

"They've only dropped three grenades around us, and that rifle fire is awfully sparse. Either there are fewer of them than we think, or they're running out of ammo." It made sense, though I hadn't taken the time to reason it out logically. Training, and instinct, maybe. The enemy had been involved in a running battle that had dragged on near the edge of forever, unable to get to any resupply—and our spec ops teams had been hitting their munitions wherever we could for more than a week.

"Could be," Taivana said. He switched channels to connect with the entire platoon. "Move forward, one squad at a time, the rest covering. First squad—go!"

I got my men up and we dashed forward, each man heading for the next available cover—however meager. Once we got to the ground again, second squad went, then fourth. Third stayed put through the first couple of rotations, since they had already been working their way toward the enemy.

One more enemy grenade landed, over to my right and ten yards behind Tonio and the lieutenant—both of whom had gone flat again after moving forward just a fraction of a second before the grenade exploded. The volume of enemy rifle fire decreased rather than increased as we moved closer. It had slackened off enough to give me the chance to look to see if either Tonio or Taivana had been hurt or killed. They both seemed to be unhurt. I saw Tonio look over his shoulder, toward where the grenade had exploded.

"Fix bayonets!" Taivana ordered on the platoon frequency, so I knew he was okay.

I already had my bayonet on the end of my rifle. A long time ago, not long after I completed ranger training,

I heard a civilian bad-mouthing bayonets, saying they were an anachronism, that they had no place in the kit of a "modern" soldier. He said something to the effect that warfare had progressed light-years since the ancient Romans with their spears and short swords, and that it was time the army got its collective head out of its collective butt and accepted three thousand years of progress.

"There's one damned good reason why we keep the bayonets, and why we'll have bayonets as long as there are soldiers," I told the guy. We were in a bar near the base where I was stationed, and we both had had too much to drink.

"What's that?" he asked, making his words a noisy sneer. I wasn't in uniform, but I guess it didn't take a psychic to figure out that I was a soldier.

"A bayonet doesn't run out of ammo, and a rifle does. Maybe a knife on the end of a rifle takes us back to the time of the Romans, or the Greeks and Persians, but a rifle without that knife on the end and without bullets takes us a lot farther back. Caveman with a club." I don't think I convinced him, but he sure as hell hadn't convinced me.

WE HAD JUST GOTTEN UP TO TAKE OUR SECOND turn advancing when Kiervauna pitched forward just a few feet to my side, hitting the ground head first. I couldn't tell how badly he was hurt, and I couldn't take time to stop. I went forward another couple of steps, then dove to the ground again, behind a rock that stuck up just a little more than my head—all the cover that was available. I emptied my rifle in the direction of the enemy, then ducked back and looked around while I reached for a new magazine. Fang was also down, on his side, with his rifle a couple of feet away from him. Neither he nor Kiervauna were moving, but that was no certain indicator of whether they were dead or alive.

Looking farther off, I could see several others down from other squads. It was easy to tell who was down because they had been shot and who was down because they had taken cover, but it's not something I can explain easily. I turned my attention back to the enemy and started firing again. When it was first squad's turn to move again, the lieutenant got up with us and moved closer to my squad. He was hobbling badly, but that did not seem to slow him down much. Tonio moved closer, too, and he didn't seem to have been hurt at all.

When I dove for cover the next time, something spun me and I landed on my back. My first reaction was surprise, because I couldn't figure out what had happened. It took me maybe ten seconds to realize that I had been hit, and longer to see that I had taken a bullet high in my left arm, near the shoulder. The wound didn't hurt at all, not immediately. I swore, but I'm not certain if the words came out or were just in my mind. I fumbled at my belt for my first-aid pouch—training came through even when my mind wasn't working right. The fingers on my right hand didn't seem to want to work either, and I ended up dumping the contents of the pouch on the ground before I could get to one of the wraparound bandages.

It seemed to take me an eternity to get the bandage wound around the entrance and exit wounds on my arm. The rest of my squad was up and moving forward again, and I was just getting the dressing in place. I grabbed my rifle in my right hand and started to get up, thinking that I had to stay with my men. On my first attempt, I stumbled and went down on one knee, but the second time I used my rifle as a crutch and made it to my feet. I wasn't aware of staggering as I moved forward, though the world was moving in ways it shouldn't have. It didn't matter. This was no time to sit and wait for the chaos to end on its own.

My left arm started to go numb; it tingled rather than hurt. There had been only an instant of pain, while I was bandaging the wound. My arm wouldn't work right, though, and I couldn't grip the forestock of my rifle with my left hand. The best I could do was hold that arm out and use it as a prop under the rifle.

Okay, I wasn't thinking straight. My vision had blurred as well, and I wasn't aware of that. I held my rifle with the butt against my side, trying to cradle the forestock with my left arm, firing short bursts at anything that might have been an enemy soldier. I dropped to the ground again, just behind the rest of my squad, scarcely aware of Nuyi at my side. He said something, but I couldn't understand the words. I wondered if my translator button was malfunctioning.

When it was time for first squad to move forward again, Nuyi tried to keep me from getting up; he did everything but sit on my chest. "Help me up," I said, and after a hesitation, he did. He stayed at my side—too close—as we moved forward.

This time we were done with the fire-and-maneuver routine. We had closed with the enemy. The tonatin soldiers of the Ilion Federation were right there in our faces, not about to back down from a dirty, spit-in-the-eye, knee-in-the-groin fight. Three of them charged Nuyi and me. Two of them fell to our combined rifle fire, but then my rifle's magazine was empty and there wasn't time to reload—even if both my hands had been working properly. Nuyi moved in front of me to close with the one remaining tonatin with his bayonet. I guess Nuyi's rifle was out of ammunition as well.

I couldn't do much one-handed with the bayonet, and I had to do a lot of fumbling to eject the empty magazine from my rifle. I gave up after a few seconds and drew my pistol, thumbed the safety off, and emptied it into that tonatin, just as his bayonet dug into Nuyi's armpit.

The tonatin fell forward, pushing Nuyi to the ground under him. Nuyi had also stuck the tonatin, low, under his armored vest. I rolled the enemy soldier off, then jerked his rifle away—the blade of his bayonet had come out of Nuyi already. Then I leaned over Nuyi, looking for any sign of life. He was still breathing, so I fumbled for his first-aid kit, dug out a bandage, and more or less shoved it into the wound under his arm. Then I pressed his arm against his side.

Right then, that was all I could do. I was suddenly dizzy—or suddenly aware of being dizzy. Vaguely, I recall reloading my pistol. Then there were two more tonatin soldiers coming toward Nuyi and me. I think I started shooting, but I really can't swear to it. I was surprised to realize that I was looking straight up at the sky. Then it all went dark.

CHAPTER 19

I WASN'T UNCONSCIOUS VERY LONG, AND WHEN I woke up, I felt more foolish for having passed out than being hurt. Right around us, the fighting had pretty much ground to a halt, and farther off, the rest of the grand battle was coming close to its end. We won, if you can call it a victory—which the politicians back home were quick to do. I was there, though, and I can't call it anything but a senseless, bloody stalemate. What settled the issue on Dintsen was not our superior soldiers, leadership, or tactics. It was simply that the occupation force left by the Ilion Federation ran out of ammunition before we did.

It was that simple. Period. Exclamation point.

The battle on the ground ended. The IFer soldiers surrendered in dribs and drabs. Away from the main battle, some of the remaining enemy units held on for several more days before they faced the inevitable. The Ilion fleet overhead was almost as slow to realize that the situation was lost and that they weren't going to be able to withdraw any of their people. It was sixty-odd hours after the end of the big land battle when the Ilion fleet headed out-system and jumped to hyperspace.

Maybe we did win in a strategic sense. Dintsen had been "liberated"—the stated purpose of our invasion—and the divotect who remained alive there could maybe breathe a little more easily, though it would be a long time before they forgot the horror and the tens of thousands of them who had been killed. But it wouldn't take too many victories like Dintsen to totally destroy an army—any army.

The Combined Chiefs of Staff of the Alliance of Light called it a major victory. They would. The politicians on maybe a hundred Alliance worlds said the same thing, loudly and repeatedly. A few bemoaned the cost—the *money*. Yeah, there were a few people who looked at that and shook their heads. But nobody seemed to be asking if it had been worth it, not that I ever heard about, anyway.

I'm not sure myself. I know why we went to Dintsen, why we *had* to go. *Genocide* is an ugly word in any language. But we should have gone in stronger, even if it had taken a little longer to start the fight. I don't see where a delay would have hurt the inhabitants of Dintsen more than we hurt ourselves by going in too soon, too weak.

Still, the 1st Combined Regiment proved itself. That was the official verdict of the Combined Chiefs of Staff. Their mouths ran over in praise of us. That wouldn't help the nearly one thousand soldiers of the regiment who died on Dintsen. It didn't make the recovery of the wounded any faster or less painful.

Fred Wilkins was dead. Jaibie had been wounded before the final fight; he almost didn't make it. Fang also came close to dying; he had taken three bullets in the chest—through his body armor, which had proved to be less efficient than advertised. Kiervauna lost part of a leg; he needed three months of regeneration treatment to grow it back. Nuyi had been lucky. He lost a lot of blood, but the bayonet had not managed to hit any vital organs. Me, my wound was almost superficial. Four hours in a medtank and I was fit for duty—the mopping-up operations and recovery of our dead.

It was two weeks later before we were pulled off Dintsen, after a divotect battalion from one of their core worlds came to garrison the place until more Alliance troops could be brought in. Colonel Hansen told us that we would be taken somewhere to get all our wounded fit, then be given furlough before we got replacements and went back to training.

The war continued.